THE SURROGATE OMEGA

PART ONE

BOOK TWO IN THE UNEXPECTED OMEGAS SERIES

JACEY DAVIS

The Surrogate Omega - Part One

Copyright © 2022 by Jacey Davis

All rights reserved.

No part of this book may be reproduced in any form or by any electronic or mechanical means, including information storage and retrieval systems, without written permission from the author, except for the use of brief quotations in a book review.

TO MY AMAZING READERS

Thank You for joining me in the Unexpected Omegas world again. This is the first part of Lake, Evander, and Logan's story and picks up pretty much where Unexpected Omega leaves off. This ends on an HFN for the characters but with no major cliffhanger.

Like book one, Surrogate Omega is an MPreg Omegaverse with on-page MPreg, so if that's not your thing, then you might want to skip this one. This is also an MMM fated mates relationship. Again, if it's not your thing, completely fine, but this may not be for you.

While Surrogate does take place in contemporary New York, this is an alternate universe, and because of that, things may not be 100% like modern day New York.

Content Warning: Content Warning: references to past child abuse, food insecurity, drugs, attempted trafficking (all off-page), and infertility of a secondary character.

I really enjoyed writing about these three men, and I hope they all resonated with you as much as they did with me!

Happy Reading!
Jacey Davis

ACKNOWLEDGMENTS

I just want to say thank you to everyone who's supported me through this. My amazing parents and sister, my husband and kids. Thank You, and I love you! And thank you to my PA, my editor Norma, Christina, who's Alpha read most of my books, my Beta and ARC readers, Kerry, who makes my beautiful covers and formats my books because I'm technologically challenged, and everyone else who has been there for me through this journey.

PROLOGUE
ERIC CIRILLO

TWENTY-ONE YEARS AGO

I don't have time for this bullshit. It's the worst part of my profession. These fucking druggies show up at all hours of the night, pounding on my door, begging for just one more hit, one more ounce, and they swear they'll get the money to me tomorrow. Fucking pathetic.

The pounding on the door doesn't go away, though. "Eric! Eric, open up! I know you're in there! I can pay you!"

Fuck, is this asshole trying to get the cops called? Sure, the chances of my neighbors doing that are slim. They all know the deal in this neighborhood, but still. I'd rather not fucking blare my business to the whole block.

Groaning the whole time, I put my joint down in the ashtray and drag my ass off of my recliner and to the front door. Of course, I already know who I will see on the other side. I'd recognize his mewling anywhere.

I open the door, and—surprise, surprise—fucking Seth McIntyre is standing at my door, eyes bloodshot and whole body twitching, desperate for another fix.

JACEY DAVIS

"What the fuck do you want, Seth? I already told you I'm not giving you another ounce until you pay me what you owe."

I back up and let him in, against my better judgment, and that's when I realize the fucker isn't alone. He has a kid with him. A little boy, no older than seven or eight. He's a scrawny thing, though; his worn jeans and faded hoodie are way too big for his body. The kid's a ginger with dark-auburn hair flopping into big light-brown eyes. Those eyes stare into me, and I swear to fuck, the kid sees into my soul. He is one of those kids that you could just tell is way too wise for his age and has seen too much shit.

Sadly, it isn't uncommon for kids in this neighborhood. My own son has the same fucking look in his eyes whenever I see him. I fucking hate it, but what can I do?

I force myself to tear my gaze from the kid and look at the strung-out asshole with him. Fuck, is this scumbag the kid's father? Just the thought of it gives me the chills. Sure, I'm not father of the year or anything, but something about Seth always unsettles the fuck out of me. I hate the fact that he might've produced some offspring.

"What the fuck are you doing here, Seth? I won't ask again. And why the fuck did you bring a kid here?" I don't even bring Ev over to this dump. I try to keep him away from this shit as much as possible.

Seth rocks back and forth as his eyes bounce around my apartment. He is seconds away from losing it. Then, before I can fucking blink, he grabs the kid's arm tight. The poor kid flinches but doesn't say a word.

"I got payment for you, Eric. As I said I would. So if you can give me just a little more, I'll leave you alone, I swear."

I roll my eyes. Same fucking song and dance. "Let me see this money first, and then we'll talk."

I don't expect him to have money; if he does, I doubt it will be the full amount he owes me. Seth never has all the money. But he doesn't even attempt to fish cash out for me. Instead, he takes the kid and shoves him in my direction, causing the poor boy to stumble and nearly crash into me.

I take a step back. No. No fucking way is he doing what I think he's doing. Just, no fucking way.

"Seth . . . what the fuck are you doing?"

"I know he ain't much, but I know how much kids go for nowadays. And he's ginger. That's gotta be worth something, right? Those queers love fucking gingers."

There is so much to unpack in that sentence that I don't even know where to start. But, one thing is clear. Seth is trying to pay his debt to me by selling me his fucking son. Or whoever this kid is to him. I'm gonna be sick.

"Fuck, Seth. Are you fucking crazy? I might be a son of a bitch, but I don't mess with fucking kids. Is this kid even yours?"

Seth shrugs and rubs his nose with the back of his hand. He's getting even twitchier. "So his mom says." Gods. "There's another one. Twins. I thought one would be enough, but I can grab the other one, too, if you need him. He's mouthier. But, I'm sure someone would be willing to train him."

I swallow back the bile that's threatening to rise. I can't fucking show this asshole how much he's getting to me. "And you think I have these connections. That I fucking traffick kids?"

The little boy hasn't moved. It's clear he's learned to stay still and quiet around his dad. Fucking sick son of a bitch. I have no idea what I am doing, but I know one thing: I can't let this kid go back with his dad.

I kneel before him and try my best not to look intimidating. But I know that isn't the easiest thing to do. I'm a pretty big fucker, and I know the piercings and tattoos on my face and neck make a lot of kids scared of me. But this kid doesn't look scared. He just looks curious.

I smile at him and try to clamp down my anger. I have a

feeling he has too much anger directed at him already. "Hey, kid, my name is Eric. What's your name?"

"Lake McIntyre." I try not to scrunch my nose. Not the kid's fault he has a weird name.

"Ok, Lake, do you like cartoons? How 'bout I find some for you while I talk to your dad real quick?"

The kid shrugs. "My brother likes *Fairly Odd Parents*. I watch with him sometimes."

"My kid likes that show too. C'mon. I'll get you set up, ok?"

Lake nods his head, that floppy red hair bouncing into his eyes.

"Yo, Eric. I ain't got all day. You giving me my shit or what?"

I fix Seth with a stare. "You can fucking wait."

Once the kid is sitting on the couch watching cartoons and drinking an orange soda, I turn back to his piece of shit dad. My mind races as I figure out the best way to handle this situation. I know I'm not letting this kid go home with him. What I'm gonna do with him, I have no fucking clue. Hopefully, his mama is better than Seth and I can just bring him back. If that isn't the case, then I don't fucking know. I just know if I reject Seth's offer, he will find someone else who will take it, and I can't let that fucking happen. I draw the line at sex trafficking. Gods.

"Hang on," I tell Seth and dig through my stash. I hate giving him more drugs. Fucking hate it. But it's the quickest way to get him out of my damn apartment and away from this kid. I'm also worried about the damn brother. Is the kid safe? Otherwise, I have to find a way to get him too.

Cursing myself mentally, I take out the stash and go back to Seth. He's pacing the room and scratching his arm. The kid is still sitting on the couch, blatantly ignoring his dad.

I shove the drugs into the asshole's hand. "Here. We're even. Get the fuck out of my house and don't come back here. We're done."

Seth looks down at the bag before shoving it in his inside coat pocket. "And we're square? You're taking the kid?"

I fucking hate the words coming out of my mouth, but what choice do I have? "I'm taking the kid."

Seth nods. "Good. It'll be good for the kid anyway. He's a fucking freak. And pretty sure he's a queer too. He'll feel right at home."

I'm not gonna punch the guy. I'm not gonna hit him. It's not fucking worth it.

"Get the fuck out of here."

Seth puts his hands out in front of him, the sign of "I don't want no trouble." "Easy, man. I'm leaving."

And Seth walks out of my apartment, not glancing at his kid once.

I slam my head against the wall by the door as I lock up after him. I'm done with this shit. I've been getting tired of being in the game for a while now, tired of not seeing my kid grow up. But this, this is the final fucking straw. How does it get to the point that people think I'd take a fucking kid as payment? Am I really that much of a lowlife? I never meant for it to go that far.

I finally push away from the wall to realize that the boy, Lake, is watching me, not the TV. I force a smile.

"Am I supposed to live with you now?" he asks calmly and matter-of-factly.

I force myself not to blurt out, "Fuck no." Instead, I say, "Is that something you want?"

Lake shrugs. "Will I still get to see my mom and River? Mom might be sad if I don't live with her anymore, but it might make things easier for her. As long as I could visit, I think it would be ok."

Fuck, this kid. "Who's River? Your brother?"

"Yeah. We're twins."

"And where is River right now?"

"He's probably at Liam Johnson's house. Mrs. Johnson was

supposed to watch us after school while Mom worked, but *he* picked me up instead. I told the school Mom said that he wasn't allowed to, but they didn't listen."

Gods. What the fuck is wrong with the school? The good news is at least the brother is safe. Everyone knows Nora Johnson in the neighborhood. She's the neighborhood mama, taking care of all the kids and half the adults as well. She's been doing it since I was a kid. She's technically Liam's grandma, but the kid calls her mama, just like most others around here.

I also know that must mean that their mama was good people. Mrs. Johnson would think nothing of keeping the kids if she thinks they don't have a safe parent to come home to. But still, I'm gonna double-check.

"And your mama? You like living with her?"

The kid's eyes get wide as he nods. "Yeah, she's the best. I know she was really tired from working all night yesterday, but she still stayed up and helped me build my science fair project. And I got first place!" The kid fishes a blue ribbon out of the pocket of his hoodie. "See?"

I can't help the smile on my face. "Nice job, kid. I bet your mama is proud. Do you know her name or where she works?"

Lake quickly rattles off the woman's full name plus the name and address of her job.

"Ok, how about this? You like ice cream? I've been craving it real bad." The kid nods, excited. "Good, so how bout we go get ourselves some ice cream, and then I'll bring you to your mama's job. I bet she'll be real glad to see you."

"That sounds good."

"Perfect. Let's go."

Twenty minutes later, we're eating overfilled cones of the best ice cream in town, and my heart fucking aches. I'm trying to remember if I ever took Ev here for ice cream, and I can't remember one fucking time. The kid isn't much older than this one here. He deserves a dad who gives a shit about him—who spends time with him.

I make a vow right then and there. Once I hand this kid over to his mama, I'm done. I'm out of the drug dealing business, once and for all. I'll go back to school, get a job, and become the dad Ev deserves. He isn't gonna just be another statistic, lost on the streets because he grew up with no one giving a fuck about him. No, all of that's changing today.

I know it's gonna be a long road, and Ev probably hates me, but I'm determined. I'll do whatever the fuck it takes. No way am I ever gonna let my son be in a position where someone tries to sell or use him. It's time for me to suck it up and be the man and father my kid deserves.

ONE
LAKE

PRESENT DAY

"Honestly, I'm surprised at how badly this is getting to her. Whenever Zo and I talked about kids, it was always hypothetical. I was never sure if she actually wanted them. But I guess now that she knows she can't, it's put it into perspective."

I'm half listening to Avery talk to my brother River and his boyfriend Cooper, but most of my attention is on the little bundle of cuteness in my arms. I never thought much about children one way or the other, and I certainly never planned to have any of my own, but even I have to admit that my niece Mirielle has me wrapped around her little finger.

Mirielle, or Miri, as River calls her, is just three months old but is already clearly in charge. When we found out that my brother was pregnant, I never expected to feel like this about his child, but the minute I laid eyes on his little one, my whole world changed.

So I understand how Zoe is feeling. But, of course, the opposite happened to me. I never expected to be able to carry my children. I'm a man, after all. But all that changed about a year ago when River accidentally got pregnant, and the world realized the Omega gene was back.

Once they started testing for it, it was logical for me to have it done. Since River is my identical twin, it only made sense. It also wasn't much of a surprise when the results came back positive.

The question is what to do about it. I don't plan on having my own children. It's one thing to dote on my niece and even watch her occasionally, but I'm not suited to be a father. It's something I came to terms with a long time ago. I'm too logical and don't always understand how most people react to certain situations. I would struggle to raise an emotionally well-rounded child. That's not to mention that my profession isn't suited for family life. Only my immediate family knows that I'm not IT for an accounting firm, but even they don't know the whole story. And it's safest to keep it that way. So no, I'll leave baby raising to River and Cooper, and eventually my sister Essie, and just be the uncle who spoils them.

But still, I can't help but think about Avery and Zoe's situation. They are newer additions to the extended Simmons family. Avery has been Cooper's best friend since childhood, and he and his girlfriend Zoe easily inserted themselves into our lives.

A couple of weeks ago, Zoe found out that she was infertile and is taking it hard. Since I accidentally found out when they were talking about it near me, an idea formed, but I don't know how to broach the subject with them.

The couple is a lot closer to River. Maybe I should talk to him first? I tend to think about situations very logically, but not everyone does. To me, the solution is simple: They can't have a baby. I apparently can. It only makes sense for me to act as a surrogate for the couple when they're ready. I never plan on having a child of my own, but that doesn't mean I should let my capabilities go to waste. But I'm not sure the best way to approach the subject.

Miri starts fussing in my arms and making faces that indicate her diaper is no longer dry. "River, I think your daughter soiled her diaper," I tell my twin, who's leaning against his boyfriend's shoulder while they cuddle together on their couch.

Riv rolls his eyes at me as he pushes himself off the sofa and goes to the drawer in the TV stand where they keep extra diapers and wipes. "I can get that for you, babe," Cooper tells him, but River waves him off.

"I got it." River takes his daughter from me, and his eyes light up as he looks at her. "Hey, there, sweetheart, did you leave a present for Uncle Lake?"

Miri stares at her dad with big brown eyes and a gummy smile as he lays out a blanket on the floor and begins to change her. Miri gurgles and kicks, clearly happy with herself for the "present," as River called it, that she left us in her diaper. That's another reason I'm not having kids. I'm not a diaper changing type of guy.

I know I should probably go back to my own townhouse, which is just on the other side of the complex, but I'm not quite ready to leave yet. It's weird. I never considered myself much of a people person. Besides River, and to a smaller extent, Dad and Essie, I keep to myself. Lately, though, I hate the idea of going home alone to my place even though I do have work to do.

River and I have always lived together, except when we were in college. It was an adjustment period when he and Cooper moved to their own townhouse together a few months ago and left me alone in our apartment. I found I hated being so far away from everyone. So three weeks ago, I moved into my townhouse in the same complex. I'm still not sure if River is happy with that development. I think he was kind of enjoying having some space away from the twin thing. He'd never say that, though. He knows how much I need to be close and would never belittle that.

Soon, though, it becomes clear that it's time to go. Avery says his goodbyes and heads out. Miri has fallen asleep, and Cooper's putting her in her crib for a nap. River's dozing off on the couch. Obviously, this is all a sign I need to leave and go back to my own life, but I still couldn't make myself move off my brother's chair. It makes no sense; I never had an issue being alone until recently. But now, I find myself dreading the solitude. The silence is suffocating, and I hate it.

I grip the armrests on the chair, trying to force myself to stand up. River opens one eye and looks over at me. "Lake, are you ok?"

I look at him quizzically. "What do you mean?"

River shrugs. "I don't know, man. You're about to tear a hole in my chair because you're gripping it so hard. Also, you've been staring at the door for ten minutes but haven't actually left. You know I can sense when you're struggling with something, right? You can't really hide from me."

I look down at my lap, not able to look in the eyes that look so much like my own. That's another thing that never bothers me much: that River and I share a face. I know sometimes River claims he's weirded out by it, especially when we are having a serious conversation. It's like his soul's being exposed by watching his own face. I never understood that until now. I feel so exposed—it's too much. I just can't look at him now.

"I'm not sure what's wrong. It makes no sense," I finally tell him because I know River's not going to give it up until I confess something.

"Why don't you try me?"

I close my eyes and lean back against the chair. "I find I'm struggling with being alone." I can barely get the words out; it makes me so uncomfortable.

I hear River sit up from the couch and scoot closer to me. I still don't open my eyes, even as I feel his hand squeeze my knee. "Lake, you know there's nothing wrong with that, right? You're going through some major changes. It makes sense you're struggling."

I finally open my eyes and stare at him. "What changes am I going through? You're the one who practically got married, had a baby, and became internet famous."

River snorts. "You realize your face is all over the internet, too, right? And yeah, all of those things happened to me, but they affect you too. It was just you and me for so long, Lake, and now I have this whole family. I moved out. I can't spend as much time with you, as much as I want to. You've never lived on your own before. Even in college, you had roommates. Of course, it's going to be a struggle. Besides, you always had issues with change."

I finally force myself to look at my brother. I want to be clear before I say the next thing. "I don't want you to think I resent you at all. Because I don't. I'm so happy for you and all of the changes in your life. I'd never try to take those away from you."

River smiles at me, and I can see genuine emotion in his gaze. I know he's not mad at me, and he knows I'm telling the truth. It's something I can just feel. "Lake, believe me, I know. I don't think that at all. And you know I don't mind that you're here, right? Dad told me that you believe I was a little upset that you moved so close, but that's not true at all. I was kind of relieved. It was weird living so far from you after all this time sharing such a small space."

I grin at River, finally feeling some of that tension leave me. "Really? I know I'm probably overstaying my welcome, but the idea of going back to my own place all alone right now is making it hard to breathe. It's not a feeling I'm used to. I don't think I like it."

River laughed. "I'm sure you don't. Lake, you know you're not alone, right? Even if you're by yourself in your house, I'm only a phone call away. So is Dad. Even Essie. She might not be as close physically, but she'd FaceTime you in a second. She always complains we never talk to her."

Yeah, but those people are my family. And then it finally hit me what my problem is. All I have are my siblings and my dad. Any friends I have are through River, so they're not just mine. I don't have a relationship or even any interest in anyone. Not that they ever would, but if my family cut me out of their lives, I'd be alone. Completely, utterly alone. And for the first time that I can remember, that scares me. I want more. I need more.

River squints his eyes at me, and I know he's trying to figure out what I'm thinking. I know a lot of people believe twins have some type of psychic connection, and River and I are no exception. I knew instantly that something was wrong when River went into labor three months ago. Long before I heard from Cooper that my brother had been rushed to the hospital, I had this overwhelming feeling of dread, and I just knew that Riv was in trouble. But, it's more a feeling than anything. We can't actually read each other's thoughts.

I force a smile. This conversation's getting too emotional for me, and I no longer want to have it. "Thanks, River. I know you're always there for me." Before he can say anything else, I add, "How do you think Zoe and Avery would feel if I offered to be their surrogate."

River's eyes nearly bug out of his head as he starts to choke. "Um, what? What kind of topic change is that?"

I just shrug. "It's something I've been doing a lot of research into after I heard about Zoe. Of course, it's all about female surrogates, so I'm not sure how it will transfer with a male, but it's been confirmed that I'm fertile. I don't plan on having a child of my own, so why not take advantage of my fertility and help out someone I care about?"

River still seems shocked. "You haven't mentioned this to them, have you?"

"No. I wasn't sure how well it would be received and thought I should speak to you first."

"Probably a good idea. I think it's amazing that you want to try this, but let me talk to Coop first, and we'll see what he thinks. He knows them the best. And then we'll go from there?"

I smile at River. "I think that's probably a good idea." I sigh. I really need to leave and get back to work. I finally force myself to stand up.

"Where are you going?"

"Home. I have some work to get done, and there's nothing else we can accomplish right now."

River stands up and gives me that exasperated look he has when I don't quite understand something he feels I should. "Lake, no one is kicking you out. Why don't you stay for dinner?"

I wave my hand at him dismissively. I know I'm not being kicked out. River would never do that to me, especially after I lamented my loneliness. He'd make me move it here if I hadn't bought my own house. And as much as that sounds good right now, I know after two nights of my niece waking up at all hours of the night, I'd be ready for my own space again. River's right. This is just an adjustment period, and I'll be back to normal in no time.

"No, it's ok. Spend some time with your family, River. I promise I'm ok."

River watches me for a long time, and I know he's trying to decide if I'm telling the truth. Finally, he nods once and wraps his arms around me in a hug. I try not to stiffen. River's always the more emotional one, and that has been compounded since he got pregnant. I awkwardly wrap my arms around him, causing River to laugh.

"Alright, alright, I get it. I'll let you go. Just please, man, if you start to feel lonely again or just want to get out of your place, give me a call. Or hell, just show up. Please."

I squeeze River's shoulder to let him know I appreciate the gesture. "I will. Thank you."

I finally leave his house and start to walk the couple of blocks to my own place. I try to clear my mind so I can focus on my job when I get back, but I keep jumping back and forth between the conversation I had with River and the possibility of me being a surrogate for Zoe. I try not to get too excited about it. She might say no. Or the doctors may not be ready to do a procedure like that with a male Omega. And even if they are, it doesn't mean it will work out. Yet, despite all of this, I can't help but hope that I will get the chance to make Avery and Zoe parents.

TWO
EVANDER

I'm so completely focused on the manuscript in front of me that I barely hear my phone ring. This thing is a mess. I have no idea how the publishers pushed it through to me. It needs a complete rewrite if anyone wants my opinion, but whatever.

Right before the call goes to voicemail, I manage to drag it out of my pocket and answer.

"Hey, man, what's up?" I ask my best friend Logan as I put my phone on speaker so I can still work and hear whatever reason Logan called me. Thankfully, I'm working from home today, so I don't have to worry about privacy or bothering my coworkers.

"Do you have a second? I got information for you."

I perk up and start to pay better attention. Logan's a detective with the NYPD, and I asked him to do some digging for me.

"Lake Simmons stops at the same coffee shop on 5th and Parker every Tuesday, Thursday, and Saturday at exactly 7:15 am. I can tell you what he drinks, too, but I don't know if you really need to know that."

"Do I want to know how you found this out?"

I completely stop looking at the manuscript I had been

editing and turn all of my attention to Logan. I'll admit it's become a bit of an obsession for me ever since news broke of the Omega gene coming back. I blame Dad, though. If he hadn't been so sure that the one twin who dominated all the news for weeks was the little boy who caused Dad to change his life, this wouldn't be happening.

Dad only met Lake once when he was eight years old. His piece of shit dad tried to sell him to my father for drugs. But, as awful as that moment was, it totally turned my father's life around. Up until that point, I had probably only seen Dad a handful of times. I had been living with my mom and whatever boyfriend she had that month. I won't lie; life was rough, but Dad had his wake-up call that day, and it completely changed both of our lives.

I always knew about Lake, although I'd never met him. Back then, he was still Lake McIntyre. Dad never saw the kid or his dad, Seth McIntyre, again. I didn't even know what he looked like. I know Dad thought about him occasionally and wondered what ever happened to him, but I never tried to find him. I figured it was impossible. Plus, I was a little scared of what I might find. I know Dad would've been devastated if it turned out that Lake was in jail or, even worse, dead, and I didn't want to be the one to do that to the man.

And then one day, I'm having family dinner at Dad's house, and right there on the screen is Lake, his twin brother River, and their asshole sperm donor, the twins completely tearing into their dad. It was fucking glorious.

That was over six months ago, and I couldn't get it out of my damn head. First, I just looked up every article I could find. Apparently, Lake's identical twin, River, was the first known Omega in 150 years. They both became internet famous for a while before the next exciting thing took them out of the spotlight.

It's escalated from just gathering information to give to my dad to needing to meet the man. But I learned quickly that I didn't have the skills to find Lake on my own. He clearly has some protections in place to keep people from finding him. After all the media leaks in the last year, like his apartment address, I can't blame him, and I'm not creepy enough to show up there. That's why I recruited Logan. It has been over a month, though, so I kind of thought Logan forgot, and while I really want to find this guy, I'm not going to stoop to extreme stalker levels by pressuring Logan.

"I won't lie; it took some digging. Your man does his best to stay off the grid. It was sheer luck that I stumbled across the coffee shop, and the barista was all too happy to give me all the information on the poor guy."

I'm a hypocrite because I find myself pissed off on Lake's behalf that this person is just dishing all his info out to some random person, probably because she knows he's connected to the Omega. Yet here I am, taking advantage of my friend's connections to find out personal information on the guy. To be fair, though, I told Logan to only find me a public place where I can "run" into the guy so I can introduce myself. I didn't ask for any personal details. It just seemed wrong.

"Thanks, Logan. I know you hate this kind of stuff, so I appreciate you doing it for me."

"You know I'd do anything for you, man. But, Ev, are you sure you know what you're doing? Something seems off with this Lake guy."

I scrunch my nose in confusion. "What do you mean?"

"I don't know. I can't really place it. His employment history says he's done IT for an accounting firm for the last six years, but even though his picture is up on the website when I reached out to the office, everyone seemed confused when I asked about him. Something's off."

I hadn't realized Logan investigated that much for me, but that's Logan for you. That is a little strange, but also, it can mean anything, and I'm not jumping to conclusions. Maybe the guy is just anti-social and never speaks to his coworkers or works mostly from home. "Did you look into it further?" I ask, a little wary about what the answer will be.

"Nah, fraud's not my department, if that's what this is. I just want you to be careful."

My heart warms at Logan's words. We've been inseparable since we were fifteen and I shared my lunch with him in the ninth grade when I noticed he didn't have anything to eat. We're perfect for each other, except for that little inconvenience that Logan is completely and totally straight. Otherwise, I'm pretty sure we'd be married by now, and I wouldn't be chronically single.

I actually considered, like, seriously, a poly relationship with Logan. I figured we could be together emotionally, not physically, and we could find a girl to complete our trio and meet our sexual needs as well.

But I never quite dared to broach that subject with him. I had no idea how he'd feel about that. And besides, even if he was ok with it, I seriously doubted the NYPD would accept one of their detectives being in a polyamorous relationship. So now, I just sit back and watch him date girl after girl while I have failed relationship after failed relationship with both men and women.

"I appreciate that, bro, but I just wanna talk to the guy, not marry him. I'll be fine."

"Yeah, ok," Logan says in that tone that tells me he doesn't believe me for a second, but I'm telling the truth. I'd meet Lake, tell him who my dad is and how much he changed our lives without ever knowing, and then I'd walk away and never talk to him again.

"Anyway," Logan drawled, changing the subject, "What are you doing tonight? This case I'm working on has been kicking my ass, and my partner is driving me up the fucking wall. I can really use a drink. And since you missed your opportunity to stalk your man this morning, I know you have two days before your next one."

I roll my eyes, even though Logan can't see me, and lean back in my desk chair. I brush my hands through my dark hair, completely messing up the style. Whatever, it rarely stays the way I want without a ton of product anyway.

I look back at my manuscript. I really should try to finish this today. The deadline to get it back to the writer is at the end of the week, and I know it's going to take me forever to write up my editorial notes and try to make any kind of sense of this thing. But . . . it's been a while since I've done anything but work or go have dinner at Dad's, and I'm getting kind of sick of staring at the four white walls of my office.

"Yeah, all right. I'm in. I probably have a few hours of work left on this manuscript, and then I can take a break."

"Sounds good. I'll meet you at your place around eight and we can either Uber or take the bus together?"

Logan never gets in the car with anyone who drinks as much of a sip of alcohol. He lost his mom to a drunk driver when he was little, and his childhood was pretty much shit after that, so he never takes the risk. Besides, we live in the city, and while he has access to cars from the department, neither of us owns our own.

"Yeah, I'll see you then. I'm surprised you're not going out with Charlotte tonight."

I try and probably fail to keep the disdain out of my voice. I really can't stand the latest girl Logan has been seeing.

Logan laughs at me. "Don't sound so excited. I'll actually start to think you like her."

I snort and turn my attention back to my computer. "There's no concern there. I think of all the girls you've dated, she's in the bottom five for me."

Yeah, ok, I'm an asshole, but Logan and I have always been

honest with each other. And it's not like he's going to marry the girl.

"Fuck, man. Your honesty is refreshing. But, don't worry. She broke things off with me the other day. Apparently, my hours are too much for her and she got mad that I couldn't spend more time with her."

Fucking bitch. I do manage to refrain from saying that. "If I thought you were remotely upset, you know I wouldn't be as brutally honest with you. But I know your heart wasn't really in it with her, so I won't pretend."

"Fuck you, man. At least I'm trying. Sometimes I think that you're planning on staying single forever. Are you trying to get into monk school? I'm pretty sure they don't approve of bisexual men with neck tattoos."

I snort out a laugh. "Monk school? I'm 99.9% positive that's not a thing. And no, I'm not trying for that even if it is. I'm just tired of sleeping around and meaningless relationships. We're almost 32 now, Lo, and we need to start thinking about something more long-term.

"Speak for yourself, man." Before he could say anything else, I heard someone speaking to him in the background. "Sorry, Ev, I gotta go. My sergeant wants to meet with me. I'll see you tonight?"

"Yeah, I'll see you then."

I hang up with Logan and try to turn my attention back to my job, but I keep thinking about the information Logan gave me. I give into temptation and google the coffee shop. It's one of those small shops with organically grown coffee beans and baristas with long dreads, but all the reviews rave about their coffee, so maybe there is something there. From everything I saw about Lake, he doesn't seem like the organic coffee type, but what do I know?

I'm so tempted to walk away from this manuscript and go to the coffee shop, as ridiculous as it sounds. I mean, he won't even be there. I know that. And as creepy as I'm being, I'm not to the point where I'm willing to chat up nosy baristas for my information. No, I'll wait the two days and take an early morning trip on Saturday. All this will be is a quick conversation. Hopefully, Lake will be willing to talk, maybe even meet Dad or at least speak to him on the phone, and that's it. I'll put this crazy obsession behind me and move on with my life.

THREE
LAKE

"Simmons, I'm going to need you to be on location for the next two weeks. We have a team going into Columbia that's going to need on-site support. We have a safe house there that has everything you need to get the job done."

I repress my sigh as I listen to my boss. I hate going on location. There's a reason the CIA recruited me as a hacker and technology expert and not a field agent; I'm not cut out for that. I don't want to spend two weeks in some hole-in-the-wall safe house in the middle of Columbia. I want to be home, in my townhouse that's only a five-minute walk away from River, Cooper, and my niece. I want to be a twenty-minute drive from my adopted father, Luke.

And despite what my boss says, I know they won't have everything I need or have it set up the way I prefer. They never do. No matter how many times I give them detailed, step-by-step instructions, they never meet my expectations.

I have no choice, though. I knew what I was getting into when I signed the contract with them. I just didn't expect there to be quite so much travel. Personally, I feel like it's a waste of the taxpayer's money. I guarantee I can complete the job just as well from the comfort of my home office as I could in Columbia.

I know better than to say any of this to my boss. Assistant Director Johnson Wells knows nothing about hacking. In fact, I'm not sure he even knows how to turn on his laptop without assistance, so I know nothing I say will matter.

I begin to mentally rearrange my schedule for the next two weeks. "When am I leaving?"

"We have a flight arranged for the day after tomorrow. Let me know if there's anything specific you need that may not be standard in a safe house, and I'll make sure it's there."

See, I knew it wasn't already equipped for me. There's no point complaining, though. "I'll email your assistant a list, sir."

"Good. You should be getting a report on what's expected of you in the next few hours. I'll let you go. Enjoy your last couple days stateside."

I hold back what I'm sure is an inappropriate comment. I'm getting better at filtering my thoughts, at least around certain people. It's a lost cause with my family, but it has been months since I got in trouble for saying something I shouldn't to my boss. I don't mean to. It's just the filter from my brain to my mouth does not always work properly.

"Thank you, sir."

Wells hangs up without saying goodbye. Rude. I'm over it, though, because now I have to see what I need to get done before I leave the country. I hate last-minute trips. I hate having to cancel plans and rearrange my workload. Oh, I'm supposed to babysit Miri for Riv and Cooper to have a date night. Hopefully, either Dad or one of their friends will be able to do it. The two of them really need a break.

There's also the matter of the dinner River has arranged tomorrow. He texted me earlier in the day letting me know that he broached the subject of possible surrogacy with Cooper, who felt that Avery and Zoe may be open to that idea. At the very least, he felt that I should discuss it with them.

However, is now a good time? I hadn't really considered how much I have to do last-minute travel in not always the most developed or safest areas. Is it even a good idea to be doing that when pregnant? I don't want to discuss the possibility with them and then have to back out because of my job.

I could possibly speak to my boss about it and see if my travel could be limited during that time. I'm not the only hacker the CIA has, after all. And like I have been trying to tell them for years now, I can do basically everything from home. I'm not sure how receptive Wells will be, though. He's known to be a major chauvinist, and he always gives any females on his teams a hard time. I'm not sure if it would be any better for me, despite my gender.

My mind is spinning, and I don't like the feeling. It makes me uneasy to be so unsure. I'm a decisive person by nature. I may do a lot of research before making any major decisions, but once I make one, I stick to it. I'm not one to waver or change my mind or even be unsure about it. However, right now I keep going over my pros and cons list, and now I'm terrified I'm not a good candidate to carry Avery and Zoe's baby. Maybe I should just drop the whole thing.

That thought doesn't sit well with me, though. I realize that I want to be their surrogate. It started out as a practicality thing, but in my mind, it's been growing to be more than that. And yes, I'm aware Avery and Zoe might shut me down. Or they might decide to wait a couple years before making a decision. I shouldn't be so set on this possibility, but I am. It scares me how much I want this already.

Not sure what else to do, I pull out my personal phone and call my dad. Ever since Luke married our mom when River and I were nine years old, he has acted like a dad to the two of us. He's never made either of us feel like an inconvenience or that we weren't as much his children as Essie is. For River and I, who only knew Seth up until that point as a father figure, it was terrifying. It took a solid year for us to stop waiting for the other shoe to drop all of the time. It took almost as long for us to stop flinching any time he reached out to touch one of us or even just stood near us. I know that it hurt Luke, but he never tried to let it show. But by the time he legally adopted us when we were eleven, River and I finally had come to terms with the fact that Luke was a real father, not Seth. He has always been there for us, and I know he can help me work out the best solution without the bias that River will naturally have, since he's also friends with Avery and Zoe.

"Hi, Lake, what a nice surprise. You never call me during the day on a weekday." Dad pauses. "Is everything ok?"

I scrunch my nose, trying to figure out how he jumped from excitement to concern so quickly. "Why wouldn't everything be ok?" I ask, curious.

"Because the only time you ever call before seven on a weekday is if there is a problem or some kind of emergency. Last time was when Riv had to go to the hospital when we found out he was pregnant."

Oh, I guess that makes sense. I shudder thinking about that day. River had been vomiting non-stop for days. Our whole apartment reeked of it. I finally couldn't stand it anymore and called Dad and Essie for backup.

"Oh, that's understandable. There's no emergency. I just have a problem I'd like your advice on."

I could hear Dad walking, and then the sound of a door opening, and then the wind. I wonder if he's at work. He "retired" about a month ago, but he's still at the office of the construction company he owns more than he's not.

"Sure, kiddo. What's going on?"

I roll my eyes at the kiddo, even if I secretly enjoy it. I'm twenty-nine years old, certainly not a kid, but it's kind of nice he still thinks of me that way.

I try to think of the best way to broach the subject, but I decide to just be blunt. That's my default anyway.

"Do you think it's a bad idea for me to get pregnant?"

There's a sputtering sound, followed by choking, and then a very long pause. Apparently, that wasn't the best approach.

"Dad?" I ask, concerned.

There's another cough. "I'm here. Sorry. You just took me by surprise. Lake, don't take this the wrong way, but are you even seeing someone? Or you know—" Dad clears his throat. He's clearly uncomfortable with whatever he's about to say, but I don't know why. "—having sex?" The last words are mumbled so lowly that I barely understand him.

I sit down in my office chair, trying to see how this is relevant to the conversation. "No, I'm not seeing anyone or having sexual relations," I tell him carefully, trying to work out his thought process. I'm legally a genius, but sometimes I have a hard time figuring out what people are thinking or the correct responses. "I'm not against sexual intercourse. I just have not found someone I'd want to take that step with."

While everyone else was experimenting and sleeping around, I was focused on my career. I never understood what the big deal was about sex. I know River loves it, but for me, it just seems to be a means to an end. If I'm not trying to have a child, why have sex?

"Gods. Ok, walk me through this, Lake. What made you start considering having a baby? Is it because of River? You know none of us would ever pressure you to have children. Sure, I'd be thrilled to have more grandbabies, but that's your decision. Just because you're physically capable doesn't mean you need to have them."

"Oh. You think I want a child? I don't mean for myself. I have been considering offering to be a surrogate for Avery and

Zoe since they can't have children. I know it may not even be possible, but if it's something I can offer them, I'd like to do that. I just don't know if maybe I'm the wrong person for this?"

Luke lets out a big breath and seems relieved. "Kiddo, that's such a thoughtful and generous offer. Regardless of if it works out, I'm proud of you for making that decision."

I can't help the small smile and the feeling of satisfaction I have. It still feels good to hear my dad tell me he's proud of me, even after all these years.

"Why do you feel you'd be a bad candidate? You're healthy. You eat well. I know you'll do your research and follow the doctor's orders. If that's something the three of you decide on, I think it's an excellent idea."

"Even if I'm in Columbia?"

"Um, what? Lake, back up a second. I'm missing something. Why the hell are you moving to Columbia?"

I roll my eyes, glad Luke can't see me. "I'm not moving to Columbia. I need to go there for a last-minute work trip, but it got me thinking. Is it responsible to offer my womb to them if I may have to leave at a moment's notice?"

"Oh, that's a very valid concern. Let me ask you, Lake. Have you discussed this with Avery and Zoe at all?"

I twirl around in my desk chair, looking at the white walls. Maybe I should hang some art. River always says my home looks clinical, but it never seemed important before now.

I realize that Luke is waiting for an answer. "Oh, sorry, I started to think about decorating my office. No, I haven't discussed it. River arranged a dinner tomorrow night with them. I was going to bring it up then, but now I'm not sure."

"If it wasn't for the travel aspect and the nature of your job, would you definitely want to do it?"

This is a surprisingly easy question to answer. "Yes."

"Then I think you need to speak with them. I understand your concerns, and they are valid, but this is something that you need to discuss with them, and the three of you need to make that decision together. Also, I know your circumstances are different, but there are laws protecting pregnant women at their employment and that require employers to make accommodations for them."

I don't say anything, but I seriously don't think those laws apply to my job. Dad knows I work for the CIA, but I'm pretty sure he thinks I'm an analyst. He's probably wondering why I need to go anywhere but is reluctant to ask.

"So you don't think it's irresponsible to want this?"

"No at all. But, Lake, what exactly do you want from this? You know that a surrogate parent doesn't have any of the same genetics as the child, right?"

Where is he going with this? "I know. I don't want my own child. I hope I can be part of the child's life as another uncle, but that's it. I'm honestly not sure why I want it so much. It just seems right."

"Then talk to them. Give them the chance to make the decision and go from there. I, for one, think you can make it work and look forward to going through another pregnancy with one of my children. This one would be even more exciting because it wouldn't be such a shock. At least we'll know what to expect."

That's true. River acted like the guinea pig. River and I aren't the only people with the new Omega gene. It seems to still be relatively rare, and so far, he's the only pregnancy, but scientists are doing more research every day, and I know it's not going to be long before male Omegas end up getting pregnant. With River, everything was trial and error, but with each one of us who chooses to have a child, it will be less and less speculative until it gets to the point where there is as much data on this as there is with female pregnancies.

"Ok, thanks, Dad. I will talk to them."

"Good. And son, I know you say you don't want children,

and that's perfectly ok, but I hope it's not because you think you'd be a bad dad. Because you wouldn't be. You'd be an excellent dad, Lake, if you ever decide to become one."

I smile even though Dad can't see me. It's nice to hear, even if it's not true. I know I'd be a terrible dad, but I'm ok with it. I know my limitations. Being a surrogate is enough.

I say goodbye to Dad after a few minutes and begin to pack while I organize my thoughts. The more I think about it, the more it feels right to at least have a discussion with Zoe and Avery. What's the worst that could happen?

FOUR
LOGAN

It's a relief when I can finally get away from the precinct. Most of the time, I love being a detective in the Missing Persons department. It can be awful, but it can also be extremely rewarding as well. But this last week has been kicking my ass. I'm ready to just say fuck it all and just bail, but then I remember how much was sacrificed so I could become a cop, and I force myself to sit the fuck down and do my job. I'd regret walking out within a day, anyway.

But still, I'm ready to go and not see the place for a solid twenty-four hours by the time I leave. I showered and changed at the precinct, so I jump right on the subway and head toward Ev's place, sending him a quick text that I'm on my way.

When I open my texts, I see the last message from the girl I was seeing, Charlotte, and I roll my eyes. No wonder Ev hated her so much. Looking back at her messages, it's clear it would've never worked out between us. Almost all of them are her complaining because I'm either late or had to reschedule or cancel a date. And sure, that's probably awful, and I can completely understand how someone would have issues with that. But at the same time, the girl was absolutely ecstatic when she found out I was a detective and bragged to every fucking body. Clearly, she just wanted the title of cop's girlfriend without having to deal with the fallout.

Just one more reason why dating sucks and hanging out with Ev is just so much easier. Ev's always understanding when we have to change plans last minute, or even when I have to bail once we're out. He's always kind of just gone with the flow, and it's made everything so much better. I know I can always count on him and his dad, Mr. C. I'd have never made it through the academy without them, and Mr. C let me crash with him when I was still a broke recruit and rookie, even when Ev was at college and not living with him.

I delete my message thread from Charlotte as I relax back in the seat, but, of course, I'm still on alert. I might come across as a chill and easygoing guy, but on the inside, I'm always ready. I'm not sure of the last time I truly relaxed.

I finally reach Ev's stop and get out to walk the few blocks to his apartment. I had only been dating Charlotte for a few weeks, so it's not exactly a surprise that I'm not devastated, but I don't feel any kind of sadness. If anything, I'm just relieved. As sad as it may be, I'd much rather spend my night drinking with my best friend than going out with some random girl, even if I get to fuck her at the end of the night. It just hasn't been holding the same appeal lately.

I also want to get a better feel on where Ev's head is at when it comes to this Lake guy. I know the story, anyone who knew Eric Cirillo even a little bit did, but it seems after Lake and his twin brother started to show up in the news and all over the internet, Ev has become somewhat obsessed. I'm not sure if he has some sort of crush on the guy or if it's strictly to do with his dad, but either way, there's something else going on there, and it's my job to look out for Ev and make sure he's safe, regardless of how bizarre the situation may be.

I get to the building and press the button to be buzzed in. It's actually fucking impressive Ev managed to snag such a swanky building, even if his apartment is small as shit. I keep trying to get him to move to Brooklyn with me, but he likes being in the city. I guess it's convenient when I need a place to crash after a night of going out.

Ev buzzes me in, and I make my way to his small one-bedroom apartment.

"Hey, man," he says as soon as he opens the door, and my chest gets fuzzy when his brown eyes light up when he sees me. I'm not exactly sure what that's about, but the last few times I've seen Ev, I've had this weird feeling in my chest whenever he smiles at me.

Ev lets me in, and I immediately go into his small kitchen to raid his fridge. I'm fucking starving. He follows after me with a snort. He's used to my antics by now. At 6'4", I tower over Ev, even if he's not a small man. But I know people always comment on how different we look when we hang, like it really matters that I'm six inches taller and 80 pounds heavier. Or that Ev is covered in tattoos and piercings, and I have one tattoo that's easily covered and that's it. Or that he has darker features than I do. What the fuck does that have to do with our friendship? It never bothered me that I was the big blond guy in the family pictures that towered over both Ev and his pops. The fact that they included me in their family and made me feel welcome was all that ever mattered to me. Mr. C's house was the only place I ever felt safe until I managed to move out and get my own place. But I've had more than one girl complain about how strange our friendship is or how odd we look together. I even had a girl or two complain that we were too close, whatever that meant. Those relationships never lasted long. Bros before hos and all that.

"Sure, Lo, you can have something to eat. Help yourself," Ev tells me sarcastically as he hops on the barstool and watches as I make myself a sandwich. I just grin at him.

"Sorry, I'm starving." He waves me off. Ev might mess with me, but I know it never bothers him how much I eat or that I eat all of his food without asking. He doesn't make a big deal about it, but he keeps food here he'd never eat in a million years, knowing it's my favorite. It's one of the things I love about him. It doesn't matter how many years it's been since I've been hungry or had to worry about my next meal. I'll always be that kid scouring dumpsters, hoping for something halfway decent to eat on a Friday after school, knowing I probably wouldn't have any other food till Monday when I came back. That Ev, and even his dad, always make sure I have enough food, even now, without ever making a big deal about it, means more to me than I'll ever be able to express to either of them.

"So where do you want to go tonight?" Ev asks.

I shrug and shove a chip into my mouth. "I don't care. You feel like dancing, hooking up, or just hanging out?"

Ev scrunches his nose. "Ugh, we are way too old for dancing and hooking up, Lo. We both have big boy jobs we gotta go to. Let's just go somewhere we can chill."

I roll my eyes. "Speak for yourself, man. I'm still young and have no issues going out drinking all night and still getting up bright-eyed and bushy-tailed for work the next day."

Ev chuckled. "Keep telling yourself that."

Eventually, I finish my snack, and we head out to the bar. Once I'm there, I'm glad Ev suggested a more low-key place. I'm more exhausted than I thought I'd be, and I'm happy to not have to battle a crowd or deal with a bunch of girls climbing all over me.

"So what do you think will happen when you meet this Lake guy? You think he'll want to meet Mr. C?"

Ev shrugs, his eyes never leaving the game on the big screen above the bar. "I mean, that's the hope. But I guess we'll see."

I open my mouth to say something when a tall blonde girl slips in between Ev and me where we sit on our barstools. She takes one glance at Ev, her face pulled up into a sneer, and then turns toward me, immediately smiling again and batting her eyelashes. She leans on the bar, attempting to get the attention of the bartender, but she's clearly trying to show her curves off, and I can't help but roll my eyes.

Normally, she's just my type: pretty, tall, curvy, and flirty. It's the perfect combination that screams quick fuck with no attachments, which is perfect since every time I try a relationship, it ends with a passive-aggressive text saying how my hours are just not working for them.

But now, with this girl? Her reaction to Ev just pisses me off, and she's not even remotely attractive to me anymore.

"Excuse me," I say stiffly. "My friend and I were talking." It's not like the bar is crazy crowded or anything; she has plenty of other spaces that she could've slid in to get a drink.

She bats her clearly fake eyelashes at me again. "Well, isn't the view better now?" she asks, her voice unnaturally husky, like she's trying too hard to get in my pants.

From behind the woman, Ev snorts, nearly shooting his beer out of his nose. I know he's not remotely phased by her comment. He knows he's an attractive guy and gets plenty of action when he wants it. Besides, she's definitely not his type. Ev tends to go for the preppy innocent-looking ones.

I shrug casually. "Not really." This time Ev really does shoot beer out of his nose, the drink spilling all over the bar top.

"Oh my gods!" the woman shrieks. It's way too overdramatic, honestly. I mean, none of the beer even fucking hit her. But whatever. It may not have been intentional, but Ev's accident does the job, and she backs away from us totally disgusted, without her drink and a potential hookup. For now. By the way at least five different guys' heads turn as she sways away from us, I'm sure she'll find someone else to satisfy her needs.

As soon as she's gone, I look at Ev, and we both burst out

laughing. Gods, he has a nice laugh. How have I not noticed that before?

"Holy fuck," Ev manages to choke out between sobbing laughter. "Could she have been more fucking obvious?"

I'm wiping tears as Ev is helping the bartender wipe the spill. He's clearly not as amused as we are.

Ev's body is still shaking with laughter, and he sucks his lip ring in between his teeth as he wipes up his drink. For some fucking reason that I can't figure out, I'm sitting here staring at his lips, imagining what they taste like. What the fuck? I don't even like dudes. And Ev is my best friend, not a fucking hookup.

But still, as the night wears on, I don't even pay attention to another girl in the place. My focus is on Ev, and I never consider leaving with anyone else besides him, even if it's to just crash on his couch.

FIVE
LAKE

I'm glad that my last-minute travel plans didn't affect the dinner River planned, at least. I'd rather not have the conversation I need to have with Avery and Zoe hanging over my head while I'm at the safe house working. This way, regardless of their answer, they will know where I stand and what their options are.

At six o'clock on the nose, I'm using my key to let myself into River and Cooper's home. I know I should probably knock, but it always seems so strange to me to knock on my brother's door like I'm a regular guest. And I do have a key for a reason.

"Hello?" I call out as I walk into their entryway and close the door behind me.

"In the kitchen," I hear Cooper's deep baritone call out to me.

Carrying the tray of cookies I picked up at the bakery earlier that day, I make my way into the kitchen. Cooper is standing at the island, stirring something in a bowl. He's holding Miri with one arm as she giggles happily, her big brown eyes wide, clearly fascinated as she watches her dad cook. I also happen to notice she's only wearing a diaper, which is unusual. Riv and Cooper typically keep her dressed.

"Hi, Cooper," I say cautiously as I make my way into the kitchen. It smells delicious. There's platters of food everywhere. Sauce must be cooking in one of those pots on the stove, because the smell of garlic and basil permeates the air. Cooper seems relaxed even though they are clearly running behind. I also happen to notice River is nowhere in sight.

Cooper glances up at me and smiles distractedly. "Hey, man. Do you mind taking the baby for me? Riv's up in the shower. This little one decided to projectile vomit all over him a few minutes ago."

I wrinkle my nose in disgust as I put my tray of cookies on the counter. "She's cleaned up, right?" I love my niece, but I do not love vomit, especially on me.

Cooper laughs. "Yeah, she's cleaned up. River's gonna bring down a new outfit for her when he comes down. But she's puke free, I promise."

I'm still a little hesitant as I take her. I *really* don't like vomit. But she smells clean, and I don't notice anything lingering, so I grab her from her dad.

"Hey, sweetie." I smile down at my niece. It took me a while to get comfortable holding Miri. I was terrified I'd hurt her somehow, but now we have an understanding. I grab a stuffed lion that's lying on the counter and go sit on one of the bar stools with Miri in my lap. I hand her the lion stuffie, which she promptly shoves in her mouth.

Once he has both his hands free, Cooper moves efficiently through the kitchen, getting the meal done. I don't bother to ask him if he needs help. I know I'll only hinder him, and holding the baby is probably the best thing I can do.

With River upstairs, and Avery and Zoe not due for another half an hour, it's the perfect opportunity to speak to Cooper about his thoughts on this situation. I know he's comfortable with it, but I'm curious how he thinks the couple will react.

Before I can ask, though, River comes huffing down the stairs. "Babe, have you seen my black jeans?" he calls from the other room.

"Which ones?" Cooper asks.

"The ones with the holes in them."

River peeks his head into the kitchen. He's only wearing boxer briefs. I've seen my brother in less before, so I don't bother looking away.

"Hey, Lake," River says absentmindedly as he smiles at his daughter before returning his attention to Cooper.

"They should be in the closet. I haven't seen you wear them in a while."

"Ugh," River groans dramatically, sounding more like a teenage girl than a grown man. "I didn't see them in there. I guess I'll wear something else." River stomps away, but Cooper is clearly distracted by trying to finish everything up, and Miri is getting fussy, so I don't have a chance to ask him about Zoe and Avery.

"The rest of her bottle is over by the fridge." Cooper jerks his head in the direction as he stirs something in the pot. "Do you mind feeding it to her?"

"Sure." I grab the bottle and settle Miri into the crook of my elbow so I can feed her her formula. She drinks hungrily as her eyes slowly start to close.

Eventually, River comes back downstairs. He must have found his jeans, or ones very similar, because he's wearing tight black ones with some strategically-placed holes on his thighs and knees. I'll never understand pants like that. Why does it cost more to have holes in your pants? I could do that myself for free. I'll stick to my khakis and button-up shirts, thank you.

I dress Miri in the little romper that River thrusts at me so that he can help Cooper finish up cooking and bring everything to the table. They're just finishing up, and I'm placing Miri in her Pack n' Play they have set up in the dining room, when the doorbell rings.

Suddenly, I'm extremely anxious, which is another feeling I'm not used to having. All these new feelings and emotions are unsettling, but I have no idea what to do with them. Even as I tell my brother I'll get the door, I'm still thinking about it. I wonder if it has to do with the Omega gene. I'm not sure how, though. I must have always had it, so why would I start changing now? Sure, River, and even Cooper, noticed some changes, but that makes sense. They created life, and they are mates, if that theory is to be believed. It's understandable that some dormant biological quirks would begin to show. But I'm not pregnant or mated. Nothing should have changed. Still, I can't deny that I have *felt* differences since being informed of the Omega gene. I just need to learn if there's a correlation.

Zoe and Avery are standing at the door as I open it. Zoe is wearing one of her colorful sundresses that she's famous for. This one is like a pink and blue tie-dye and comes to mid-thigh. She's wearing a blue cardigan over it that matches the blue in the dress. Her usually wild hair is pulled back in multiple braids today. She smiles wildly at me and looks much more relaxed than last time I saw her. Maybe I shouldn't bring up the surrogacy. I don't want to upset her again.

"Hey, guys, come on in."

"Hi, Lake," Zoe says as she leans in and kisses me on the cheek. I fight the urge to back away. Zoe is always affectionate, and typically, I don't mind when it comes to her. Actually, it feels nice. I just wasn't expecting it, and my mind is still on the conversation to come.

I shake Avery's hand. He's holding a covered tray of . . . something. "Zo made fresh beer bread and spinach dip."

I take it from him with a smile, trying to hide my awkwardness. Like my brother, he's wearing black jeans, but his don't have holes in them. He's wearing a dark-blue Henley that matches the color of his eyes.

"Hi, guys!" Cooper calls with a smile from the hallway. "Perfect timing, dinner's ready."

Zoe bounds into the room, more energetic than I have seen her in a while. She wraps her arms around Cooper and kisses his cheek as well. Cooper laughs, and even I understand why River was so attracted to him, even before he knew they were destined for each other. He's so comfortable in his skin, and his deep voice definitely isn't hurting anything.

"Hey, Zo. You seem to be in a good mood today."

"I am! I just got a part in the new revival of *A Chorus Line*!"

River bounds into the room so fast my head spins and wraps Zoe in a hug, spinning her in a circle. "Oh my gods, Zo! That's fantastic!"

"I know! I go in next week to start learning the choreography, and we're supposed to open up early in the new year. I'm just a part of the chorus, but I'm the understudy for the character of Sheila Bryant!"

There's a lot of cheering and celebrating for a while, and I carefully stay out of it. I know River notices, but he also knows I'm uncomfortable with too much touch and social interaction, so thankfully he doesn't say a word. Finally, everyone settles down and starts to head into the dining room. Before I enter, though, Cooper grabs my shoulder to hold me back. He leans in and speaks quietly so we're not overheard. "Go ahead and still talk to them. She may tell you she needs to hold off, or no altogether, but I think they'd appreciate having the option."

I nod at my sort of brother-in-law, grateful he took the time to tell me this. I hadn't been sure, again, if I should just leave it alone, but I trust his opinion on the subject.

It takes a while, but finally we all settle into our seats and begin eating. The food is delicious. I'm not sure how much of it River cooked, but I'm surprised at both of them. River's always been a better cook than me, but I've never seen him make homemade raviolis and meatballs, along with an assortment of appetizers. The meal is paired with red wine, but I refrain. I barely drink, and I certainly wouldn't when I have to be up so early the next morning to take an international flight. I need my head clear. I won't even have time to stop for the latte I always get on the days I go into the office since I have to be at the airport at five am. I definitely don't want to be groggy.

I'm not sure when to bring up the subject. In the first twenty minutes or so, the conversation is strictly dance and Broadway, which are two subjects I know nothing about. I make a mental note to look up *A Chorus Line* later so I can at least be somewhat knowledgeable. Finally, there's a lull in the conversation. River kicks my leg under the table and gives me a meaningful look which clearly means *now's your chance.*

I take a minute to gather my thoughts and try to decide the best way to approach this. Then I decide to just go for it and approach it as myself. They know me well enough by now to understand my quirks.

I look at Zoe, who smiles at me behind her wine glass, her brown eyes sparkling. When she realizes I'm gearing up to speak, she scrunches her nose and looks at me with curiosity.

"What is it, sweetie?" she asks me.

I take a deep breath. "I'd like to be your surrogate. That is, if you do decide you want a child and you want me to be that person."

Avery starts choking on a meatball. Cooper bangs on his back, trying to hide his amusement. Zoe just stares at me, her eyes wide, her mouth gaping.

Surprisingly, despite nearly dying, Avery recovers first. "Do you mind running that by us again?" he asks, his voice a little shaky.

I look over at River, who looks half amused and half

exasperated, but he does nod encouragingly. Apparently, I still need to work on my delivery.

"Sorry. This might not be the best timing, but I'm going away for two weeks, so I wanted to give the two of you a chance to think about it. I know you two have been struggling with infertility. I recently found out that I am, in fact, fertile. I have been doing a lot of research, and while I'm clearly not a woman that all of the research is geared toward, I do feel like it is possible for me to carry your child if you are interested, and I am happy to do so. I even spoke to the scientists at the Omega project, and they believe it's possible."

Both of them still seem so shocked, so I continue speaking, not entirely sure if I'm making this worse or better for them. "I understand you need time to discuss it. And I just want to let you know the offer does not expire. You just got that amazing job, so I understand you may want to wait. That's completely acceptable. If at any time you decide you would like me to be a surrogate, I am happy to do so."

Avery is just blinking at me like I'm from an alien planet. Zoe has tears in her eyes, but I'm not sure if they are happy or sad. Since she still hasn't said a thing, I ask, "Are those good tears?"

Zoe laughs while River snorts. "Yeah, sweetie, they're good tears. I'm just so overwhelmed. That's the sweetest thing anyone has ever done for me."

Avery seems to finally shake off the shock and drags Zoe's chair closer so he can wrap her in his arms. They don't look like they'd be a couple. Zoe is always so bright and shines, even when she's sad. And it's not just her bright dresses that light up a room. Avery is a lot more reserved. Everything about him is a lot more unassuming. But, it clearly works for them. It's obvious how much they love and support each other, even to me.

"Seriously, Lake, that's super generous of you. You do

understand we'll need to discuss it, just the two of us, right? I don't think we can give you an answer today."

I wave off his concern. I figured that. "I know. Which is why I wanted to tell you now. Like I said, I'm going to be out of the country for a few weeks." I pause. "Which, if you decide to do this, we will have to discuss my job and its impact. But it's irrelevant if you decide against it completely."

With her eyes still shining brightly with tears, Zoe unwraps herself from her boyfriend's hold and circles the table to hug me. I find myself hugging her back immediately. She's just infectious like that.

"Lake, seriously, thank you. You have no idea what this means to me, to us. Just having this option is a weight off my shoulders. We never would have been able to afford surrogacy the traditional route, and adoption is extremely expensive. I'm not sure if my non-traditional incomes would impact the chance of getting accepted. This gives us the chance to have a baby, and I'm so, so grateful."

I smile into Zoe's hair and hug her tighter. There's a warmth growing inside me that I enjoy. I'm glad I can give them this option, even if they choose not to take it.

SIX
EVANDER

It is now 7:45 am on Saturday morning and there is still no sign of Lake Simmons. Logan is adamant the barista told him 7:15 without fail. Yet, he's not here. I'm not a morning person. I've never been one, and the weekend is the only time I can ever indulge in sleeping in. I sacrificed one of my two days I can ever sleep past 7 am to meet this guy, and he's not even here.

I know I'm being irrationally angry. Lake doesn't even know who I am, let alone that I planned on ambushing him while he's getting his morning coffee. But at this moment, I want to be irrational. I'm fucking tired, and I refuse to buy a $6 coffee on principal, so I'm starting to get a headache behind my eyes.

I decide I'm going to stay till 8 and then bail. Maybe I'll try again on Tuesday. Or maybe I should take this as a sign that I'm a fucking ridiculous creeper and leave the poor guy alone, though I know that's unlikely. Besides my own obsession, that I can't even understand, I think about how excited Dad was when I told him I'm going to reach out to Lake. I know he's desperate to at least check in and see how he's doing. Dad was beyond relieved when we saw that stream and he learned that their mother finally managed to get away from Seth, but I know he needs more closure than that.

My phone vibrates, and I scowl when I see it's Logan. *Did you talk to him?*

I don't feel like texting because I'm pissed and grouchy and fully intend to take it out on Logan, even if it's not his fault, so I call him.

He answers on the second ring. "What happened?" I can hear a lot of voices around him, and I realize he's probably at work. I suddenly feel like an asshole. I don't need to bother Logan with my problem that shouldn't even be an issue.

"He never came. Sorry, I shouldn't have called without making sure it's ok. I'm a little irritable."

Logan barks out a laugh. "I'm guessing you refused to buy one of the insanely overpriced coffees?"

How does Logan know me this well? "You guessed right."

"Are you sure you didn't just miss him? The barista was adamant he comes in every single Saturday."

I roll my eyes even though he can't see me. "Yes, *Logan*, I'm positive he didn't come in. No one who even vaguely fits his description has been in this coffee shop."

"Fuck, man, I'm sorry. Why don't you ask the barista? She seemed to know everyone's story."

"And tell her what? I used my best friend's resources as a cop to stalk this guy, and I know he comes here on Saturdays but he hasn't shown up. Do you know why?"

Logan sighed. "No, Ev, that's not what I mean, asshole. Why don't you just tell her you're supposed to meet him here and wanted to make sure you hadn't accidentally missed him."

I grumble even if it's not a bad idea. I really don't do well without coffee. I probably should've known I couldn't bring myself to buy a cup at a shop like this. I'm actually surprised that Lake does. Not that I know the guy, but I know we had a similar upbringing, at least in our younger years. Before Dad cleaned up his act and got custody of me, there were many nights I went to bed hungry. And even when I did have food, a lot of the time it was boxed mac and cheese and cereal. Even after Dad came and got me, it took a few years before he worked himself up the ladder enough at the auto shop, which he eventually bought, for us to have enough money to be comfortable.

That would always stick with me. Even though I made decent money now, and both Dad and I were financially stable, I'll always remember what it was like back then, and it stops me every time I consider making an expensive purchase. The only things I ever spend money on that are strictly for myself and not practical are my tattoos and piercings.

I turn back to the conversation since poor Logan is clearly waiting for me to say something. "Yeah, maybe I'll do that. I'm gonna give him till eight, then I'll ask her. If she knows nothing, I'm gonna bounce. This was probably a bad idea anyway."

"Nah. I can understand why you wanna talk to the guy. If it doesn't work out, you can always try something else. He doesn't have social media, but his twin does. You can reach out to him that way."

I think about it, but I don't know. It seems inauthentic, especially since all of this Omega stuff came out. I'm sure the poor guy is getting bombarded in his DMs. If he even sees mine, I doubt he'd take it seriously.

"Alright, I'm gonna let you go, Lo. I'll give you a text and let you know how it goes."

"You do that. Later, man."

"Bye."

I hang up and glance at the time again. 7:57. Close enough. There seems to be a lull in the crowd, so it's the perfect time to chat up the barista. In fact, she's eyeing me already. I know she sees the gauges in my ears, my nose and lip ring, and my tattoos and thinks we'd be compatible. But strangely enough, guys or girls who have similar tastes to me don't usually hit my buttons.

I don't know why exactly, but there's something about a straight-laced person being attracted to or turned on by me that really does something for me. Doesn't mean I won't use her obvious interest for my own gains right now. I know, I can be an asshole. Sue me.

The barista smiles as I walk up to the counter, and I fix her with my best charming smile. "Hi." She beams at me, and ok, she's pretty cute. She's in her mid twenties, probably, with dreaded hair pulled back into a ponytail, bright blue eyes, a septum piercing, and a sleeve of tattoos on both arms. Her smile, though, is pretty gorgeous. "What can I get for you?"

I smile back at her, leaning on the counter so that my biceps are on display. I know I have nice arms. "Sorry to bother you, but I have a quick question."

Her smile dims a bit, but she nods politely. "Of course."

"I'm supposed to meet a guy here." I think quickly on my feet when her smile dims even more. "We went to school together as kids and were close but drifted as we got older. Just connected again on Facebook, you know? Turns out we live in the same area and both could use some more friends." I emphasize the word friends. "We were supposed to meet up. Apparently, he comes here all the time. But he was supposed to meet me at 7:15 and he's still not here or answering his phone. I just wanted to make sure I didn't miss him."

Her smile returns, though I can see her still trying to asses whether I'm gay or straight. "Oh sure, I know most of our regulars pretty well. Who are you looking for?"

I shrug, trying to stay casual. "His name is Lake. He's got reddish hair, usually some facial hair, and is a little under 6 ft tall, I think."

The barista's eyes widen. "Oh Lake! He's a sweetheart. Yeah, he's usually here by now. 7:15 on the dot. He's never late. And I can only think of a handful of times when he didn't come in."

I make sure not to sound too interested. "Oh, when was that?"

"Well, when his niece was born." She rolls her eyes. "I'm sure you've seen all of that drama on the news, but he missed a few days for that. We were all dying for the gossip too. Not that Lake is one for gossip, but he did show us a few pictures of the baby. She's adorable. She has red hair just like they do."

I stop the eye roll just in time. I'm sure the kid is adorable, but I don't really care right now. "I'm sure she is. What about the other times?"

"Hmm. I guess he has last-minute business trips sometimes."

"Business trips?" I ask, genuinely curious.

"Yeah. He didn't tell you what he does for a living?"

"Not really, just said he's in technology."

She nods like this makes sense. "Yeah, that's what he tells us too. There's been a few times where he just doesn't show up for a few weeks, and when he gets back, he just says he had an unscheduled business trip. We always try to get more information, but Lake really isn't much of a talker."

I get more and more fascinated by this man the more I learn about him. I think about what Logan says, how he feels he might have some secrets under the surface, and I'm starting to agree. It's hard to see what last-minute business trips that last a couple weeks a guy in IT for an accounting firm would have. But then again, I know absolutely nothing about IT or accounting, so maybe I'm wrong.

I smile at the barista. "Oh well, maybe something came up. I wish he'd texted me though."

She shrugs. "Yeah, that sucks. Lake's always been a little off, though, when he comes to social interactions, so I wouldn't worry about it too much. He'll be back around eventually."

I smile like this is a relief while my mind is whirling. I know the logical path. Give up. Maybe contact the brother on social media and see what happens. Stop being a fucking stalker. Am I going to do it, though? Honestly, I'm not sure.

"Thank you. I appreciate your help." I start to walk away but the barista speaks up.

"Wait!" I turn around patiently. She was very helpful after all.

"Since you got stood up, maybe you'd like to stick around a bit? I go on my break in ten. I can treat you to a coffee? I know the price is insane, but they are pretty good."

My instinct is to make an excuse and bail. I don't want coffee with this girl, but I stop myself. It's been way too long since I've been on anything even resembling a date. She seems sweet, and she is cute, even if she isn't my normal type. There's no reason not to stick around. Plus, coffee.

"Sure, that sounds great. My name is Evander, but most people call me Ev."

The girl smiles. "Hi, Ev, I'm Lucy." She holds out her hand, and I chuckle as I shake it. It's not exactly how I planned my morning to go, but hell, it sure could have been worse. I make the decision to give up on this whole crazy thing with Lake Simmons. We both have our own lives, and I don't need to complicate them by trying to blend them together. I'll have coffee with Lucy, and if things go well, maybe it'll turn into more. Anything further than that, well, I guess I'll have to see what happens.

SEVEN
LOGAN

"That's it, babe, so good," I say distractedly to Kayla, who currently has her lips wrapped around my cock. We're lying in my bed, and typically a blowjob from Kayla is exactly what I need when I'm pent up like this, but I can't stay in the moment.

All I can think about is Ev, and more so the guy Lake who keeps eluding him. When Ev first asked me to look into the guy, I did it strictly as a favor for Ev and his pops, since I owe them everything. But the longer this goes on, the more I have to say, I'm intrigued. Ev is getting desperate, and though he tries to play it off like it's not a big deal, I know he's bummed he still hasn't seen Lake after two weeks of trying.

I promised myself I wouldn't look into the guy any further. It's not my fucking business. But Ev can't let the dude go, which is so fucking strange. It's like ever since he saw him on TV, my best friend's been brainwashed or something and all he cares about is finding Lake. And I might think it's stupid and a waste of time, but Ev is my best friend and I love him. So, if it's important to him, it's important to me too.

And I won't lie, the longer it goes on, the more I'm intrigued by the whole thing. It's the mystery of it, I think. Or at least that's a large part of it. I am a detective after all. But I don't know. Whatever invisible hold this guy has on Ev seems to have extended to me, and I'm not sure what to do about it.

Kayla pulls off my cock, and I realize, with some guilt, I completely forgot she was here. She frowns, but it's more out of concern than annoyance. "Logan, are you ok? You're completely zoned out."

I feel my cheeks redden as I smile sheepishly at her. "I'm sorry, Kay. I'm just a little distracted. I didn't mean to be a total asshole."

I know Kayla's not upset. She pulls away completely and sits next to me on my bed, her legs criss-crossed. Kay and I actually met in the academy and hit it off. It all started when she invited me over to dinner and her Korean mother made us the most delicious traditional dishes I ever had. Honestly, I can probably become friends with anyone if they feed me good food, but we discovered we genuinely enjoyed each other's company as well. We've never been more than friends and fuck buddies though. When both of us are single and have an itch to scratch, we're that for each other, but neither of us have any interest in taking it further.

Kayla takes my hand and pins me with one of her looks. It's the one that has you instantly spilling your guts to her, even if you didn't want to. Her pin-straight black hair is pulled back into a ponytail but is falling down her front, covering one of her small breasts. Kayla has a thin build, narrow, and compact, but a lot of muscle is hidden in her small frame. It doesn't matter that she is only 5'3", she could've kicked all of our asses in the academy. She had my 6'4" ass on my back more times than I could count.

Unfortunately, a career with the police department didn't work out for Kayla, and now she's a private investigator. In fact, it was Kayla who got most of the information on Lake that Ev asked for. I'm not sure why I didn't just tell him that. He knows and likes Kayla, but I kinda want him thinking I handled it completely on my own for him. I know, I'm a fucking jackass, but I just wanted to do something for him for a change instead of the other way around.

"Do you want to talk about it?" Kayla asks. Since it's clear sex isn't happening, she leans off the side of the bed, grabs my T-shirt, and puts it on. It's big enough to be a dress on her and covers everything. Taking the hint, I get up and put my underwear back on before climbing back on the bed.

I cringe, not wanting to tell Kayla what I was thinking about while she sucked my dick, but I know she won't leave it alone. "I was thinking about Ev and that guy Lake."

At first, Kayla scrunches her face in confusion, but I see when she realizes what I'm talking about. "Oh, the brother of the Omega you had me look up?"

"Yeah, Ev's still trying to see him, and the whole thing is messing with me for some reason. I don't really get it."

Kayla bites her bottom lip as she tries to think of what to say next. "Babe," she says carefully, and I know I won't like whatever she's about to tell me because she called me babe, which she very rarely does. "Do you think maybe you're jealous?"

The thought is so absurd that I laugh. Like, actually fucking laugh out loud. Jealous? Of what? I've never even met the guy. Hell, Ev hasn't either. He's read a couple of online articles and a sad story about his childhood that he told at that protest that ended up going viral—that's it. And even if Lake becomes more than that, why the fuck would I be jealous? Ev is my best friend, not my fucking boyfriend.

Kayla narrows her eyes at me, clearly irritated by my outburst. "I don't see what's so damn funny," she says haughtily, her nose pointed in the air like a fucking nineteenth-centruy noblewoman.

"I'm sorry, Kay, I'm not laughing at you. Just, what could I possibly be jealous of?"

Apparently, this doesn't soothe her annoyance at me, because Kay grabs a pillow and smacks me upside the head with it.

"Hey!" I scream, covering my face for protection as she hits me again. I don't care how much bigger I am than the woman, she's fucking scary.

"Ugh, I just can't understand how men can be so dense."

Once I'm no longer under attack, I pull myself up so I'm leaning on my elbow. "Babe, I have no idea what you're talking about."

She throws her hands in frustration. "Yeah, that's exactly what I'm talking about. Logan, you're in love with Evander. Seeing his attention so focused on someone else, even if it's someone he's never met, is affecting you. You're used to being the most important thing in his life, and somehow, this stranger is starting to upstage you. Of course you're going to be distracted."

I blink at Kayla, trying to process everything she just said. Leave it to her to just drop bomb after bomb with no fucking warning.

I couldn't even make sense of her words. I'm in love with Ev? Like, in love? He's my best friend, and honestly more than that, almost like a brother. Of course I love him. But I'm not *in* love. The woman is fucking insane. First off, I'm straight. I don't like dick; I've never liked dick. I've gone to gay bars with Ev before, and even watched a gay porn or two, and it never ever did anything for me. And thinking of Ev like that. Just, no. Right?

I mean, yeah, he's a good-looking guy. I'm not blind. And he's so fucking smart. And sure, there's times I crash at his place and I like to watch him curl up in his oversized chair and read as I play video games. But that's just because he always looks so at peace with a book, and I like seeing him happy. And the jealousy part? That's insane. Ev has had both girlfriends and boyfriends before. Hell, I've fucking wingmanned for him at bars, and I've never been jealous. Why would this guy he never met, a guy we have no idea if he's gay, straight, in a relationship, whatever, make me jealous?

But Kayla's just sitting there calm as fuck, the little shit, waiting for me to come to terms with her words. Which I won't. Because she's wrong and the whole thing is dumb. Maybe I am distracted by the whole situation, but none of those are the reasons why.

"You're out of your mind," I tell her.

Kayla just shrugs, unbothered. "Maybe. But I know what I see. Maybe one day the two of you will see it too."

She's just pissing me off and confusing me now. I have the sudden urge to kick her out of my apartment and go to Ev's place, which would only confirm her stupid ass opinion, so I will not do that. So instead, like a little kid, I just pout at her. "Can we please just drop it?"

She shrugs. "Sure." Kayla looks down at me and my now obviously soft cock. Fuck. I didn't even get an orgasm out of this shit night, and I'm not in the mood anymore.

"Wanna watch a movie?" she asks me.

Needing the distraction, and happy to move off the topic of Ev and me, I hand her the remote off my nightstand. "Sure, you pick."

I scoot up the bed and arrange the pillows so that we can be propped up a bit. My apartment is pretty basic. I never really understood spending money on things like decorations or pictures. I need a bed, a couch, a couple TVs, a coffee table to eat on, and I'm good. Ev forced me to get a small dinette table as well because, and I quote, "I can't live like a barbarian." But I only use it the rare times Ev or Mr. C come over.

But pillows, for some fucking reason, are my weakness. I have way too many on my bed, and the fancy shit too, the orthopedic ones that are always cool and take forever to lose shape. I also keep super comfortable throw pillows on the couch for anyone who crashes or if I fall asleep there watching TV. Maybe it comes from the fact that I didn't have one for like eight years of my childhood, but that's my one splurge.

I rearrange them so we're basically in our own little movie pit. Once I'm settled, I open my arm so that Kayla can snuggle in with me. We might not be more than friends and fuck buddies, but I fucking love to cuddle. She's so small and compact, she fits perfectly into my massive side.

Kayla flips around the channels for a while before she finds something that works and puts the remote to the side. We lie there, cuddled up to each other, laughing and making fun of the movie, and little bit of intimacy is doing someting that sex wasn't able to do. It takes my mind off of Ev. At least for a while.

EIGHT
LAKE

I lean my head against the headrest and my eyes start closing on their own volition. Thank gods my Uber driver isn't a talker. He has a low-key alternative playlist playing softly through speakers, and honestly, it's perfect right now. It's exactly the type of music I play when I'm having issues sleeping. Of course, I don't actually want to go to sleep right now. Falling asleep in a stranger's car is not acceptable.

I was supposed to be in Columbia for two weeks. It's been nearly four. The whole operation was a disaster, and of course, the organization didn't have half of the things I needed. Due to the circumstances and location, I only had minimal communication with my family back home. When I realized I'd be longer than two weeks, I managed to send out one text to River, letting him know I was safe but temporarily delayed and to let Dad know. I told him I'd try to keep him updated as best I could. I received a return text telling me to be careful and that they all loved me, and that was it.

It's shocking how much I missed them. There's no doubt now that I'm going through some kind of change, though I still have no idea why. I can't bring myself to go back to my empty home now, even if it's the most logical thing. After all, it's nearly 11 at night, and no one knows I'm back. I know Dad is definitely asleep, and no doubt River and Cooper are as well.

It doesn't stop me from giving my Uber driver River's address instead of mine. If everyone is asleep, I'll just peek in on them, see my niece, and then leave.

As we near the townhouses, I pull out my cell phone. It's still off, but it's time to face the music and see what I missed in the last few weeks. It'll at least keep me from falling asleep for the last ten minutes of the drive.

Once my phone is booted on and off airplane mode, I'm bombarded with missed calls, unread emails, and text messages. Most of the calls are spam, though there is a phone call from Albert Rooke, the lead doctor with the Omega Project. They are the ones handling most of the testing and researching regarding the gene. I called them before my trip to hear their thoughts on a possible surrogacy. It seems that Dr. Rooke has some information he wants to share with me. I quickly put an alarm in my calendar to call him tomorrow when it isn't so late.

I also have a message from Zoe asking if the three of us can meet up when I'm home. It's 11 pm on a Friday, so I know Zoe is up since she bartends. I quickly send her a text letting her know I'm back and to see if they want to meet up for coffee tomorrow. I get a thumbs up emoji back and *11am good?*

I shudder at the thought of getting such a late start to the day, but I realize most people don't want to be up at 7 on a Saturday. Since I'm just returning, I get tomorrow off, so it's not like I have to go into the office. I reluctantly agree to the time. At least I'll be able to get my mocha latte from Dream Beans Cafe tomorrow. I missed my treat I typically indulge in three times a week while away. I know the whole thing is absurd. The place is such a cliché hipster coffee shop with its overpriced drinks, decor, and even the baristas, but I love it. The place is my guilty pleasure.

Finally, my driver turns into my neighborhood. At the last minute, I change the address and tell the driver to go to my house instead. He doesn't bat an eye. I tell myself it makes more sense. I know that River checked on things a few times and hopefully watered my plants, but I should unpack, take a shower in my own bathroom, sleep in my own bed, and make sure everything is good with my own eyes. Since I'm not meeting Avery and Zoe until 11, I have plenty of time to stop by my brother's for breakfast to see him and my niece. I quickly put in another reminder to call Dad first thing, to let him know I made it home safely. He's always up early, even on the weekends.

The Uber driver pulls up in front of my unit. I paid and tipped through the app, so I thank him for being the perfect driver and automatically give him a five-star rating. I turn off the alarm at the keypad and enter my home. Of course, it looks exactly like it did when I was here last. River knows how particular I am. And while he's not especially neat or organized, he knows to keep my space the way I prefer it. After a quick glance to make sure everything looks good on the first floor, I make my way upstairs, dragging my suitcase with me. My office is still locked, which is expected.

Like the rest of the house, my room looks untouched. I know River opened my windows daily to air it out, which I appreciate so the house doesn't have the closed-off smell. I leave my suitcase by the door and immediately start stripping. By the time I have my travel clothes off and in my hamper, the exhaustion is finally starting to hit me, and I'm happy I decided to go home instead of going to my brother's. I eye my suitcase but decide to take a quick shower before even considering tackling that. Maybe it could wait till morning? Though I know in reality I'll never be able to sleep knowing I still have tasks to complete.

I keep my shower short, just long enough to get the sweat and stink of a long day of travel off. As I'm washing my cock and balls, I consider how long it's been since I last masturbated. Did I do it once during my trip? I can't remember, which disturbs me. It's not something I ever get much pleasure from, more a necessary task, like cutting my fingernails or brushing my teeth, but still, I usually try to orgasm at least once a week.

I look down at my limp cock as the water rushes down around me and decide I can wait one more day. If I take any longer in here, I'll be at risk of falling asleep in the shower. I take one last glance at my neglected dick before rinsing and shutting off the water.

Once I'm dressed in a pair of boxer briefs, sweats that River left before he moved out that somehow became mine, and an old MIT T-shirt, I quickly finish the rest of my chores before I crash. I don't even start a load of laundry, just throw all my dirty clothes into the washing machine to start tomorrow. It makes me a little shaky. I know I'm going to toss and turn all night thinking about the dirty clothes sitting in the washing machine, but I'm afraid I'll fall asleep before I can get them in the dryer. There is nothing worse than wet clothes sitting in the washing machine all night. That musky, moldy smell, ugh. It gives me chills just thinking about it.

I reluctantly turn away from my laundry room, go back to the bathroom to brush my teeth, and then head back to my room. After setting an alarm for the morning, I immediately climb into bed, and it's only seconds before my eyes begin to close. As much as I miss my family, sleeping in my own bed is really nice . . .

The next morning, I'm up early and feeling refreshed despite the fact that I didn't get a lot of sleep. I have plenty of time to do my laundry, run a couple miles on the treadmill, masturbate, and still be at River's in time for breakfast. I didn't inform him that I'm home yet, wanting it to be a surprise. Hopefully Miri slept well enough last night. I do not want to deal with a cranky River.

Once I start the washing machine, I climb down to the bottom level of my place where I set up a small home gym. Working out is another new development for me over the past few months. It never seemed important before, but even I have to admit I'm getting older and all of those hours in front of a computer are catching up with me. While I do have an impressive set of dumbbells, I found the treadmill most effective for me. I'm able to listen to my music or an occasional audiobook on days I need to disconnect and relax. On days I'm deep into a project, I can look over notes while I run or listen to reports through my AirPods. It just feels more productive to me. Besides, I'm never going to be the bulky type of man. I'm always going to be on the thin and lanky side, and I have no issues with that.

The morning flies by, and before I know it, it's time to head over to River's home. I already texted my dad to tell him I'm home, and he invited me over on Sunday for a family dinner with River, Cooper, Essie, and, of course, Miri. I happily accepted.

I'm dressed in my casual clothes, even though I know River will make fun of me, but I'm comfortable in my dark-gray khakis and my lighter-gray sweater, thank you very much. It's a brisk morning, but still warm enough that I can walk. October is so hit or miss in the north. Sometimes it's incredibly warm, and on other days, it can be snowing. Today I'm fine in my sweater without an additional jacket.

I decide to ring the doorbell since River doesn't even know I'm stateside again. After the second ring, I hear River grumbling, "I swear to the gods, Cam, if this is some random leather Daddy you invited to my home first thing in the morning . . ."

"That was only one time! And it wasn't in the morning!"

"Same idea." I can hear River grumbling all the way to the door as I try to process what I'm hearing. Why is Cam over at River's so early? Did he spend the night? I'm not sure how I feel about this. We've always had a strange relationship. I know he's an amazing friend to River, so I respect him for that, but the small man is just *a lot* to deal with, and I typically don't have the patience for it.

Before I can think any more about it, though, River opens the door. Whatever protest that's on the tip of his tongue stops short as he sees his own reflection staring back at him.

"Lake! I didn't know you were back!" He steps aside so I can come in and then immediately hugs me. I awkwardly tap his back until he finally releases me.

"I just came back last night. I wanted to surprise you."

"Well, I'm definitely surprised. It's so fucking good to see you. I was getting nervous because you were gone for so long."

I wave away his concern. I'm never really in danger with my position. They'd actually have to find my location to hurt me, and I'm just too good for that. But I know from prior experience that River won't listen to reason. Neither does Dad and Essie. I think it's a waste of energy, but I can't exactly force them to stop worrying.

"I'm glad to be back. Is Miri awake? I wanted to say hi to you guys and my niece before meeting Avery and Zoe for coffee."

River's eyes widen. "Oh, really? This is a new development." River heads into the kitchen without another word. "Coop, did you know Lake's meeting with Zoe today?"

Cooper is sitting at the island looking utterly exhausted. Miri sleeps peacefully on his chest while he stares at his coffee like it holds all of the world's secrets.

He looks up at the sound of River's voice. "Did you say something, baby?" he asks, his voice rough, like he didn't get any sleep. "Oh hey, Lake, when did you get back?"

I smile at my basically brother-in-law. The idle thought has me wondering when they plan to make that part official. I know they planned on waiting a while, but now that they are pretty sure they are fated mates, I don't really see the point. Not that they ask me my opinion.

"Just last night." I turn toward my brother. "And he probably doesn't know. I just messaged them late last night."

"Know what?" Cameron enters the kitchen looking as worn as Cooper, which makes me wonder exactly what happened here last night. He's wearing bright pink leggings and a long black T-shirt that falls to his knees. That makes me realize that River and Cooper are still in their sleep clothes. Even Miri is still wearing a little pajama romper with sleeping lambs on it. I guess that makes sense; it's still pretty early after all.

"That I'm meeting with Avery and Zoe for coffee later."

That news finally wakes Cooper up a bit. "Oh, that's great. I didn't know that they came to some kind of decision."

This worries me a little bit. "They haven't discussed this with you?"

Cooper shrugs, unworried. "Nah. It's not exactly my business. I'll find out later, I'm sure."

I look over to Cam, who's pouring himself a cup of coffee. "Did you spend the night here?"

Cam looks surprised by my question, though I can't understand why. "You didn't tell him?" he asks River, accusation in his voice.

River just grunts as he grabs a carton of eggs out of the fridge. "No, I didn't tell him. I had exactly one text message conversation that lasted two texts while he was gone. I wasn't wasting that to tell him you got kicked out of your apartment and are crashing here."

"What!" I ask, alarmed.

Cam shrugs like it's no big deal. "There was just an argument between my roommates and me. We'll get it settled and I'll be back there in no time."

Cooper rolls his eyes in a way that says he doesn't agree, but he doesn't say anything. I decide I don't actually want to know.

Once everyone is settled and the food is cooked, we all sit down to a surprisingly delicious breakfast. I'm more of a shake or coffee and protein bar type of guy most mornings, but sometimes it's nice to have a complete breakfast. Eventually Miri wakes up, and I get to spend some time playing with my niece before I have to leave to meet Avery and Zoe. I'm anxious about the whole thing. I still can't believe how much I want them to say yes, but I tell myself I won't be disappointed if they say no or want to wait. Either way, it's finally time to get an answer and move on from all the uncertainty.

NINE
EVANDER

It's been nearly a month, and not once has Lake shown up at the coffee shop. Now, I know, I know, I sound crazy. But no, I'm not still waiting for him, not really. I'm here waiting for Lucy to end her shift. And the fact that I always make plans to meet her here on Saturday mornings and usually hang out her entire shift under the pretense of working? Well, that means nothing.

Lucy and I discovered pretty quickly we're not compatible. We're both too dominant in bed. I briefly considered bringing Logan into the mix, but I can't actually picture him being submissive at all, so I dropped it. Despite this, Lucy and I have become good friends over the last month. It's kind of nice. The only people I ever talk to are my dad, Logan, and my coworkers occasionally. With Logan's insane and unpredictable hours, it's nice getting close to someone I can always rely on to be available when they say they will be.

I fessed up about a week ago why I had been asking about Lake. At first, Lu was a little pissed at me, but she got over it quickly once I explained the story. Lucy has no family to speak of, so I invited her to Sunday night dinner at Dad's the week before I told her the truth. She fell in love with the man immediately and got on board with the "meet Lake Simmons" plan. She even agreed to text me if he happens to come in on one of her other shifts. Now the guy just has to show up.

I'm starting to wonder if maybe he found another coffee shop or moved. I'm reluctant to bring Logan back into it. I'm pretty sure it's not completely legal looking for the guy like this, and I don't want to cause any issues. But I'm not sure what else to do.

I'm staring at the new manuscript I'm supposed to be editing but completely spacing on when the bell above the front door of the shop rings. It's habit to look up, and I have to double take when I see the lanky man with auburn hair, brushed back to stay out of his eyes, walk into the shop. He's with two other people, which I know is a change in routine, but I barely notice them. All I can focus on is the man who's now walking to the counter, gesturing to the menu as he speaks to his companions in a low voice I can't quite hear. I'm glad I'm sitting in a booth that faces both the counter and the door so I can get a clear look at his face, though.

"Lake!" Lucy exclaims loudly while giving me a meaningful look. I dip my head once in acknowledgement, letting her know I already realize it's him. "We've missed you."

The man looks up from the menu to where Lucy is practically hanging over the counter to speak to him. He smiles, but it's kind of awkward, like he doesn't know what to do with the attention. His shoulders are stiff, and I have this urge to go over there and massage them to help him relax, which is fucking crazy. Great, I've had eyes on this guy for less than a minute and I'm already certifiable.

"I've missed this place too," Lake responds, and I can't help but notice he refers to the place, not the people. He has a nice voice though. It's not very deep, but it's soothing. "Sorry, I had a last-minute business trip and just returned."

A trip that lasted an entire month? I suppose that's possible. Is that normal for an IT guy? Honestly, I have no idea.

"Oh, well, I'm glad you're back." Lucy beams, and I know it's genuine. She's just one of those sunshiney people who is always like that. It'd be annoying if I wasn't becoming so fond of her. "Do you want your usual?"

This time Lake's smile seems genuine. "Yes, please." He glances over at his two companions. "What can I get you guys?"

The woman smiles up at him. She's pretty, with long braids pulled up in a ponytail, and her light brown complexion is perfectly smooth. She's about three inches shorter than Lake and has a killer body. She's wearing a long-sleeve orange maxi dress.

"I'll take a vanilla latte, iced, please," the woman tells Lucy. Lu punches the order into the register and looks at the other guy. He's holding the girl's hand and seems distracted. They are clearly a couple, but he seems the exact opposite of her in every way. He's the tallest of the bunch and slightly bulkier than Lake, though not by much. His light-brown hair is perfectly styled, and he's wearing black pants with a black Henley.

"Just a regular coffee, cream, no sugar, please."

As Lucy gets their orders together, Lake turns and gestures toward a booth, one that's directly across from me. It's the first time I get to see his face, and holy fuck, the cameras did not do him justice. The man is gorgeous and so fucking perfect. Damn, all I want to do is mess him up. Destroy that perfection. My dick agrees as it makes an effort to come to life in my jeans, and I'm regretting wearing such tight pants.

I take a sip of my coffee that I now get for free (thanks, Lucy) just to give myself time to get myself together. I'm getting way ahead of myself. All I want to do is introduce myself to the guy, ask him to meet my dad or at least talk to him, and then get out of the guy's life.

But that doesn't stop me from watching him with his friends. I'm pretty sure that's all they are to him. While the woman seems fairly affectionate, I think that just might be in her nature. Lake sits on the opposite side of the booth from them and seems to be acting somewhat formally, like he doesn't know what to expect. Meanwhile, the other two are obviously a couple with how the man has still not let go of the woman's hand.

Luckily, Lake sits facing me so I can try to not so obviously watch him over my computer screen. I know, I'm a fucking psycho. But I've come this far, and I just can't stop myself. Like, at all.

Lake's one of those guys who will always have a baby face, and if it wasn't for the well-groomed dark-red beard, he'd probably still look like a teenager. I wonder if that's why he always keeps the facial hair. Or maybe it's so he and his brother don't look identical anymore. Or maybe he just likes it, who knows? Either way, it does nothing to hide his porcelain skin or his high cheekbones. Fuck. I shift slightly, trying to unobtrusively adjust my jeans.

Lucy brings their drinks over, and Lake smiles at her with genuine warmth in his eyes. I'm a little too far away to make out the exact color, but they're still beautiful, and Gods, what am I doing?

As Lucy walks away, she eyes me meaningfully, and I give her a little nod in acknowledgement. As much as I'm itching to speak to Lake, I'm not going to interrupt his time with his friends.

The first minute or two, the conversation is friendly. They ask him what time he got back into town, and the female tells Lake she's glad he came back safe. Came back safe? The more I learn about Lake, the more questions I have. *Not important, Ev. You're not gonna get in a personal relationship with this guy. Stop worrying about the details that don't fit.*

After a minute or so, the conversation changes direction. I try not to listen, I really do, but they're not exactly whispering. Ok, maybe I'm an asshole, but I also know I'm not the only one listening. Lucy and her coworker are practically hanging over the counter, not even hiding their interest. Since this is the first time Lake ever came in with anyone else, everyone is curious.

"So, since you reached out to me, I guess you made a decision, or at least have some questions?" Lake asks, his voice serious.

I try to turn back to my work, but the woman answers him, and I find myself listening again. "We definitely have some questions first. I won't lie, Lake. I haven't been able to stop thinking about your offer the entire time you were gone. Gods, that is the sweetest thing anyone has ever done for me. I know it's a huge risk for you, and for you to be willing to do something so selfless . . . Both of us are really touched."

Lake looks down, clearly uncomfortable. "It's not much of a risk. Yes, things went wrong toward the end of River's pregnancy, but we have more knowledge now. And since this will be planned, the Omega Project and whatever doctors of our choosing will be with us every step of the way. I feel very comfortable with that portion of this."

My mind is racing, and I give up all pretense of working. My eyes are glued to Lake's mouth, the way his lips move as he is speaking. I know he's not trying to be, but he looks so freaking sexy, and all I'm doing is imagining what else those lips can do.

The woman reaches out and squeezes Lake's hand. "What are your concerns, honey? Let's start there since you'd be the one carrying the child. If there are any doubts, we should start there."

Carrying the child? While there's a lot of speculation, the Simmons brothers never confirmed whether Lake also had the Omega gene. Most of the rumors assumed he must, identical twins after all, but nothing has been proven. If I'm understanding the conversation, then he must also be an Omega. My dick twitches again, apparently really enjoying that idea. I'm not sure why, I never even considered having kids of my own, but it brings out a possessive streak in me I didn't know I have. Which, I know, makes no sense, but whatever.

Lake's lips thin as he takes a sip of his coffee. "It's not exactly a doubt, but I am concerned about my job. As you saw, I do have to travel last minute, and it's often out of the country. I am willing to speak to my boss about it, but I'm not sure how receptive he will be. The man is known for being sexist and giving women a hard time concerning maternity leave and modified assignments. I doubt he'll be more accommodating with me. It was his supervisors that pretty much forced him not to fire me when everything happened with River. That, and I know too much."

For the first time since the conversation started, the other guy contributes, laughing as he speaks. "Jesus, you sound like a fucking spy, Lake."

Lake just shrugs, but something shines in his eyes. The other guy continues, "Personally, that and Zoe's new role are the only two things that are keeping me from saying yes outright. Zo and I discussed this a lot, and the more we spoke, the more we decided we would love for you to be our surrogate, and sooner rather than later, but this role with *A Chorus Line* is contracted for at least a year. Depending on the timing, neither of us want her to be stuck doing shows eight times a week and not have a chance to bond with the baby. And I won't lie, the travel makes me nervous. I don't want you to be on the other side of the fucking world with no way to contact us when you go into labor."

Lake's face is serious. "It's a valid concern."

"How about this? You said you contacted the doctor in charge of the Omega Project, right?"

"Dr. Rooke, yes. I actually have to reach out to him today. He called while I was away."

"Ok, so let's see if he's willing to meet with us, along with the fertility doctor, and OB or whoever else would be involved with this. We can see how valid this possibility really is, have all the uncertainties and dangers laid out for us. If they believe it's plausible for you to carry our child, we can then make decisions on timing and if there's a way for you to get your assignments modified without causing issues. But honestly, those are secondary right now. We need to make sure it can even happen."

Lake seems excited about this. "So, if all of the details are worked out, you'd actually want me to be a surrogate for you?"

The woman, Zoe, squeezes Lake's hand again. I feel a stab of irrational jealousy and push it down. "Yes, sweetie, we're honored you offered, and we'd love for you to be our surrogate."

The conversation dies down after that, and I manage to get a couple pages of edits done while still keeping an eye on them. I'm hoping to catch Lake, either alone or as they're leaving. I don't want to just walk up to their table if I can help it.

Finally, they begin to clean up their empty cups and start to head out. The couple scoots out of the booth first, but Lake is following them to the door, and I know it's now or never. I jump to my feet and follow them to the exit of the coffee shop. Right as the man's hand is on the door, I call out, "Lake?"

The three of them turn around, and instantly I see Lake's expression turn from questioning to hard. The guy lets the door close and comes to stand next to Lake. Zoe is shooting daggers at me already.

At first, I'm thrown by their instant hostility. I mean, nothing about them has been aggressive before this. But then I remember how much the brothers have been harassed by the media, and I realize that they're suspicious.

"Yes?" Lake asks, his voice stern.

"Hey, I'm sorry to bother you. I'll be quick."

The man's eyes narrow. "Listen, buddy, he's not answering any questions. Don't you have someone else to harass?"

I glare at the man. I'm not someone who's easily intimidated, and besides, I'm speaking to Lake, not him. I'm not going anywhere unless Lake says so. "I'm not sure who you think I am, but I'm not a reporter or any other kind of media. My name is Evander Cirillo."

It's clear the name means nothing to Lake, but he gestures for me to continue. "You don't know me, but you do know my father."

I see confusion cross his face. From this close, I can see his eyes are brown, but there are specks of gold throughout. It's so mesmerizing that it's hard to keep focus on the conversation.

"You father?" he finally asks.

"Yes, I know this is nuts, but just hear me out, ok? My dad, his name is Eric Cirillo."

Again, no recognition, which makes sense. I doubt my dad told him his name back then, and even if he did, it makes sense that a scared eight-year-old boy wouldn't remember.

"When you were young, you met my dad. We both heard the story you told on TV to that reporter. The one about what your dad tried to do to you and how the drug dealer brought you back to your mom." I don't mention any details; it's not really my place.

Lake's expression darkens, and his friends move closer to him, but he does nod. "That's my dad. You changed his life that day. He stopped dealing drugs, got clean and legitimate. He started to be the dad to me I always wished he were before that. I know you don't owe either of us anything, but after we saw you on TV, both my dad and I just wanted to reach out to you, tell you thank you. I know it's probably a crappy memory for you, but I thought you deserved to know you had an impact, and there hasn't been a day that has gone by in the last twenty years that my dad hasn't thought about you and prayed you were safe."

I shrug, not sure really where to go next. Lake's just staring at me, and it doesn't seem like the conversation is going the way I hoped it would. "Anyway, that's all. I'm sorry to take up your time." I give them all a small smile and nod. "Have a good day."

I turn awkwardly back to my table, hoping they walk out the door and I can just forget the whole thing.

I don't look up as I pack up my things as quickly as possible. Lucy will understand if I bail. I still haven't heard the door open or the bells ring, and I'm just imagining them staring at me. It's awkward as hell.

Just as I'm about to make my escape, a throat clears behind me, and as I turn, I see Lake. He seems uncomfortable, but he does hold his hand out for me to shake. "I'm Lake Simmons." And I can't help but laugh as I take his hand.

"Hi, Lake, nice to meet you."

TEN
LAKE

I'm standing in the doorway of Dream Beans Cafe, still in shock and trying to get my bearings. I'm about to consider the whole thing a scam and walk out when Zoe stops me. The name he gave isn't familiar. If the drug dealer from over twenty years ago gave me his name, I honestly don't remember. Anyone can pretend to be related to him, and I wouldn't know without doing further research. It's a smart and easy way to gain my trust, honestly, because while I don't think about the man every day, he certainly crosses my mind on occasion, especially in the last few months since I told the story.

Zoe loves things like this, though, and won't let me just walk out. In the time it takes me to process what just happened, she has Google up and is pulling up the name the man gave us. Evander Cirillo. She's not me when it comes to technology, but she's still a millennial, and within seconds has three separate social media accounts up as well as a website from a publishing company where he's listed as one of the senior editors. Nothing through my very quick glance says anything about him being a reporter, or even having a blog. His social media accounts are basic: pictures of him hanging with friends, on the beach, a few at some book signings. Nothing that screams content creator in any way.

It could be a fake name, of course, but the picture on the publishing website is definitely the man in front of me. He's only an inch or two taller than me, but with a more muscular frame. The way his black sweater fits snugly around those defined arms and his chest makes me think he might work out a lot. His light-brown eyes had a steely focus and determination in them when he spoke to me. I had a hard time focusing on anything but them, and the same ones are staring back at me in this picture. While I know from experience that can be faked, I can't think of a good reason why it would be.

Before I know it, I'm walking up to the man. Evander, he said. He has his back to me as he packs up his belongings. The sleeves of his sweater are rolled up, revealing a colorful sleeve of tattoos on both arms that come down to his wrists. He also has tattoos on his neck that go to right below his ears. Only his face seems free of the markings, and I have an idle thought, wondering how much of the rest of his body is covered. He doesn't look much older than me, maybe his early thirties, and I keep thinking back to that conversation I had with that man that day when I was a kid, trying to remember if he said he had a son. It's possible, but a lot of the details are fuzzy from that whole experience. While there are no tattoos on his face, it doesn't mean there are no modifications. He has a ring in both his lip and nose, as well gages in his ears that are about ¾ of an inch. His dark, nearly black hair is long on the top and buzzed shorter on the sides. He has it slicked back, and I have to admit, he pulls off the whole look. His dark facial hair is neatly trimmed and accentuates his full lips, almost as much as the lip ring.

This is the second time I've ever felt anything but indifference toward a person, and it's a strange sensation I'm not sure I enjoy.

Evander notices my presence as I awkwardly hover around

his table. He turns and looks at me, surprise evident in his eyes. He definitely expected me to walk out without so much as a word.

Social interactions do not come naturally to me. So, I do the first thing that comes to my mind and stick my hand out toward him. "I'm Lake Simmons," I tell him, which I know is idiotic considering it's clear this man knows exactly who I am.

Despite that, the smile he gives me is genuine, and I feel warmth pooling in my belly. It's such a strange sensation that I'm not sure how to process it. Maybe it's something I ate? I can't shake the feeling that the butterflies that are swarming around in my stomach are because of this man, not indigestion.

I notice when a person is objectively attractive, typically. I can acknowledge that a person is good-looking—both men and women—without actually feeling any type of attraction toward them. In my nearly thirty years of life, I've never felt anything more than a disinterested acknowledgement of someone's looks, nothing more. I've never had fantasies about my teachers or professors like so many other young men. I always thought that plastering my walls with posters of people I found hot was a waste of time. But for some reason, it seems more with Evander. I may have only met him for a few short minutes, but the desire to get to know him better is strong.

Evander returns my shake. "Evander Cirillo." He gestures behind him to the table. "But most people just call me Ev. Do you want to take a seat?"

Ev. I don't know why, but it doesn't fit for me. Evander seems to just roll off my tongue better. I don't say anything though. I'm sure this stranger does not need me criticizing his nickname of choice.

I glance over at Avery and Zoe. Zoe has her phone out, and seconds later, I feel mine buzz. I smile apologetically at Evander before looking down at it.

Go ahead and talk. Do you want us to wait for you?

Rather than respond, I shake my head and wave in the direction of the door. I'll be fine. I don't need them hovering while I talk to this man. I'm sure they want someone who can look after themselves carrying their baby. They don't need to chaperone me.

Zoe seems unsure, or at least reluctant to leave the show, but Avery guides her out. I turn my attention back to Evander, who's leaning against the booth, his hands casually in his pockets with an amused expression on his face. I feel a blush spread across my cheeks as I force a smile. "Sure, thank you. I'm sorry about that. My friends just want to make sure I don't want them to stay close."

Evander frowns at that. "I understand why you doubt me, but I promise I'm not trying to get a story or anything out of you. I just want to talk."

"You wouldn't be the first person who said that in order to exploit my brother or me in the last year, though." There's a brief flash of some emotion, maybe hurt, before it smooths out.

"Well, people are assholes," he replies. He's still standing by the booth, I guess waiting for me to make my decision. With a small sigh, I sit down. What's the harm, really? And if he is telling the truth, well, I admit I'm more than a little interested.

"Do you have any proof?" I hear myself asking. "That you are who you say you are? I'm sorry if it seems ridiculous, but people have gone to great lengths to talk to us. That story went viral, and half the world knows it now. I need a little more."

Evander wrinkles his nose, not in annoyance, but like he's thinking. "Um, I think I have a picture of my dad and me from back then. One of those things he posted on Facebook for one of my birthdays, you know? It might be a couple years after, but he still looked the same, if you think you remember."

I shrug, unsure. "I might."

As he pulls out his phone and begins to search for the picture, his eyes widen. "Oh! Wait, let me think. Dad has spoken about that day so fucking much. I'm sure there's something I know . . ."

He's still scrolling through his phone, searching for the picture when he looks up at me. "Oh! *Fairly Odd Parents*! That's what he put on the TV for you, right?"

The memories start to flood in my mind: *sitting on a beat-up brown couch with strange stains on it, Dad getting agitated and angry in the background, the man with the friendly smile who got angry when Dad grabbed me,* Fairly Odd Parents *playing on a small TV resting on top of a crate.*

While I'm lost in my memories, Evander finds the picture he's looking for and shows me the phone. I know I'm supposed to be looking at the older man, but my eyes drift toward the boy smiling in the picture. Even younger and without all of the tattoos and piercings, it's obvious this is a younger Evander. He's probably around 12, his dark hair short with the tips styled upward. He's wearing black pants and a black hoodie, and even at that age, the rebellion in his eyes is obvious.

But I'm supposed to be looking at the man, not his son. I stare down at the dark-haired man in his early thirties, and I'm immediately shot back in time. I only usually remember bits and pieces of that day, but it's clear now. I know this man is telling the truth. His father was the one that saved me. He probably didn't know it at the time, but that instance was the one that finally gave Mom the courage to take River and I and run far enough that Seth couldn't find us, at least not for years. By the time Seth did, Mom was already dead, and Riv and I were practically adults.

I look up at Evander, who's watching me, his eyes full of emotion. "You're telling the truth," I tell him quietly.

His smile lights up his face, and I have that warm sensation again. I love that something I said made him smile, which is a strange thought. I file that away to think about later.

"Yes. Yes, I am."

I clear my throat. "How is your dad?"

"Good. Really good. He owns a couple automotive shops now. He still lives in Brooklyn, though, and I typically see him once a week for dinner."

I smile at that, glad it worked out for them. "My brother and I try to have dinner with our dad once a week too." By the look on Evander's face, I know I need to clarify. "Our step dad adopted us when we were kids. We both call him Dad. He deserves the title. Our sister Essie comes when she's home from college too."

Evander's features turn serious. "I'm relieved that your mom was able to get you and your brother some security in your childhood. I know it's something that always worried Dad—that she hadn't managed to get away."

I shudder at the thought. I know River thought about it sometimes: what our life would've been like if Mom didn't finally run far enough and hadn't met Luke. I didn't see the point. I know I'd be dead by now. Seth was always harder on me than River, and I didn't have the ability to gauge his moods and react accordingly like River always did. He'd have killed me long before I reached adulthood.

"I would like to meet your dad, if you think he'd be ok with that?"

A smile lights up Evander's face again. It makes him look so much younger. "Dad would love that. Are you free next Sunday? You can come for dinner. He'd really enjoy that."

I pull out my phone to look at my calendar and see that I'm free. "Yes, I'm free that day. I would like that."

Evander sucks his bottom lip into his mouth, his tongue absently playing with his lip piercing. "Perfect. Give me your phone, and I'll put in my number."

I shock myself when I hand it over. No one takes my phone from me. Well, I'll check it for any devices or tracking apps when he leaves. For some reason, I don't believe the man in front of me is like that, but I can't be too careful. This is my personal phone, not my work one, but I still can't risk someone finding any type of classified information, so I always have to be cautious.

But Evander is quick. He angles it toward me so I can see him texting himself so that he has my number as well. "I'll talk to you later in the week, and we can iron out the details."

"Ok." I look awkwardly toward the door. I'm still a little overwhelmed by the day and need to get out of here and decompress. Between the news that Avery and Zoe would like me as their surrogate and then meeting Evander, I'm exhausted. And while part of me doesn't want to leave the man, a larger part of me knows I need to.

Evander seems to understand this because he hands my phone back with a smile. "Alright, I'll let you go. It was really nice meeting you."

The feeling in my core is back again. "It's nice meeting you, too." Not knowing what else to say, I stick my phone back in my pocket, wave awkwardly, and run toward the door. I have no idea what these feelings when I look at Evander are, but they are leaving me unsettled, and I just need to get out of here.

ELEVEN
EVANDER

"So he just ran away? That's fucking weird, man," Logan tells me as he shoves a piece of steak in his mouth.

I glower at my best friend. I have no idea why, but I have this irrational urge to protect Lake, even if he doesn't need it. "It wasn't weird. I think he was just overstimulated."

One of the other editors I work with sometimes is like that. After a long meeting or when we have a particularly demanding client, Lizzy needs to just step away and decompress by herself. I've worked with her long enough to know the signs, and Lake has a similar vibe.

"Why, I thought you two just talked?"

I roll my eyes at Logan. I love the guy, but he can be totally clueless. He's the kind of guy who just lets stress roll off his back. He's a beast in any type of dangerous situation, and I'd never want to hurt someone he cares about, but once the dust settles, he's immediately back to his carefree self.

"Yeah, but I told you he was with friends. They had an important conversation before I interrupted him, so I'm pretty sure he was already overwhelmed and I just added to it."

Logan tilts his head in interest. Just then, my dad and Lucy walk onto the porch where Logan and I are talking. For years, Sunday dinners were just Dad and me, but at some point, Logan joined, and even Lucy has been to the last two.

Lucy is holding a tray of drinks, water bottles, refills on our beers, and a pitcher of a dark-purple drink filled with fruit.

"Lucy made us sangria," Dad says happily as he follows her out, also holding a tray. I know he loves how these dinners evolved. Even if it's been twenty years, I know a part of him still feels like he has to make up for the beginning half of my childhood, and knowing that my friends feel like his home is a second home for them, too, even as adults, eases that guilt slightly.

"Oh sweet, you're the best, darling," I say as I stand and take the tray from her. Logan rises from his seat to take the tray my dad is holding, his mouth still full of food. It looks like my dad brought out a couple different types of salad, corn on the cob, and watermelon slices.

Logan and I put the food on the outdoor table as I laugh. "Dad, you realize it's October, right? Where'd you even get watermelon?"

Dad just shrugs. "It's never too late in the season for an outdoor barbeque. And no barbeque is complete without watermelon." Which isn't even remotely an answer to my question, but whatever.

"I think it's awesome, Mr. C," Logan says as he piles his plate with potato salad. Until Logan met me, food wasn't always easy for him to come by as a kid. It's how we became friends, actually. I caught him trying to steal my lunch, but instead of telling on him, I shared it with him. That night, I went home and told Dad about Logan. From that day on, Dad began making me two lunches, one for me and the other for Logan. He never even said anything, just handed me the extra bag and said, "In case your friend is hungry." That was it.

Because of his childhood, Logan has a tendency to

overindulge. It's like his brain is still programmed to eat as much as he can just in case it's a while till his next meal. Dad is always happy to indulge him. Luckily for Logan, he's 6'4", 250lbs., and insanely active, so he can eat as much as he wants without worrying about it.

Once we're all settled and drinking the best fucking sangria I ever had, Logan turns the conversation back to Lake. I'm not sure why he's so curious, but since I can't get the damn man out of my mind, it's not exactly a hardship to talk about him. I already told Dad about Lake wanting to meet him next week, and he's ecstatic.

"What was this conversation he had that was so serious?"

"I'm pretty sure it's not your business. I felt guilty enough listening in."

"He's going to be the surrogate for his friends," Lucy interrupts, not even remotely phased that she's sharing personal information about a virtual stranger. "Isn't that the sweetest? That's going to be a good-looking baby, too. That was a gorgeous couple."

I had to agree. While objectively attractive, the couple with Lake didn't do anything for me. My mind keeps going back to Lake in his pseudo-professor attire, with his tight smile and those serious golden-brown eyes.

Logan's blue eyes widen in surprise. "Shit, really? I didn't even know dudes could do that."

"Clearly he's been tested for the Omega gene," Lucy says in that tone she gets when she thinks she's smarter than everyone else. Basically, she reserves that tone for Logan. I've never heard her use it on anyone else.

Logan grabs a piece of watermelon. "Yeah, no shit. Doesn't mean he can carry someone else's kid, though."

Lucy sips her sangria with a smirk on her lips. "I got the impression they weren't sure yet either. I think they're waiting to speak to a doctor."

"Gods, Lu. Let the man have some privacy."

This time she does flush sheepishly. "Sorry. You're right. I saw you got his number."

Lucy's eyebrows waggle seductively.

I roll my eyes, trying to ignore her implications and how happy I am to have that saved in my phone, even if I know it's strictly for practical purposes. "Yeah, so I can give him the time and address to Dad's." I eye my two friends. "Neither of you will be here for that dinner," I tell them seriously.

Logan falls back in his chair with mock hurt. "What? C'mon, Ev. You'd never even have found the guy without me. I don't get to meet him?"

"No," I tell him. I know Logan. He's going to interrogate the shit out of the guy, especially since some of his personal information doesn't add up. I don't want that to happen. I get the feeling Lake won't handle that well, and I don't want him to run now that I finally found him.

Dad speaks up, and thankfully he agrees with me. "I think the first time should just be Ev and me. It's probably going to be an emotional night, and I don't wanna overwhelm him or make him uncomfortable." Dad smiles fondly at Logan as he sighs dramatically, but he agrees.

"I'll drop off leftovers to your apartment on Monday," Dad promises Logan.

Logan beams at this. "Thanks, Mr. C, you're the best."

I see the smile on my dad's face as he settles back in his deck chair. I know he thinks of Logan as another son, and even if he insists on calling Dad Mr. C, I know he's the closest thing Logan has ever had to a real father.

As the night continues, I can't help but count my blessings. Sure, it would've been nice if Dad was in my life the entire time. I'd have loved my mom not to be a crack addict alcoholic. But even with that, I got lucky. It may have taken longer than I'd like, and a small part of me wished Dad managed to turn his life around just because of me and didn't need another kid almost getting sold to be a wake-up call, but I'd take it. He did turn his life around before it was too late, and that's more than most people get.

Lucy has a date that night, so she leaves shortly after we're done eating. Logan has a rare day off, and we decide to take advantage of it. Dad always keeps the spare bedroom open, so I can crash at any time, and makes sure there are clean sheets on the pull-out couch in the living room so Logan can crash if he needs to. We decide to take advantage of that, and long after Dad goes in for the night, Logan and I sit on his back porch and drink. We have way more than we should for a Sunday night when I have to work at 8 am, but whatever.

In a lot of ways, Dad's place will always be home, way more than my apartment. I got extremely lucky and managed to get one of those rent-controlled apartments in the city so my rent isn't ridiculous. It's still way too high for a tiny one-bedroom apartment, but definitely manageable. Still, it's never felt much like home to me, and my room at my dad's house will always feel more like mine than the other one.

It's a little after 1 am when Logan and I finally crash. He stumbles his way onto the pull-out that my dad already has set up for him. He doesn't even take off his shoes. My eyes are blurry and everything's double, but I somehow manage to make it to the couch. Logan somehow sleeps through my clumsy attempt at pulling off his boots. I consider taking off his jeans too. I know for a fact he only wears boxers or nothing to bed, but I'm pretty sure I don't have the coordination for that.

It's basically just instinct that gets me up the stairs to my bedroom. My dad's door is closed, but I can still hear his snores. I snort as I push the bathroom door open to piss and brush my teeth. My dad has to be the loudest snorer and deepest sleeper in all of Brooklyn, though it was convenient in my teenage years when I snuck in my girlfriends, and even one guy, without him noticing.

"Holy fuck, I shouldn't have drunk so much," I mutter to myself as I piss. I practically fall onto the sink, but I manage to wash my hands and brush my teeth. I'm one of those people who has to brush my teeth every night and every morning no matter what. It doesn't matter how drunk or tired I am. I'm brushing my teeth. It's a fucking disgusting feeling if I don't. I strip out of everything but my boxer briefs, leaving the clothes in a pile in the bathroom, and stumble into the room I sleep in at Dad's, making a mental note to clean up in the morning.

I crash into the bed, also already all set up for me, and I think I'm gonna pass out immediately, but I don't. Instead, I'm just lying here, staring at the popcorn ceiling and thinking. I can't believe I actually met Lake. After years of him just being an arbitrary figure, one that impacted my life so much even without a face to go with the image, it's strange finally meeting the man in real life. A good strange, though. He's quirky, intense, a little odd, and so fucking adorable. Every time I think about him, my cock takes notice. I had a lot of fucking alcohol, so I'm not exactly hard, but I still palm my dick as the image of Lake fills my mind.

He's not in the gray professor outfit. Well, not the sweater at least. He's still wearing the pants, though, because let's be honest, his ass filled those out nicely. He's shirtless and I'm staring at all his smooth, pale skin. In my imagination, he has no ink, no piercings, and no scars, just perfect untouched skin screaming for me to mark it up. He's standing next to my bed with that awkward smile on his face, as if he's waiting for me to tell him what to do next.

I slide my briefs down so my semi hard-on pops out. I'm blindly reaching for the lube because I don't want this image of Lake to leave me. "Take off your pants," my imagined self tells him. He blushes but pushes his pants down slowly. It's not meant to be seductive, though. He's just awkward, and I fucking love it. I want to ruin him, destroy that little bit of innocence that's in his eyes.

I beckon imaginary Lake onto my bed as I pour some lube onto my hand. I wrap my hand around my cock, imagining it's Lake's. "You like that?" I'd ask him as he pumps me.

He'd nod shyly. "I like the piercings," he'd say. I smile, like he's really there.

"Yeah, baby? I bet you'd like them even better inside of you. I hear the Jacob's Ladder feels fucking amazing as my dick fills you up. It's a totally different sensation."

I moan and rub my fingers along the piercing like it's Lake's hand. Despite all the alcohol, the fantasy, as innocent as it is, is enough for me to pop a boner. I close my eyes, desperate to keep it going for as long as I can. In my fantasy, Lake shudders at the thought and shyly looks away. He's still in his underwear, but there's a wet spot on the front, and I can see his cock bulging.

"Are you nice and hard for me, baby?" He'd nod and bite his bottom lip, and I'd see just how shy he is. "Let me see."

He'd blush but still obey me as he'd push his briefs down and let me see his goods.

I moan and thrust up into my hand. "Can I taste it?" Lake would ask, and I'm obviously not going to turn that down.

I pump myself harder as I imagine Lake's luscious lips wrapping around my dick. I coat one of my fingers on my other hand with a combination of pre-cum and lube and push up enough so I can get my hand behind me. I wonder idly if Lake tops or bottoms, maybe both. Fuck, I'm not even sure if he likes guys, but in my fantasy, I just can't imagine him topping me.

As I slide a finger inside my hole, it's not Lake or even myself that's fingering me, but Logan. I have no fucking idea how he invaded my fantasy, but it wouldn't be the first time. I normally try to force him out, but this time, I don't. It's Logan's big, rough finger that's invading me now. He's not gentle as he forces his way in, putting a hand around my throat. It's not strong enough to hurt me, but enough to let me know I'm no longer in charge of my own fantasy.

My eyes roll to the back of my head, and I'm so fucking close. Fuck, what an image. Lake's sucking me off, tentative at first, but as he becomes more confident, he finds his stride and is doing all the things that get me to the edge. Logan is taking complete control of everything, pegging my prostate with his finger, telling me that soon it'll be his cock filling me up . . .

I'm almost there, just a few more pumps and then I'll be orgasming, when my door opens. "Ev, who the fuck you talking —oh, oh, fuck."

Logan is standing in my doorway looking completely shell-shocked. I know I should move my hands, or gods, at least cover myself the fuck up, but I can't. I'm too close to the edge to stop myself.

The cum starts shooting out as Logan stands at my doorway, his mouth gaping and his eyes wide. He's not horrified, though. As my orgasm rips through me, an involuntarily whimper leaves him. His lips part and he palms his own dick through his jeans.

What's happening here? I finally finish having one of the most intense orgasms I've ever had from masturbating. My head crashes back onto my pillow as I pull my finger out of my hole and release my oversensitive dick. Fuck.

Logan is still just standing there, and I know I should do something, say something. We'd seen each other masturbate before, when we were horny teenagers trying to figure shit out, but never like this. And never when I was just fantasizing about him. The cum is cooling on my belly, and I know it'll start getting itchy soon.

"If you're staying, do you mind handing me some tissues? It's starting to get sticky."

Logan doesn't move, and I'm concerned maybe I went too far. Maybe we should just act like it never happened. But eventually, Logan blinks and takes a step into the room. He almost seems like he's in a trance, but he has the sense to close the door behind him. It's not that Dad will wake up, but still. No reason to take the chance.

His movements are slow and unsure, but his pupils are blown and his hand is still cupping the obvious bulge in his pants. I watch his movements as he heads toward the bed, but he doesn't reach for the tissues. Instead, he walks right up to the bed and awkwardly climbs on.

"Logan?" I ask, unsure of what he's doing.

He kneels in between my spread legs, still not answering me, and stares down at my spent cock and cum pooling on my belly.

"What were you thinking about just now, when you came?" he asks, his voice rough, and fuck, does it turn me on. What is going on? Am I still in my fantasy? I have to be, right? Or dead. There is no fucking way my straight best friend, who I've imagined in my bed more times than I can count, is really here right now.

I have a brief worry that he's still really drunk and has no idea what he's doing, but no, his voice is steady and his eyes are a lot clearer than I'd expect for how drunk he was earlier. He's turned on, but he's clearly in control and coherent. He's watching me with his intense blue eyes, and I can't decide if I should stop this and check in. I have no idea what he's thinking. But I can't. Even if this is my imagination, or just a one-time thing, I can't turn this down.

"You," I finally tell him, my voice quieter than I want it to be.

"Oh, yeah?" he responds. His smile is lopsided and kind of sweet, but there's a look of possession in his eyes that gives me the chills. Gods, how many times have I pictured Logan possessing me?

I nod, unable to speak at first. I clear my throat as Logan comes even closer. "You and Lake."

There's a flash of surprise that runs across his features before he controls it. His smile transforms from sweet to absolutely savage.

"I knew you had a thing for him." He looks back down at my cum.

"Can I taste it?" he asks, which surprises the fuck out of me.

"It's probably cold," I say dumbly. But hell, if this is his first time tasting male cum, I don't want it to be a bad experience.

"I don't care."

Fuck. He's gonna get me hard again. I'm in my thirties now, so I don't exactly have the quickest recovery time. I realize Logan's still waiting for me to answer, and I nod.

I expect him to use his fingers to grab it, but no. This fucker who I've had a crush on since I was fifteen, who never gave any indication of liking guys at all, let alone me, leans forward and licks my cum. Fucking licks it. And he's not at all tentative either. He starts at the small puddle right above my pubes, but he slides his tongue down, his nose grazing my skin. He hesitates right before my dick, and I'm about to tell him not to worry about it, when his tongue dashes out and tentatively licks my cock. I don't think it's out of hesitation so much as fear I'm too sensitive, which I appreciate.

I just stare at him in shock as he licks me completely clean. I'm so turned on again, and I know if this was ten years ago, I'd be hard. Now, I'm just lying here, unsure what to say or do. I want to touch him but I'm scared if I do, he'll somehow disappear. Part of me still feels like this might be some elaborate dream. But as his tongue rubs against my piercings, I think there's no fucking way. My dreams are never this detailed.

He finally gets his fill, and I see the moment when the panic sets in. His eyes are wide and he crawls a few inches away from me, though he doesn't try to get off the bed.

"Logan, it's ok," I tell him. And it is. I'm not sure what happened here, but if this is all I ever get from him, it's enough.

He's still my best friend, and nothing ever will come between that.

He just nods. "I'm sorry." His voice is harsh. "I-I don't know what just happened."

I force a smile. I wonder if he ever thought of himself as bi. I don't think so, and if that's the case, then I'm sure what happened is a shock for him.

"It's ok. You don't need to apologize."

"I liked it." His voice is barely above a whisper, but the lump in my throat starts to ease.

"Good, me too."

He eyes the door. "I'm gonna . . . I'm gonna go."

His hand is palming his dick again, and I see he's still hard, but I know there's no way he's ready for reciprocation.

I feel a stab of hurt in my chest that he wants to leave, but I understand. He probably hasn't been having wet dreams about me since we were fifteen like me. "You can't drive. It's been a night and you drank a lot. I can wake up Dad to take you or call you an Ub—"

But he cuts me off. "No! I'm not leaving. I don't know what happened, and I need a fucking minute, but I'm gonna just go back on the couch. I'll be here when you wake up, ok?"

I smile, feeling reassured. "Yeah, ok."

Logan then does something even more shocking than eating my cum. He leans over and kisses me on the lips. It's not more than a peck, but I'm still processing it as he clamors off my bed and leaves the room, closing the door behind him.

I stare at the door for a long time, but he doesn't come back in, not that I expect him to. A quick glance at my phone shows me it's nearly three and I have work in the morning. I have to get sleep, even if I can't imagine sleeping after this night.

But eventually, my eyes get heavy and close, and my last thought is, what the hell just happened?

TWELVE
LOGAN

I have no idea what time it is, but I've been staring at the ceiling fan in Mr. C's living room for hours. The sun is starting to come up, and I know it won't be long before Ev and Mr. C are up and going about their business to get ready for the day. Still, I can't fucking sleep.

What the hell did I do in there? Gods, I don't know what came over me, but when I walked into Ev's room to see him sprawled out on his bed, his hand on his dick, his other hand just finished fingering himself, I fucking lost my mind. In that moment, I'd never seen anything sexier. Not one girl I've ever been with looked like Ev did with cum cooling on his belly, his hair mussed, his cheeks flushed, looking positively debauched. I couldn't look away no matter how hard I tried.

And I did try. I wanted so badly to look away, close the door, go back to the pull-out couch, and forget I ever saw the man like that. But I didn't. Fuck, I couldn't. My dick was hard as a rock and straining in my jeans, and all I wanted to do was grab Ev and kiss him, muss him up even more. What the fuck was that thought?

Then I did it. I ate his fucking cum. What's wrong with me? I never even tasted the stuff before, but it's not nearly as disgusting as I expected it to be. At least not Ev's. It was like I was in a trance or something, but I wanted nothing more than to be a part of that experience.

When he said he had been picturing both Lake and me, I couldn't deny the image appealed. Just from the little I've seen and heard about Lake, he seems so buttoned up, the kind of guy Ev loves to ruin in bed, and instead of being jealous, like Kayla said I was, I felt turned on. So fucking turned on.

When it was all said and done, though, I didn't know what to do. Reality hit me like a fucking freight truck, and I needed to get out of there. I wasn't ashamed, and honestly, I didn't even regret the whole thing, but I needed a minute to get my thoughts together. I ran out of the room, hastily jerked myself off in what had to be the quickest masturbation session I ever had in my life, and then crawled into the pull-out bed in the living room where I proceeded to question every decision I ever made in my life.

What does this mean? Am I bi? I don't think so, but I can't deny the attraction I felt toward Ev, at least at that moment when I saw him in the bedroom. But what would stem from it?

I know Ev and I are solid. If we decide whatever that was is a one-time thing, then that's all it will be. We'll still be friends. I'm fucking confident in that. Our friendship is not that fragile. And besides, I'd be fucking miserable without the man in my life, and I know he feels the same way.

Do I want to be more than friends with him? Surprisingly, the thought doesn't freak me out at all. I'm not exactly sure what I want, but I'm not having some kind of identity crisis or whatever. The guys in my unit might make a few cracks if I start dating a guy, but I wouldn't be the only cop who likes guys too, and I know it would be mostly harmless. Anyone who does make a big deal about it, I can handle.

I hear an alarm go off, a groan following it, and I know Ev is up, but I haven't slept a wink. The other concern is Lake. It's clear he and Ev have some kind of connection and he's interested in him, even if he just met him.

It's crazy quick, but I know my friend well enough to see when he has a genuine interest in someone, and that's the case with Lake. He likes the guy. My mind goes to a story I read online about how fated mates might be coming back now that the Omega gene is back. It seems fucking ridiculous, and at the time, I laughed at it. Fated mates? That's some magic bullshit that doesn't exist. The Omega gene isn't some kind of magical property. It's a genetic thing. Science.

But thinking about how quickly Ev latched onto this Lake thing once he saw him, it makes me question the whole thing. And where does that leave me? Does Ev want to forget this whole thing happened and pursue Lake? Is there room in his heart for both of us? Do I even want to be a part of that? So many questions, and I have no fucking answers.

There's footsteps coming down the stairs, and Ev peeks down the hallway and startles when he sees me watching him. He's hesitant and kind of awkward, and I don't know if it's because he regrets last night or he's worried I'm in the middle of a freak out and am about to lose it on him.

"Hey," he says tentatively as he finally walks out of the hallway. He's already dressed, and I guess he's going into the office today because he's wearing dark-tan khakis and a royal-blue long-sleeve polo shirt. His office is pretty casual, but they still can't wear jeans or hoodies and T-shirts, Ev's usual apparel.

He tilts his head toward the kitchen. "Do you want some coffee? I have a fucking monster hangover, and I figure you must too."

Now that he mentions it, yeah, my head is fucking pounding. I don't know if it's from the alcohol last night or the lack of sleep . . . or the fact that my mind is going a thousand miles a minute.

"Yeah, sure." I reluctantly climb out of bed as I hear the shower go on down the hall. Mr. C must be up too. I know he won't care if I stay and sleep in, but it seems weird right now, especially when Ev is acting like this.

It's like he's purposely not mentioning last night, and I'm not sure why. I decide to bite the bullet and be the one to clear the air. It's fucking uncomfortable right now.

"About last night . . . ," I start in the most horribly cliché way possible. Gods, what are we, in some cheesy Lifetime movie?

Ev startles and looks up from where he's fumbling with the coffee pot. It's strange seeing him look so unsure. I've never seen him like this before. "Yes?" he replies reluctantly, like he's afraid where this conversation is going.

I wish I knew where his head is at, but at this point, I have to just plow through and hope for the best. Like I said earlier, I know we'll be fine. We just have to see where we stand now.

I'm silent while I try to think of the best way to phrase this. I'm still really fucking confused, and I know we need to have a real conversation without Ev's dad around the corner and with longer than the short time before he has to leave for work. I can't leave everything completely unsettled either. "I don't regret it," I finally say.

I physically see all the tension leave Ev's body. His shoulders relax and he fucking deflates, a small smile on his face. "Oh, thank fuck. I was kind of worried you were freaking out, having an identity crisis, and never wanted to see me again."

I can't take it anymore and stalk toward Ev. He watches me with cautious eyes, but there's something more there, like maybe he's a little turned on. I cup both his cheeks with my hands. "There will never be anything that would cause me to not want to see you again, ok? Nothing in this entire fucking universe can cause that to happen."

Ev's eyes darken as he nods around my hands. I let him go. "Ok," he whispers, his voice a little breathless.

"I won't lie and say that I'm not fucking confused. Because I am. I have no idea what came over me last night. I've never felt anything like that before. But I don't regret it, and I wouldn't change it."

Ev smiles up at me before sucking his lip ring between his teeth. "Good, I wouldn't change it either."

The coffee pot finishes and he goes over to pour us some mugs. I notice he pours a third for his dad as well. He immediately starts doctoring them all up and I have to smile. He doesn't even need to ask; he knows exactly how each of us likes our coffee.

"I didn't know you were attracted to guys." He says it casually, but I know it's not a casual question. He's probably wondering why I've never mentioned it to him.

"I'm not. Or, I don't think I am. I've never had the kind of reaction I did to you last night with any other guy. I've never even gotten hard thinking or looking at another guy before. Maybe it's just a you thing. I don't know."

Ev grins at my words. "I can live with that." His face sobers. "So what does this mean, exactly?"

"I don't know. I'm not freaking out at the possibility of being with you. Like, it almost seems natural, you know. That is, if that's what you want. I am a little overwhelmed. I literally laughed in Kayla's face when she suggested I liked you and I was jealous of you and Lake a few weeks ago, and now I'm here eating your fucking jizz. So, I might just need a minute to process all of this."

Ev squeezes my shoulder. "Of course, man. I'm a little overwhelmed myself. I'm not going to lie, I've thought about it hundreds of times over the years, but I never really expected it to happen. So yeah, it's a lot. Kayla really thought you were jealous of Lake? I barely know the guy."

"Yeah, but something's there; you can't deny it. Even you admitted he was part of your fantasy last night."

Ev shrugs, trying to keep it casual, but there is a slight blush to his face. He tries to hide it by drinking his coffee. "What do you think about that?"

"About what? Your crush on Lake?"

Ev blushes again but nods.

"I don't know. At first, I thought Kayla may be right and I was jealous, but I don't feel that way anymore, just intrigued. And confused. So fucking confused."

Ev bursts out laughing. "Yeah, me too. You know how I said I didn't want you to come to the dinner next week when Lake's here?"

"Yeah," I reply, hiding the hurt in my voice. At the time, I wasn't sure why it hurt so much to be left out of the dinner except for the fact that I've always considered Ev and Mr. C my family, but maybe there's more to it.

"I've changed my mind. If you want, I'd like you to be there. I think it might be good for you to meet him in person, see if you feel and see what I do. I think there might be something there between us, but it's nothing compared to what I feel for you. I want you to be on board with it, even if we stay nothing more than friends."

I squeeze Ev's hand and rest my forehead against his, feeling at peace. That's what I want more than anything—to be fully a part of Ev's life. Even if we never do anything sexual again, for him to want me to be there and meet a guy who's clearly important to him, that means fucking everything to me.

"I'd love that."

A throat clears behind me, and on instinct, I go to step away from Ev, but he grabs my hand as he nods toward the coffee cups. "Morning, Dad, I made you some coffee."

I'm not sure what I'm expecting when Ev's pops catches us, but it's not this. I mean, we weren't even doing anything, but the moment was clearly intimate, so I expected some kind of reaction. But Mr. C just grunts and heads toward the steaming mug. "Thank you, Ev. You know I need my coffee in the morning."

We're still standing there holding hands, and I know he notices because he glances down, but he doesn't say a damn thing. And really, what do I want to say? He's not like my sperm donor. He knows full well that Ev is bisexual and never bats an eye, but he practically raised me. I expect for him to have something to say if he sees us holding hands and standing insanely close like some kind of couple.

But instead of commenting on whatever this is, he goes, "Ev, you have time for breakfast? I was gonna put on some eggs and bacon."

Ev pulls away from me to dig his phone out of his pocket. "Yeah, I've got some time. Breakfast sounds good. I'll help."

And just like that, the whole thing is over and I'm left floundering, wondering why I'm the only one making this into a thing.

THIRTEEN
LAKE

"Are you sure you don't want me to come with you?" River asks for the thousandth time.

It's the day I'm meeting Eric Cirillo and having dinner with him and his son, Evander, as well as another man that Evander just called Logan. I'm a little anxious over the dinner, but River is about to lose his mind, and I don't understand why.

"I'm not sure what you're so concerned about. I am perfectly capable of having a meal on my own."

We're in the bedroom of my townhouse while I pick an appropriate outfit. River is sprawled out on my bed and not helping me at all. Miri is asleep in the Pack n' Play I bought for my home so River and Cooper didn't have to keep moving it back and forth. River rolls his eyes at me as he tosses a rolled up pair of socks up and down idly.

"Lake, you're about to go to a strange man's home, one you only met once in your life as a child twenty years ago. And oh yeah, he's a drug dealer."

"Was. He was a drug dealer, River. You have to know I did an extensive background check on both Eric and Evander before confirming the details of this meeting. He's been clean since that day. Not even a parking ticket. No signs of drug use or dealing. Evander also has a clean record. He's an editor for a publishing company."

"Doesn't mean he's not a psychopath," River replies dryly.

"River, I assure you, I'll be fine. I'll keep my phone on me at all times, keep alert, and let you know as soon as I'm home, ok? But I don't need you to come with me. Believe it or not, I don't need a babysitter."

"Ugh." River sighs dramatically and throws the ball of socks at me. At least they're clean. "I know that. I'm not trying to babysit you. I'm just worried. This whole thing pulled all the crazies out of the woodwork. On top of that, I know you're more at risk because of your job. This whole thing just gives me chills. I'd feel so much better if I were there. Please."

I don't really know what to say about it. I mean, I don't mind River coming with me. In a way, it would be nice for him to meet the man that helped jumpstart our new life. But I don't want him to see me as this inconvenience he has to monitor because I'm unable to assess people on my own.

"They'd need to find out about my job for them to pose a danger to it. That's not happening."

"Lake, if you really don't want me to come, I understand and I'll do my best to wait to hear from you. I know you're more than capable of handling yourself. That's what you're thinking, isn't it? That I think you can't judge people or a situation and need me to watch out for you?" I hate this twin thing sometimes. "Well, I'll always look out for you, but it's not because you can't do it yourself. It's because you're my brother and I love you."

Ugh. He's going to win this one, isn't he? And honestly, having him there to navigate the social aspect isn't the worst thing. Also, I am concerned about the one person involved I hadn't been able to vet, the man named Logan.

"I'll text Evander and see if his father minds you coming

along. I don't want to bring a guest to a dinner party without permission."

River beams and jumps up and hugs me. "You don't know how relieved this makes me. Coop has something going on at work tonight so he won't be home till late, but Cam's home, so I'll see if he can watch Miri. I just baked a couple apple pies today, so I'll bring one with us, since I'm basically inviting myself."

I sigh as I finish up the text and continue to get dressed. When did River become an avid baker? I wonder if his newfound obsession is because of his adjusting hormones or just a new hobby. Before I can ponder on this too much, my phone rings, and I see a new text from Evander.

Dad says the more the merrier.

I look up at River. "He says it's ok if you come."

"Oh good. I'd be a nervous wreck otherwise. Ok, let me run back, get the baby settled, and get changed. I'll be back in time."

"Alright. I'm going to shower. You have a key."

River nods and bounds out of the room like he's nine and I told him he gets to go to an amusement park. It's strange, but I shrug it off. I'm glad I'll have my brother there. The whole meeting with Evander left me unsettled, and I'm glad to have someone I love and trust on my side.

I take a quick shower and dress in a pair of black slacks with a royal-blue button-up shirt. I'm lacing my shoes up when my security system buzzes. The code is entered, so I know it's River, and seconds later, I hear his footsteps pounding up my stairs.

River's slightly more casually dressed than I am, but he still looks good. He's wearing his work pants, which are a pair of khakis, and a dark-gray sweater. He's shaved and has his hair slicked back, so we don't look exactly the same, thank gods.

River whistled. "Damn, look at you."

I feel myself flush as I glance in the mirror. I look fine, I think. My hair is tamed and kempt, my beard trimmed, my clothes neat. I don't see what River is talking about.

"I mean you look good, bro."

I blush again. "Oh, thank you. You do too."

River grins. "Good, thanks. I left the pie by your front door so we don't forget it. I feel kind of bad that I invited myself. I'm probably overreacting. Cooper said I've been getting like that lately. I'll understand if you'd rather I stay here."

"No. I'm glad you're coming. Now let's get going so we're not late." River rolls his eyes but follows me back downstairs, grabbing the pie as we head out. He's used to me being anal about timliness and doesn't argue.

Neither River nor I enjoy driving into New York, but we felt like it would be better to have our car there just in case we do need to leave on short notice. I honestly believe there will be no issues, but it's better to be safe than sorry.

As we're driving, River glances at me. "So I hear you're meeting with Dr. Rooke next week and a fertility doctor he recommended. I guess regardless of what happens, the first step is that Zoe needs to freeze an embryo, and since the process hasn't even been started yet, they will get everything rolling then." Zoe and Avery decided that they'd freeze their embryos regardless of if I am a good candidate for surrogacy. That way, if they do decide in the future to have a child, even with someone else carrying the baby, they will be ready.

"How're you feeling? Between that and this whole thing . . ." He gestures in front of him, and I assume he's talking about the people we're about to meet. " . . . that's a lot of changes, and I know that can be overwhelming for you."

That's an understatement. It's always taken me longer than most to adjust to any type of change, and there has been a lot of it over the last year, but these most recent developments are more exciting to me than anything.

"I think I'm ok, actually. I feel prepared for the surrogacy, wherever that takes us. And as far as this meeting, I think it will be good. It's strange, but I had an unusual reaction to Evander. I'm curious to see if it's the same this time."

River side-eyes me as he drives, his nose scrunching in confusion. "What do you mean unusual?"

"I'm not sure. I just had this strange warm fluttery feeling in my belly the whole time."

"Like butterflies?" River is grinning, and I'm not sure why.

"I guess? But I wasn't particularly nervous."

"You don't only get butterflies from nerves, you know."

I glance at him, and he's smiling so hard, I'm surprised his face isn't aching. "What else do you get them from?"

"Lake, I think you might've been attracted to the man."

I frown, considering this. Have I ever really been attracted to someone before? Not to the point where I had a physical reaction, no. I can admit Evander is a good-looking man, but I know River means more than that.

"He was attractive, yes. Is that what you mean?"

River sighs like he's exasperated. "Lake, I mean you were turned on by the guy."

Turned on? "Like, did he give me an erection?"

River snorted. "Gods, Lake, I don't think I've ever heard it phrased that way. You can be turned on without having an erection."

"I'm not sure exactly what you're talking about, but I will admit I'm intrigued by the man."

"Alright, that's probably good enough for right now anyway. Let's see if you still feel that way after tonight."

After a while, we drive into a residential neighborhood. All of the houses are small, individual two-story homes. "I think it's this one," I tell River as he drives past it. He glances toward it and nods. Ok, let's try to find parking.

One of the nice things about our townhouse complex is we

have driveways and guest parking. Parking in the city is just as bad as driving in it.

Luckily, it doesn't take long to find a spot that's only a few houses down. It's a cute neighborhood. I can hear some kids playing outside since it's a warmer day. I wonder if this is where Evander grew up. We walk up to the house. There's a fairly steep staircase leading to the front door. The first thing I notice is how well kept it is, with a little flower bed below the windows. There's a plastic pumpkin on each step leading up to the front door.

It opens before I can knock, and we're greeted by a huge man that fills most of the doorway. He's holding a bowl of chips that he's munching on as he stands in the doorframe with a smile.

"I'm guessing this isn't Evander," River whispers to me. I described the man and showed him a picture from when I vetted him. I shake my head. Since this clearly also isn't Eric, I'm assuming this is the third man, Logan.

"Hey!" he says cheerfully. "Lake and River, I take it." I see his dark-blue eyes bounce from each of us, probably trying to figure out which one is which. "I'm Logan. Mr. C and Ev are just finishing up dinner out back. It's so nice out, Mr. C wanted to squeeze in one last outdoor dinner before it gets too cold."

I'm still a little shell-shocked by this man. I'm not sure what I expected, but his presence is so overpowering, it's almost overwhelming. Even though he is relaxed and friendly, there's this undercurrent of danger there.

River seems to have recovered quicker, as he steps up to the man, his right hand extended. "I'm River. It's nice to meet you. Thank you for letting me come so last minute." He doesn't elaborate as to why, and Logan doesn't ask.

His eyes are on me, assessing. I clear my throat. "You must be Lake, then." He steps back enough so we can walk into the home, but he's so close I can practically feel his breath on me as I slide by him. I force myself to get it together and look him in the eyes. He's another very attractive man, but he's completely different from Evander. Even as I'm captivated by his dark-blue eyes, I notice the rest of him. He's blonde, but the cut is short and efficient, almost a military style. His facial features are as tough and masculine as his build, which adds to the whole image. His nose is slightly larger than what's probably conventionally attractive, but it doesn't take anything away from him.

He smiles at me, amused I still haven't answered his question. His jawline is impressive, and I have to jerk my eyes away from it. "Oh yes, I'm Lake."

River is eyeing me suspiciously, but he turns back to Logan. "I brought a pie, homemade apple. I hope that's ok."

Logan beams, and that weird sensation in my stomach I had with Evander reappears. "Oh, sweet! I love apple pie. I'll put it in the kitchen for now, and I'll lead you out back."

The house is cute and well kept, though clearly outdated. I have to imagine that most of the furniture is the same as it was when Evander was a kid. I'm pretty sure this is his childhood home. There's small touches that show that a child grew up here, like notches in the wall with a growth chart and pictures of a much younger Evander. There's even a few with what must be Logan, though he was much much skinnier back then.

As Logan places the pie in the small kitchen, River catches my gaze and sees I'm staring at a picture of Evander, his father, and Logan at what must have been their high school graduation, as both boys are wearing graduation caps and gowns. I glance at the older man in the middle of the two teens and can see the pride in his eyes. There's a very similar picture of Luke with River and me in his home.

River turns back to Logan. "I take it you've known the Cirillos for a while." He nods toward the picture. I'm shocked by the question but glad he asked it. I'm curious about the relationship between this man and Evander.

"Oh yeah, Ev and I have been best friends since we were fifteen. Mr. C's like a father to me. I'd never have graduated or made it through the police academy without them."

Police academy. I make a mental note of that so I can vet him later. "Oh, are you a cop?" River asks with interest, and I'm even more glad he invited himself along. Social situations have always been difficult for me, but trying to have a conversation with Logan is even more so. His entire presence leaves me flustered.

After leaving the pie in the kitchen, Logan pops another handful of chips in his mouth as he gestures toward the sliding back door where I assume Evander and his father are. "Detective, actually. I work in Missing Persons."

I force back a swallow. Detective. I'll have to be careful what I reveal about my job, though that did answer some questions for me. Once I left the cafe last weekend and had a chance to think, I found myself wondering how Evander found me at all. Now, I can only assume he used some of Logan's resources to look for me. I'm not sure how they found the cafe, but I'll leave that question for later.

"C'mon, let's head back. I know Ev is excited to see you again." And there's that flutter in my stomach. River eyes me meaningfully as he follows Logan out the door and to the back. I'm not sure what his look means, but clearly he knows something I don't. There's no time to ask him about it, so I follow them outside.

The outdoor area is pretty typical for urban New York, for those lucky enough to have one at all. We walk out onto a deck that's raised above the ground. It's huge, and all I can think is that Dad would love this. He always complains about the lack of outdoor space in his home. Below the deck is a tiny patch of grass that's closed in by a beat-up old fence. The deck is well maintained, and there's a very impressive patio set that can easily seat ten people.

Standing near the grill are two men who easily could have been confused for the same person based on build and presence alone from behind, except that one of them has colorful tattoos crawling up their neck, and the other one's dark hair is speckled with gray.

"The guys are here," Logan calls as he ambles toward a big red cooler that's in the corner of the deck. He's oddly graceful for such a large man.

The two men turn around, and I get my first look at Evander since last week. Not much changed, obviously, but I still instantly feel that warmth again, and the feeling just gets stronger as he smiles at me. He has his dark hair slicked back again, and it looks like he changed the open gauges to closed ones that look like big black buttons. I'm actually surprised I noticed that. I'm not usually the best with details, but something about Evander has me memorizing everything about him. He's dressed more casually than we are, in dark jeans and a dark long-sleeve Henley.

"Lake!" he says excitedly. "I'm so glad you were able to make it." His eyes linger on me a little too long, and I have to fight the urge to look away. Eventually, he does and turns his smile toward River.

"You must be River. I'm Ev." He sticks out his hand toward my brother, who accepts it with a smile.

"Nice to meet you. Lake's been talking about you all week. Thank you for letting me crash the party at the last minute."

The other man, Evander's father, walks up to us. "Don't be ridiculous. We're happy to have you. The more the merrier."

Memories come flooding back to me as I look at Eric Cirillo for the first time in over twenty years. He's older, of course, with crinkles around his eyes and gray in his hair and beard, but not much else has changed. He and Evander look so much alike it's startling. Yes, I'm aware I'm an identical twin, but I look nothing like my biological father, and while we resemble our mom, it's nothing compared to the two of them. I'm getting a perfect glimpse of what Evander will look like in his fifties.

Eric's eyes are warm and a little wet as he takes me in, and his smile is genuine. I remember that smile. It's the same one he gave me as he ordered me an ice cream cone before bringing me back to Mom. "Lake, oh my gods, look at you. I'm so glad to see you."

I smile at the older man and start to offer him my hand to shake, but before it's even an inch away from my side, Eric takes the two steps necessary to enter my personal space and envelops me in a hug.

FOURTEEN
EVANDER

I'm not exactly sure what I expected to happen when I invited Lake to dinner. I expected it to be just Dad, Lake, and me; that's for sure. I definitely didn't expect to have Logan and Lake's twin brother here acting like overprotective fathers making sure their daughter comes home from prom with their virginity intact.

"Lake, Ev told me you were on an extended business trip. Do you take a lot of those working for the accounting firm?"

"So, Evander, how exactly did you know Lake goes to that coffee shop all the time? He doesn't exactly plaster it on social media."

And so it went, on and on. I stand up and grab another beer, making sure to get one for my dad and Lake too. I'm not sure if Lake even drinks, so far all he's had is water, but judging by the uncomfortable look on his face, he's willing to start tonight.

Besides the ridiculous posturing, the night is actually pleasant. I teared up at my dad and Lake's reunion. It seems like a piece of my dad has settled tonight at seeing that Lake is happy, well adjusted, and safe. Seeing Lake again, I won't lie, it does something for me.

He and his brother may be identical twins, but while I can acknowledge that River is an attractive man, I don't get the same tightness in my gut that I get every time I look at Lake. He certainly doesn't make me hard just by existing, but when River isn't interrogating me, he is a very warm and likable man. And without even trying, he makes it obvious Lake is hiding something.

River immediately warmed to my dad, showing him pictures of his daughter and his mate, as he called him, Cooper. He told him all about his job as a physical therapist, their home across the Hudson, he and Lake's little sister Essie, and their adoptive dad Luke. He was extremely open and honest, which makes Lake's evasive measures about his employment even more obvious.

"So where'd you go to school, Lake?" Logan asks as he scarfs down his third cheeseburger. I roll my eyes and look at my dad, who's just staring up at the night sky like maybe the gods will come down and smite him, ending this endless interrogation.

And I know the question seems innocent, but not out of Logan's mouth. He may seem casual now, but he's in full detective mode, which honestly kind of sucks. I was really hoping he'd meet Lake and immediately fall for him like I think I did. Logan and I are in this weird place now, and I want it resolved immediately. Nothing seems to change with our friendship, but all of that easy affection we share with each other is gone, and I know it's not coming back until we decide if we're gonna be more to each other than just friends.

A lot of that depends on the man sitting across from me in one of my dad's deck chairs though. Because the longer I spend with him, the more I feel this connection between us, and it will be hard to walk away from that. I will for Logan, but I don't want to. All I want to do is close this distance between us and wrap the man in my arms—and then get Logan to shut up and wrap his arms around the both of us. That would be fucking perfect. But it is clearly a fantasy.

"MIT," Lake responds.

"Oh wow, that's impressive. What's your degree in?" Logan asks.

"Lo, chill with the third degree," I snap at him, over this whole thing. He looks over at me, and I can see some guilt in his eyes. Good. He needs to fucking relax. This isn't an interrogation.

"Ok," he says after a breath. "Sorry, Lake, I get carried away with myself sometimes."

Lake looks a little confused but smiles slightly, and damn does he look adorable like that. "It's ok. I can tell how close you and Evander are, though Evander came looking for me, not the other way around."

Well fuck, he has us there. I stare pointedly at Logan. The man has a point. If anyone should be getting interrogated, it's us. And while River did, to an extent, he seemed a lot less nefarious about it than Logan does. It's Logan's job, though, and I understand that sometimes the lines blur.

My dad takes this opportunity to change the subject, thank gods. "So, besides work, what else is going on with your life?"

Lake seems to take this question extremely seriously and ponders it for a while before his face lights up. And fuck, my dick takes notice of that look. "Oh, I may be a surrogate for friends of ours."

We all already know this, since I'm a fucking stalker who can't mind my own business, but we all have the sense to act surprised. And honestly, I think we all do have questions.

"That's amazing, Lake. I'm glad you're able to do that for your friends," my dad says diplomatically. He's not one to press for information. I think it comes from years of being a drug dealer and working on the streets. The culture was very much *don't ask no questions and don't see nothing you're not supposed to*. It's probably why he didn't say anything when he walked into the kitchen and saw Logan and I holding hands and touching each other in a way we never have before. It was nothing inappropriate, but I know he must've been curious. But Dad was the king of minding his own business, and I know he is just waiting until I finally come clean.

"So, does that mean you're an Omega?" Logan asks, who is not the king of minding his own business. "Are they sure you're able to do that? I thought there were all types of requirements for being a surrogate, even when it's a female."

"Gods, Logan," I mutter under my breath. My dad pushes my half-finished beer toward me, and I finish it in two swallows.

Lake isn't offended though. If anything, his golden-brown eyes twinkle with excitement. This is clearly a subject he's comfortable discussing. "Yes, I was tested shortly after the gene was discovered in River. It was only logical, of course. As his identical twin, chances were pretty high. What's actually fascinating is how the gene is presenting itself in Essie, though. She's a female, but her blood tests show some differences in her DNA from regular non-Omega women, though there's no difference in her anatomy. They aren't sure what that will mean yet. The doctors suspect that any differences won't present themselves until after she has a baby. That seems to be what happened with River. He was completely normal until after his pregnancy, and now they are noticing some changes—"

"Lake, stay on subject," River chides gently, and I have to smile. At Lake's blush and River's eye roll, I imagine this is a common occurrence between them.

"Sorry, sometimes I get excited when discussing subjects I find interesting," Lake replies with a slight blush to his cheeks.

I glance at my dad and Logan. My dad's eyes are glistening with amusement and some kind of fatherly affection. And Logan, most of that animosity he has been showing toward Lake all night is quickly washing away. I can't quite place the look on his face now, but he has slipped out of cop mode, finally, and is now the Logan I know and love.

"That's ok," I tell Lake, smiling at him reassuringly. "I'll be honest, I haven't been paying too much attention to the science behind this—" Because I was too busy stalking you. "—so it's interesting to me."

Lake beams at me like I just told him he won the Nobel prize, and the affection I feel toward this man increases. "Anyway, we have a meeting with the scientists in charge of the Omega Project this week, and we'll see the plausibility of them being able to implant the embryo inside my uterus and of me carrying a pregnancy to term."

My dad looks at River, his expression serious. "I saw a bit on the news about your own delivery. There were some complications, right?"

River shudders. "Yes, though a lot of that came from them having no idea what to expect. I'm hoping that if Lake is able to carry the child, they'll have more knowledge on the whole thing."

It makes sense, but I have the inexplicable urge to tell Lake he can't be a surrogate, which is insane. But I hate, like, absolutely fucking loathe, the idea of him possibilly putting himself in danger, even if the risk is low. I literally have to bite my lip to the point that it's bleeding to keep from shouting my thoughts out loud. What the fuck is wrong with me?

"Have any of you been tested?" River asks. "I know they are opening the tests up to the public now." Yeah, in fact, a few politicians are pushing to make them mandatory and for anyone that tests as an Omega to have to have it listed on their license. Why? I really have no fucking clue. I'm sure it's a power and control thing.

"I have," Logan replies lazily, scooping some more pasta salad onto his plate. Dad and I don't bat an eye, we know how Logan eats, but I see both River and Lake eyeing the man discreetly. I get it though. It takes some getting used to. "Everyone in the department was required to. I am not an Omega, but they did notice some differences in my blood, kind of like with your sister, I guess. Though they think, if anything, it's the start of an Alpha gene." Logan shrugs. "They want me to get further testing but I haven't gotten around to it."

"I have as well. My employer was offering it for free, so I figured why not. I have no Alpha or Omega traits. Just plain old human here," I explain.

"Nothing wrong with that," Lake says, his voice a little husky.

"Yeah, that's how Avery and Zoe tested too, the friends Lake may surrogate for. My best friend, Cam, has the Omega gene, which is no surprise to anyone, honestly. If anyone looks like the Omegas from back in the day, it's definitely Cam," River tells us conversationally. The man can talk, and I wonder if he's always like this or if he's just glad to be out of the house and talking to people over the age of one.

"What about your . . . mate." Dad stumbles over the word, which I get. I'm still not sold on the fated mates bullshit.

River smiles. "I know it's weird. I just don't have a better term for it. Coop and I thought the fated mates thing was crazy too, but the more I got to know him, the more it just fit. And since we're not married or engaged yet, I feel like that term is the only one that makes sense. We're more than just boyfriends." River has a hazy look in his eyes as he thinks about his lover, the kind of look that normally would make me want to vomit, but today it makes me feel warm. What the fuck?

"And to answer your question, originally his tests showed no differences. That was when I was still pregnant. But after the baby, we both started to notice some changes. It's like having a child to care for and protect brought out some latent instincts inside both of us. When he retested, his genes had some more of the original Alpha qualities. Though, like you, Logan, it's not exactly the same as it used to be."

The conversation shifts again, and most of the rest of the night is spent with us talking and getting to know each other. It's crazy, but it feels like we're meant to all be one big family, though my feelings for Lake and Logan aren't exactly brotherly. But I feel a connection toward River too. Again, nothing sexual or romantic about it, but I somehow know that we were meant to meet him as well. That we should all be one big family, like a pack. It's an odd thought, but it fits.

Eventually, River and Lake have to leave. Dad invites them back and tells them to bring their father, Luke, as well as Cooper, River's daughter, and if Essie is around, she's also invited. Dad hugs the twins like they are his long lost children and then takes his leave. River looks at Logan and me, his gaze assessing before nodding slightly to himself.

"Why don't you say your goodbyes. I'll meet you in the car," River says quietly to Lake but loud enough that I hear him. Lake looks confused but agrees. After River says goodbye and thanks us again, he walks down the front steps and toward his car, leaving the three of us.

Being alone with the two men immediately changes the atmosphere of the room. It seems to be charged with the sexual tension that was a low undercurrent all night, but without our chaperones present, it's heightened.

Lake's eyes widen as he takes the two of us in. Even Logan is staring at him hungrily, and I wonder when the change happened, taking him from hard-assed detective to horny lover, but it's here now.

I've never seen a grown man look more innocent than Lake right now as his gaze bounces from me to Logan. Has he ever been with a guy? Or with anyone? He admitted to being single tonight, but we didn't learn much else about his sexuality. The way he's staring at us now, with a mix of innocence, confusion, and just a bit of lust, makes me wonder if he has any experience at all. The thought that he might be a virgin, that no one has touched him before, turns me on in a way that surprises me. What the fuck? I've never felt like this before, but I find myself wanting to be possessive of this man.

"Um, guys, I'm sorry. I don't understand what's going on here."

Logan's grin is feral, and holy fuck, that's hot as hell. My dick starts straining in my pants, and I wish I wore my looser jeans. "Don't worry, Little Bird, we'll show you."

FIFTEEN
LOGAN

I have no idea what came over me, but from the second I laid eyes on Lake, he felt like mine. It is a fucking bizzare thought, but there's no other way to describe it. The way he froze in Mr. C's doorway when he first saw me, his eyes wide, his mouth parted slightly? Fuck. It sparked all of these instincts in me I didn't know I had. And I knew. I just knew he belonged to me.

The feeling is different than what I feel toward Ev. Maybe it's because I've known Ev forever and I've spent most of that time thinking of him as my brother. Seeing Ev all spread out on his bed like that, like a fucking dessert I needed to devour, my feelings definitely shifted. Over the week, my love for Ev has begun to slowly morph from brotherly affection to something more potent, more consuming, but there's no desire to possess him, to own him. It's scary, and probably fucking wrong, but it was the first thing that popped into my mind when I saw Lake.

Of course, that didn't mean I couldn't give the guy shit. Whatever initial attraction I had toward Lake, however powerful, was just that, attraction. But Ev already has feelings for the guy, even if he barely knows him. I could see it from the moment his eyes caught Lake and his whole face lit up. That happens for very few people.

At least for now, my loyalty to Ev comes first. So yeah, I interrogated the guy. And fuck, he was cute as he kept avoiding my questions and trying to change topics. He's definitely hiding something, but as the night wore on, I decided I didn't care. My instincts are rarely wrong, and they tell me Lake is a good person. I seriously doubt he's some secret crime lord or something, so whatever it is he's hiding, I'll let him keep that secret, for now.

Lake is staring at Ev, and right now, his expression is a mixture of fear, curiosity, and confusion. My poor little bird, he has no idea what's going on, does he? A thought occurs to me that he might be a virgin, but is that even possible? He's nearly thirty years old. Well, I guess that means nothing. I'm fucking thirty-two, and I've never even considered that I like men as well as women. Yet here I am, in the small foyer of Mr. C's house, closing in on two men and very fucking turned on.

I've spent the last couple of days trying to see what's going on with me. I watched gay porn. I paid attention to all the men around me, but none of it did anything for me. Some of the porn was hot, I'm not gonna lie, but I didn't get as horny from that as I am right now with two men who are fully dressed and doing nothing remotely sexual.

After a minor identity crisis, I've decided it doesn't matter. I couldn't care less if I'm bi, or pansexual, or straight. Why do I need a label? What I do know is I want more than friendship with Ev and that Lake turns me on in a way that's never happened with a female before. I'm too old to be worried about what that means. I never gave a fuck about society standards or what anyone thought about me. And sure, the guys I work with might give me a hard time, but they can go fuck themselves. I know what I want, and I'm going to take it.

Lake's eyes bounce from me to Ev, and then back again. "Um, guys, I'm sorry. I don't understand what's going on here."

I smile and take a step toward Lake. He takes a step back. His pouty bottom lip is stuck firmly between his teeth. My poor little bird looks rattled. "Don't worry, Little Bird, we'll show you."

Lake's eyes get even wider, and he glances toward the door. Maybe I'm pushing him too far? Before I can back off, though, Ev shoots me a dirty look. "Easy, Lo. You're freaking the guy out."

Ev closes the gap between him and Lake and gently takes the man's chin in his hand. They are about the same height, but Ev is more muscular and a little bulkier than Lake, making the man look smaller than he really is. "Hey, are you ok, Lake? Logan didn't mean to scare you. He can be a big brute sometimes, but he's totally harmless."

I shrug. I probably should be offended, but Ev's not wrong. I think I may have underestimated how little experience Lake has, or maybe he doesn't feel this attraction between the three of us. After all, I was kind of an asshole to him most of the night. I wouldn't blame him if he wanted to stay away from me. I smile slightly. Well, if that's the case, I'll definitely enjoy the chase.

Lake's head cocks to the side like he's trying to figure out Ev's words. "Hmm? Oh, Logan didn't scare me. I'm just unsure what's going on. River left so I can say my goodbyes, which makes absolutely no sense. We already said goodbye. Why do I need to say it again? Then you two are acting very strangely. I know I should understand what's going on, but sometimes I don't pick up on social cues. So I apologize if that's what's happening."

Oh, my sweet, pure, little bird. I see the pure adoration on Ev's face, and I know he feels the same way. We are probably the wrong guys for this. We're going to eat this poor man alive. But the thought of it being anyone else makes me all itchy and agitated. No, Lake's mine. I don't understand this feeling, but I know for an absolute fact that these two men in this room with me belong to me, and I will make that happen.

Ev's expression turns serious. "Lake, Logan and I are very attracted to you. I know it's very sudden, and we barely know you, but I knew from the second I saw you. Hell, even before that, I felt a connection to you, and it's only getting stronger. Logan and I are trying to figure out what's going on between us, but I think he's feeling this same connection."

I nod. "I am. It's fucking bizarre. Just last week, I was straight and fucking my way through every available female in New York, but I feel it."

Ev just shoots me a dirty look and rolls his eyes. What? He turns back to Lake. "I think your brother saw there's some interest here. That's why he left to give us some time alone. What we want to know is, do you feel it too? If you don't, that's totally fine and we'll back off." Ev shoots me another look and I put my hands up defensively. What does he think I'm gonna do? I don't pursue people who aren't interested in me.

Lake seems to consider this question. He's quiet for so long it's starting to freak me out. What if he doesn't feel this? Or he does but doesn't want anything to do with us? My chest tightens at the thought. I force myself to calm down. I'm just fucking horny. That's all.

"Is that what I'm feeling? This butterfly feeling in my stomach every time I look at you two?"

Oh, my heart fucking melts. "Lake, you've been turned on before, right? Like by a man, or a woman, or both?"

"I'm not sure. I can acknowledge when someone is good-looking, and I've certainly masturbated before, but I'm not sure if I've ever been truly attracted to someone. My brother suggested I should watch porn before, but it did nothing for me."

"No one has ever gotten you hard?"

"I had a girl give me a blowjob in college. She was able to

get me hard and I ejaculated, but it seemed more because of the action than any feelings toward the girl."

Hmm. Is Lake ace maybe, or demisexual? I suppose it's possible. "What about a guy?" I ask Lake.

"Again, in college, my roommate jerked me off once. I did orgasm, but I felt nothing toward the man. I have gotten erections before, obviously, I just never had any desire to act on them. After college, anyone else who offered, I turned down. I felt nothing toward the people, and I don't believe meaningless sex works for me."

I'm quiet as I try to process this. "Ok, well, I'm not talking about sex," Ev replies. He's not? "At least, not right away. I'd like to get to know you better as more than a friend. I want to take you out on a date. Fuck, I want both Logan and me to."

I blink. I never really thought about the logistics of this outside the bedroom, though I should have. I've only just realized I like dick at all. Am I ready to publicly date two guys already? I decide pretty quickly that yes, yes I am. I've had more than one girl comment that I should just date Ev. If he's that important to me, why not make that a reality? And Lake, he just fits with us. We'll see what happens long-term, but for now, I absolutely want to see where this goes.

Lake seems surprised by this development. "You want to take me out on a date? Like, to dinner?"

Ev shrugs. "Sure. Or whatever we decide to do. It doesn't have to be dinner."

"I've never gone on a date before," Lake tells us. He doesn't sound upset about this, just factual.

I can't stand on the sidelines anymore. I step into their personal space and lower my head so that our faces are very close. "Let us take you out on your very first date, Little Bird. I swear we'll make it special."

Lake blushes and shifts uncomfortably. Fuck, maybe he's going to say no. But, he looks up and meets both mine and Ev's eyes. "Ok. I'd like that." Oh thank gods. "Not tomorrow though. I'm meeting the specialists with Avery and Zoe."

Oh right. The surrogate thing. I still have to work my feelings out on that. I can easily picture Lake with a round belly full of baby, even if it's not my child, but I am concerned about the dangers associated with it. I force myself to stay silent, though. We are definitely not at the point that I can have any opinion on the subject.

"How about next Friday night? That's your night off, right?" Ev asks me.

I shrug. "It's supposed to be."

"Yes, Friday night is good. Will you text me the details?"

Ev smiles affectionately. Man, these men are fucking cute. I just want to scoop them both up and throw them in my bed. "Of course, sweetheart."

Lake looks ready to leave, but Ev gently stops him. "Before you go, can I kiss you?"

Lake freezes, his pupils blown. I wonder if he's going to just run, but instead he nods slowly. Ev's smile widens as his eyes darken, and I witness the most erotic thing I've seen in my life.

The kiss isn't much, it's pretty innocent, actually, but my dick is about to explode in my pants. Ev leans forward slowly, probably giving Lake a chance to back away. He doesn't. One of Ev's hands comes up and cups the back of Lake's head. Lake shivers and tentatively touches Ev's shoulder just as their lips touch. I don't even think there's tongue, and the kiss doesn't last long, but I swear to fuck, I see sparks flying.

Eventually, Ev pulls away, and Lake blinks at him in a daze. Fuck, my little bird is so sweet, and there's no way I'm letting him leave without my own taste.

I turn him so he's facing me. "Can I have a turn?"

Lake can't speak, but his nod is very clear consent. I tip his head up with a hand on his chin and devour his mouth. Fuck, I wasn't lying. Lake even tastes sweet. He's a little hesitant, and clearly inexperienced, but it's somehow the best kiss I've had in my life. The only thing that would make it better is if Ev's involved.

I blindly reach out toward my other man and turn my head to face him. Ev gets the hint, and his lips are on mine. There's none of that hesitation that Lake has. Ev knows what the fuck he's doing and what he wants, and it's so damn hot. At the same time, we both turn back toward Lake and begin kissing him. We're going to destroy this man, and it's going to be glorious.

Eventually, we all need air. We pull away at the same time, all of us panting like we ran a damn marathon. Lake looks positively debauched, his perfectly maintained hair all mussed up, his lips red, swollen, and spit slicked. I have to resist the urge to take him right here in Mr. C's foyer. But no, Lake deserves more than that. And so does Mr. C. It's bad enough I ate his son's cum one room over. I won't fuck a virtual stranger in his front room. But damn, do I want to.

"I-I have to go. I'm sure River is wondering where I am."

I seriously doubt that. They may be identical twins, but they clearly have different personalities. River is not the sexually naive man Lake is. But I let it go. Lake needs some time to process whatever just happened. So do I. I know I should be freaking out more than I am, but everything just feels so right, like I finally figured out where I'm supposed to be, and I'm not going to question that.

Ev pops back into reality quicker than I do. He leans forward and kisses the top of Lake's head. "Thank you for that," he says softly. "Drive safely, and please just let me know when you get home? So I don't worry?"

Lake nods. "I can do that." His eyes bounce between the two of us once more, and I think he's going to say something else. But instead, he just clutches his left wrist in his right hand and turns toward the door. "Bye, and um, thank you." And with those final adorably awkward words, Lake runs out of the house and down the stairs toward wherever River is parked.

Both of us watch until we can no longer see him. I turn toward Ev, my mouth partially open, about to speak, when Ev literally pounces on me, his fingers clutching strands of my hair as his mouth covers mine.

SIXTEEN
LAKE

River eyes me suspiciously as soon as I get into the car, a strange expression on his face.

"What?" I ask.

River snorts. "What? Seriously, Lake? You're in there forever and come out looking like you had a quickie in Mr. Cirillo's living room." River's mouth drops open and he covers it dramatically. "Oh my gods, *did* you have a quickie in his living room?"

I can only assume he means sex. "If you're referring to sex, then no, we did not do that." I tilt my head toward him. "Is it even possible to have penatrative sex in that short amount of time?"

River starts the car with a shake of his head. "I didn't necessarily mean penatrative sex, as you put it, but yeah, you'd be surprised how quick some guys get off. I wouldn't expect it from those two, they look like they know what they're doing, but you never know."

I stay silent, trying to process his words. They both made some comments that make me think they may have been considering some type of sexual relationship with me, and I'm unsure how I feel about it. It's never been something I've considered too much one way or the other. But for some reason, I can imagine eventually being comfortable enough with the two of them to get there. That's a thought for another day.

"They asked me out on a date," I blurt out after minutes of silence.

River glances my way, that strange smile back. "Oh yeah? Both of them?"

"Yes, is that strange?"

River shrugs. "It's not the societal norm, but I don't think it's strange. I never really understood why anyone else cared about a complete stranger's personal life. Cooper and I aren't hurting anyone fucking each other and making babies, and you wouldn't be hurting anyone if you date two men. There will be people who respond negatively to it, just so you're aware. But if it doesn't bother you, and you don't feel forced, then there's no issue with it."

I think about what River says. I definitely want to pursue more with Evander and Logan, though I'm not exactly sure what that means yet. Does it bother me that there's two of them? No, it feels right. And generally, I don't let other people's opinions of me affect my decisions, but there are a few people I do care about.

"Do you think Dad would be upset?"

River shakes his head. "Nah. He might be a little surprised, especially since you never showed any interest in anyone before now, at least that we know of, but he won't be upset. He'll like them. I'd just make sure you tell him you're interested in them before he meets everyone for Sunday dinner. You don't want him to be blindsided."

That makes sense. "But he won't be disappointed?"

River scowls. "Fuck, no. Lake, Dad is so proud of you, and

nothing short of murdering someone would change that. Even then, it would probably depend on the circumstances. He'd never, ever be disappointed in you for liking two men."

River seems so confident that I start to believe him. I think Dad and River are the two people in the world I'd never want to disappoint. They mean too much to me. My mind thinks of Evander, but I push that to the side. Too soon.

"What about Essie? And Cooper?"

"Essie will be jealous as fuck. And Cooper couldn't give two shits about that kind of thing as long as you're happy and they treat you well. You might have resistance from the public, and I don't know how the NYPD will feel about it, but your family has your back, Lake. You do what feels right. And before you ask, Avery and Zoe will not change their mind if you decide to date two men at the same time. They are the most open-minded people I know, and besides, their relationship is open."

That's news to me, but I can't say I'm surprised. I feel like some of the stress is starting to ebb away. I'm worried slightly about my job, not because they'll care if I'm seeing two people, but because anytime anyone starts a serious relationship, it's a huge vetting process. Until it's complete, we have to keep everything a secret. I hate it, but we're nowhere near the point that I'm subjecting them to that.

"They kissed me," I blurt out again, and River laughs.

"I was wondering when you'd get to the good part. There was no way you came back looking like that just from getting asked on a date. How was it?"

How was it? That's a good question. It was overwhelming, and addicting, sweet, hot, and wonderful all rolled into one. "It was very good," I reply diplomatically.

River snorts again. "Very good? That's all I'm getting?"

"Yes."

He chuckles. "Ok, then. I guess that'll have to do."

I'm glad he doesn't push for more. When we get back to our complex, he asks me if I want to go back to his place or mine, and I tell him to take me to my home. I need some time to process everything that happened. Plus, for some reason, I have an erection. And while it went down some from the car ride, it's still quite uncomfortable and I need to take care of that. I masturbated yesterday, and I typically don't need to every day, but today seems to be an exception. I'm assuming it's because of the scene with Evander and Logan.

Once I'm inside, I quickly text Ev to tell him I made it home like he asked. The thought that he's concerned about my safety gives me that warm fluttery feeling, which reminds me, once again, of my erection. After I have taken care of my needs, I try to process everything that happened tonight. It was overwhelming, and I definitely need some time to myself to regroup. Meeting with Eric was amazing, but it did open a lot of old wounds that I had buried deeply. Even discussing it on television during River's baby shower didn't expose those scars like seeing Eric did. I'm so glad that the situation was the push the man needed to get his life in order. He seems to be an amazing man and a great father to Evander, and I'm glad he got to finally experience it, even if it took longer than it should have.

It's a shame that Seth didn't have the same revelation, but it doesn't bother me much. I have much better than Seth now. For his own sake, I wish Seth had gotten clean and made something of his life, but River and I hit the lottery with Luke as our dad, and I'd never change that.

I think everything is going to be raw for a while as I remember more of the past, but I know it will be healing for me.

Of course, that wasn't the only or even most overwhelming part of the night. Logan and Evander. I'm not sure what to make of the whole situation. I went into the night wanting to explore that strange feeling I got when I saw Evander, only to realize I have it with Logan too. The man is intimidating in a way I've never experienced before.

My smaller stature has never bothered me. I'm smarter than most people and use that to keep control of most situations. However, something about Logan makes me feel out of control, but not in a bad way. Just different.

And Evander. Evander makes me feel safe. Another feeling that's strange to me. How does a virtual stranger make me feel safe? And why? I'm not in danger or a nervous person by nature, but I find myself relaxing on a whole new level with Evander.

Sleep evades me as my thoughts race, and I kind of wish my meeting with Dr. Rooke wasn't tomorrow. I need to work. To just throw myself completely into my assignments and not think about anything else. I'll have to just manage for a little while longer.

I eventually give up on sleeping and decide maybe I should work for an hour. It should be enough to calm my brain, and then I can get a few hours of sleep before the meeting. One hour turns to two, which turns to three, and before I realize it, my alarm is going off, it's time to get ready to meet Avery and Zoe, and I didn't sleep a wink. At least I'll have time to get a coffee at Dream Beans Cafe before I go.

I muddle my way through my morning routine before trudging into the coffee shop. My favorite barista, Lucy, is there. She lights up when she sees me. "Lake! It's so good to see you. How did last night go? I messaged Ev but he hasn't answered."

I blinked, trying to make sense of her words. "How do you know about last night?"

"Oh! Ev and I are friends. We've only known each other for a little over a month, but we became close. I've been to a couple Sunday dinners at Ev's dad's before. They're nice, right?"

I'm starting to wonder why Lucy's my favorite. Is she always so energetic and bubbly? "Yes, they are," I respond. That's the appropriate response, right?

Lucy looks at me curiously as she makes my drink. Did I order, or does she just know it? Of course she knows it. Wow, I really should've slept last night.

"And everything went well?" I'm starting to wonder exactly how much she knows, but I let it go. I'll ask Evander later.

"Yes, it went well, thank you. I don't mean to be rude, but I have an appointment soon. Maybe we can chat more next time?"

Lucy looks embarrassed as she nods. "Of course! Sorry, let me finish up your drink, hang on."

Lucy quickly hands me my coffee, and I pay and thank her and leave the shop. I'm meeting Avery and Zoe at the office since it's in the city, so I need to hurry up and get on the train before I miss it.

Zoe and Avery are already there when I finally arrive. I've only been to the building once before, when I took my Omega test. The availability of the tests are becoming more widespread now, and even primary care physicians are offering the test in some locations, but when I took it, you had to travel to the Omega Project building in order to get it done.

There's nothing special about the building. It looks like every other one in New York, similar to my own. That's what government buildings are always like: unassuming so people don't question them.

Zoe hugs me as usual when she sees me. "Are you ready for this?" she asks. Today, Zoe is wearing a long-sleeve dress that reaches her ankles. It's covered in some colorful geometric pattern. And as usual, she looks beautiful.

"Yes," I tell her, even if I'm a little anxious. "Are you?"

She nods somberly. "Yes. I'm sure we're all a little worried. But, I'm excited too. Let's see what's in store for us."

It turns out all that is in store for us today is a lot of testing. Zoe and Avery start the process needed to freeze their embryos. After some brief introductions and a rundown on what to expect, Zoe and Avery are whisked one way and I'm taken to the other side of the building. I get blood work done, again, as well as fill out extensive paperwork. They do a physical and take some internal scans of my uterus. I'm asked hundreds of questions.

When we're finally done, I think we're all exhausted, and my lack of sleep is only a small part of that. I'm ready to crash when I finally make it back, but I do manage to pull out my phone and send a group text to Dad, Essie, and River to let them know I'm ok and the process is started. I tell them it will probably be a couple of weeks before we know if we can proceed to the next step.

As I'm putting my phone away, I get another text. This one is from Evander. My heart skips a beat as I open it, and I see another number is also part of the chat. I guess it must be Logan's.

Hey, sweetheart, we know you had your appointment today, and we just wanted to check in and see how it went.

Yeah, is our little bird knocked up yet?

I shake my head. Yes, that's definitely Logan. My heart warms at their messages, though. I don't know why I'm reacting to a text so much but I'm genuinely touched that they contacted me and remembered my appointment.

I also have so many questions, like why does Logan call me Little Bird? But I'm too exhausted to worry about that now.

I respond quickly. *Yes, my appointment was this morning. I'm back now and exhausted, but everything went well. It was mostly just testing. And no, I'm not "knocked up," as you so crudely put it. The process is not that quick. Thank you for reaching out. I'm very tired, though, and am going to sleep, so if I don't answer, that's why.*

There, that covers everything, right? I immediately get two messages back before I can even put my phone on do not disturb.

Sleep well, sweetheart. We'll talk later, once you're awake.

Logan's starts with a smiley face emoji with its tongue

sticking out. Then he replies: *Good night, Little Bird. I hope you dream of us.*

I roll my eyes. He is utterly ridiculous. However, I find myself smiling as I climb into bed, and once my eyes close, I do, in fact, dream of them.

SEVENTEEN
EVANDER

My alarm going off wakes me up from one of the deepest sleeps I've had in a while. Groaning, I try to roll over to grab my phone and shut it off but find that I can't move. Logan has the majority of his massive body thrown across mine. His muscular thigh is resting across my stomach, his head on my chest, and his arms are wrapped tightly around me.

Since I can't move, I take a moment to admire his body. Logan is all muscle, and it's obvious how much he works out, but he doesn't look like one of the roided-up bodybuilders. On him, it looks natural. Unlike me, he only has one tattoo, a small piece dedicated to his mom, who died when he was little. Besides that and a few scars, his skin is completely smooth and unmarked. My eyes roam down to his ass, and damn, what an ass it is. He's wearing a tight pair of briefs—neither of us is ready to sleep completely naked together—but it does nothing to hide his tight rounded cheeks. Or the erection pushing into my stomach.

My alarm is still blaring, and I have no idea how Logan is sleeping through it. He's a cop. I would've thought he'd be alert even in his sleep, but apparently not. I manage to free my arm from Logan's clutches and finally get my phone. Once the alarm is off, I close my eyes and just enjoy the moment.

Logan showed up at my doorstep at 2 am last night. Apparently, the really rough case he was working on just shifted from Missing Persons to Homicide, and he was taking it hard. It was a seven-year-old little girl, so I get it. I'd never seen Logan cry, though, so when I stumbled to my door half asleep and saw him standing there with bloodshot eyes and blotchy cheeks, it really fucked with me.

We didn't do anything besides cuddle until exhaustion finally took Logan. It just didn't feel right without Lake here. We need to talk and all get on the same page. Besides, everything still feels so new with Logan. Sometimes I forget I can hope for more than just friendship with him.

I need to get up, though, which is easier said than done. Thankfully, I'm working from home today, but I still need to get started. I'm glad Logan has the day off so he can get some rest and regroup from his rough night. The best part about all of this is it's Friday, the night of our date with Lake.

As excited as I am, I'm pretty nervous about it. I've never tried to date two people at the same time before. I have no idea how this is supposed to go, especially when one of those people is my best friend. And Lake. I'm not sure how to even express my feelings for Lake. He's so unique, and I never quite know how he's going to react to a situation. He's so pure and honest, and it makes me want to hold him close and never let him go.

I was shocked when he said this would be his first date, and I'm excited to see what Logan has planned for it. Logan is still sound asleep when I get out of the shower, so I throw on a pair of black sweats and a black Nirvana T-shirt I've had since I was a teenager and stumble into my kitchen in desperate need of coffee.

I hate to fucking admit it, but the stuff I have here isn't as good as the coffee at Dream Beans. Fucking Lucy and her organically grown beans. Speaking of Lucy, I feel guilty that I brushed her off all week, and as I let the caffeine do its job, I pull out my phone and text her.

Hey, babe. Sorry I've been an asshole and ignored you most of the week. I've just been trying to process everything. I've got a date tonight, but are you free Saturday?

It takes less than five seconds for the three little dots to appear on the screen. Was she waiting for this?

Oh, finally, you remember I exist <smiley face with tongue sticking out>. I guess I can find some time to squeeze you in tomorrow. Wow, sarcastic much? *And wait, did you say date? With Lake?!?!?!*

Yes, and Logan.

I send it and wait. In the time it takes me to drink one sip of my coffee, my phone starts ringing. I hide my smile as I answer my phone.

"Hello?"

"You little shit! You just casually throw in that you're going on a date with Logan and think I won't notice? When the hell did you and Logan become a thing?"

I have to bite back my laughter. "Gods, Lu, it's brand new, and besides, there's not much to tell yet. We're not even a thing. I don't exactly know what we are, but all I can say is that it makes me happy."

Lucy squeals into my ear. "This is so exciting! I know I just met you guys, but the minute I saw you and Logan together, I thought, oh, this is why there was no chemistry between Ev and me, because of this guy. Then I just sat back and waited to see if y'all would ever get your heads out of your asses. I'm glad I didn't have to wait long."

"You're ridiculous, Lu. We're taking our time. Logan thought he was completely straight until a week ago, and now he's interested in two guys. And Lake, he's special, but also completely innocent. We're going to go slow, and I'm fine with that."

"But, you're going on a date tonight, right? So that's a good start."

I smile as something settles inside of me. "Yes, it's a really good start."

"I want all the details. Who's planning it? Where are you going? Do you plan to get lucky tonight?"

"Get lucky? What are we, 60? And I don't know. I'm certainly not going to say no, but I don't think we're ready for that. Logan's planning it. I wanted to, but he insisted."

"Aww, that's adorable. So, he's not freaking out?" she asked.

I rummage through my cabinets as I think of my answer until I find the cereal I was looking for. Grabbing a bowl, I pour some cereal and milk inside before answering.

"I don't think so. Logan has always taken everything in stride and rolled with the punches. It doesn't seem like he's handling this any differently."

"And how about you?"

My face scrunches in confusion even if Lucy can't see me. I lean against the counter, the phone resting between my shoulder and ear, as I eat. "Me? Lu, I've known I was bi since I was thirteen."

"Yeah, I didn't mean that. But you and Logan have been besties for what, fifteen years?"

"Eighteen, actually, but yeah."

"That's a long time to be that close to a person that you clearly are attracted to. And don't deny it. I saw it the first time I met Logan."

She's not wrong. I let myself forget about it for a long time, but Logan was my first crush, and it never completely went away. "So it's probably a bit of a shock that he's suddenly interested in you as more than friends. And then add in whatever is going on with Lake—it's a lot."

I sigh and shove a bite of cereal into my mouth. I really need to get better about my eating habits. And the gym. I typically work out four days a week, but the last couple of weeks I've been slacking. Ugh, when did life get so complicated? And why does Lucy have to be so brutally fucking honest and completely burst the bubble I've built around me?

"I haven't thought about it much. It's not like he purposely pushed me to the side. I do wonder what changed though. But it feels right now, so I'm not going to dwell on it."

Lucy is quiet for a moment before answering. "That's fair. I really am happy for you, but don't bottle it in. If you need to talk to me, or hell, even Logan, about how you're feeling, you need to do so. You know Logan's not going to get mad at you for expressing your feelings."

She's right. Logan would never hold it against me. But there's no need to rock the boat. I know he'd never mean to hurt me, even if he did. I don't want to make him feel guilty. He's going through enough.

Since I know Lucy won't accept that answer, I just say, "Thanks, Lu. You're the best." Lucy snorts, knowing I'm deflecting, but she doesn't call me on it.

"I gotta go, babe. I have to get this project done before tonight," I tell her, and it's not even a lie.

"Yeah, ok. I'll let the lame excuse go for now. Have fun tonight, and seriously, I want details. Don't shut me out for a week, ok?"

"I won't. I really am sorry about that."

"I know you are. It's fine. Talk to you later."

"Bye, Lu." I hang up with a chuckle and turn to dump my empty bowl in the sink and crash right into Logan. Literally.

"Oh, hey, Lo," I say awkwardly, complete with a little wave. *Wow, real smooth, Ev.* Times like this have been extremely uncomfortable between Lo and me for the last few days. For the most part, it seems like nothing changed, but then there's times like right now, which feel like the morning after, even though we didn't fuck or do anything remotely sexual, and I don't know how to handle it. Plus, I have no idea how much of that conversation he heard.

Logan doesn't seem to have the issues I'm having, which is so typically Logan. Once he commits to something, he just goes for it without thinking too hard about it. He just smirks at me, tips my chin up, and kisses me chastely on the lips. He tastes like toothpaste, which I'm thankful for because I don't do morning breath.

"Good morning," I whisper, my voice husky.

"Morning. Do you mind if I snag some coffee before I head home?"

I roll my eyes. Maybe he's not as comfortable as I thought. Logan never asks before he takes food at my place. "Since when do you ask?"

Logan just grins. He's pouring himself a mug, but his eyes are on my open cabinet, and I know he sees something he wants to munch on as well. "I was just trying to be polite."

"Well, don't. It's weird. You know you can have anything I have, Lo. And you don't need to leave. I don't mind you being here while I work."

"I got a couple things I need to get done before our date tonight. I just got a call, and I need to go into work for at least a few hours. I need to get all the files for the case over to Homicide." His voice catches, and the happy-go-lucky act disappears for a moment. "I'll be back in time for our date."

I walk closer and, on instinct, wrap my arms around Logan. He sighs into my embrace. "You know I'm not worried about that. Obviously I want you there, but I understand your job comes first. I have a feeling Lake would understand too. It seems like he often has last-minute changes as well."

Logan just grunts. I know he's trying to let go of whatever Lake is keeping from us. We barely know the guy. He's entitled to secrets, and both of us are pretty sure he's not hiding criminal activities, so we'll let him tell us in time. But Logan is a detective at heart, so it's not exactly easy for him to not investigate.

"Well, either way, I planned this date, and I won't miss it." Logan pulls a box of Pop-Tarts out of my cabinet. He's only wearing a pair of briefs that are so old they're practically see-through.

Why is that so fucking hot?

It's weird because even though I always thought Logan was hot, nothing felt this sexually charged before. I mean, the guy is just eating a cold Pop-Tart in my kitchen, for gods' sake, yet I'm popping half a boner from the sight. Ugh, I need to get to work.

"I'm going to head into my office. Just lock the door behind you."

"Ok," Logan tells me around his half-chewed pastry. It's so adorable that on instinct, instead of leaving, I close the space between us, clutch my hands in the hair on the back of his head, and kiss him.

Logan's taken by surprise and freezes. It only takes a moment for his brain to catch up, and Logan quickly swallows his bite before taking control. I only meant to give a quick peck before going to work, but apparently, that's not going to happen. Logan's big hand wraps around the back of my neck as he pulls me closer, not letting me go. Logan's tongue brushes against my teeth, and I part my lips, allowing him in.

I feel actual sparks run down my body as Logan completely devours me. The only kiss in my life that has ever come close was with Lake the other night. I don't know what that says about me or us, but when we finally part, I feel like I'm in a daze, and I'm so fucking turned on.

Logan is staring at me, his eyes completely clouded with lust as he pants, trying to catch his breath. His cock is practically bursting out of those little briefs. It would be so easy to take this further. To tell work I'm running late, drag Logan back into my bed, and have our way with each other until we're both satisfied.

It takes all the strength in me not to do just that. I feel very strongly that this isn't just going to be Logan and me in this relationship. And if that's the case, then we owe Lake a conversation before any combination of the three of us goes further than we just did. Hell, that fucking kiss was already more than I anticipated.

Logan seems to understand how hard it is for me to turn around and go to work because that possessive, turned-on look morphs into a smirk. "Don't you have to go work, babe?"

Oh, that cocky little shit. But he's right. So I adjust myself so I'm a little less uncomfortable and turn around, finally forcing myself out of my damn kitchen.

Logan is chuckling to himself as I leave. "Have a good day at work!" he calls after me, and ugh, I just want to go back and throw something at the guy. Then I find myself laughing as I finally close the door to my bedroom slash office. Logan is literally the only person that can make me go from a horny teenager who wants to jump him and have my way with him to absolutely driving me nuts. And I wouldn't want it any other way.

EIGHTEEN
LAKE

Since I already worked in the office today, I told Evander I'd meet him and Logan at his apartment for our date. They offered to come to New Jersey, since I'm the only one who has to keep coming into the city, but there's no point today.

I'm strangely calm, and I feel like maybe I shouldn't be. I received texts from River and Cooper in a group chat, then a separate group chat from Avery and Zoe, another text from Essie, and a phone call from Dad. Even River's friend Cam messaged me, which is really strange, since I don't think he particularly likes me. I still don't know the full story as to why he's living with my brother, but he's still there and shows no sign of leaving.

All of these well-wishes are confusing me. Maybe this is a bigger deal than I think it is? Or maybe they just aren't used to me expressing any interest in another person? Either way, the only nerves I have are because I'm probably going to have to cancel.

Assistant Director Wells threw this assignment on my desk ten minutes after four, and it was a mess. Whichever agent had this assignment before me either purposely sabotaged the case or is completely inept at their job. Either way, they were caught as soon as they tried to infiltrate this system. Not only that, the hackers on the other side used our intrusion as a way to get in too. And now, not only does Wells want me to stop these hackers before they break through our walls, but he wants me to somehow salvage this mission and find a way back in.

It's not completely impossible, of course, but it's going to be hours and hours of work, and I will completely miss my first date. I'm not sure what to tell them, either. Will they believe that a regular IT guy would have this kind of emergency? Probably not, and I'm a terrible liar. It's one thing to lie about my job on paper, but to lie to their faces or over the phone? They'll see right through it.

I don't want to cancel. It confuses me some, but I'm actually looking forward to this. I consider calling River and asking for advice, but I really need to work this out on my own. So, as soon as I'm in a good place where the systems can run on their own for a while, I tell my assistant to keep an eye on things while I make a personal phone call, and I walk outside the building to get some privacy.

I dial Evander's number and he answers on the third ring. "Hey, sweetheart. It's nice to hear from you."

I clear my throat, unsure what I'm actually going to tell him now that he's on the phone. "Hi, Evander."

Ev chuckles a bit, though I'm not sure why. Then he seems to catch some of the tension in my tone because he says, "Oh gods, Lake, you're not canceling, are you?"

I swallow back some of my guilt. He sounds devastated. "I don't want to."

"But you're going to anyway?" he asks cautiously.

"I can't give you any details, but I know you both already figured out I don't actually work for an accounting firm."

Evander's voice seems overly formal as he answers, "Yes, we suspected."

"I'm sorry. One day I'd like to tell you what I do, but I can't today. There's an emergency at work. One that quite literally could be life or death. It's going to take me hours to work through this. I won't be able to get away." I pause, expecting Evander to say something, but he doesn't.

"I'm sorry. I actually was looking forward to this."

Evander is quiet for so long I think he disconnected, but no, he's still there. "Will you get a break to eat?"

I have no idea what he's talking about. "There will be lulls when I can walk away, yes. And I have two very capable assistants that can be trusted once I wade through these early parts."

"How long do you think you can get away, Lake?" Evander asks patiently.

"Maybe a half an hour? Forty-five minutes?"

"Ok, Logan and I will bring food to you." Before I can protest, Evander continues, "I'm assuming we can't come into the building?"

"That's correct."

"Is there anywhere close by we can meet? A park or something?"

I'm still trying to process exactly what's happening, even as I rattle off the name of a small park with picnic tables and benches for eating. There's even a section with fire pits so it won't be as cold to eat outside.

"Perfect. I know of an amazing Greek place not far from there. Do you like Greek food?"

I'm so overwhelmed, not having expected this conversation to go like this at all, but I do manage to squeak out a "yes," to Evander's question.

"Is eight still ok? Or should we wait to hear from you?"

"Um, I believe eight's ok. If I need to change it, I can let you know."

"That sounds great, sweetheart. I'll let Logan know."

What just happened? He's not upset? He's not going to grill me about my job or the assignment? I don't ask any of these things. The only thing that somehow comes out is, "He won't be upset? I know he had plans."

Evander laughs. "Sweetheart, Logan is a detective with the NYPD. I can't even count how many times he's had to cancel or reschedule plans or how many girls broke up with him because his schedule was too unreliable. He's the last person to give you shit about a work commitment."

The tension in my shoulders starts to ease. I was concerned my first chance at romance was going to be dead before it began. The warmth in my belly spreads again, but now I'm finally starting to understand what it means.

"Thank you." I practically whisper it.

"There's no reason to thank me, Lake. I'm not going to ask about your job right now because I understand you can't tell me anything. But one day, if things go the way I want them to, I hope you'll be able to tell us the truth."

I swallow down the emotions threatening to well up. How did I manage to meet a man so understanding? I think of all my coworkers who are married or in relationships, even the analysts who don't have to hide their profession, and all of them are given a hard time regarding their hours. I'm not naive enough to think it'll never happen, but that he's willing to give this a chance means everything.

"I understand. And I hope to be able to tell you one day too. There's a system regarding that. Once we're at that place, I will give you and Logan all of the information."

"Thank you, sweetheart. That's all I ask. Ok, I'm sure you have to get back. If I don't hear from you, Logan and I will meet you at that park at eight. If anything changes, just text one or both of us."

"I will." I hang up and make my way back up to the office, feeling so much lighter. I still feel bad I'm making them change their plans, but hopefully, one day, we will be able to have the date Logan planned. For now, I'm just relieved they're still willing to see me at all. I quickly set an alarm for 7:50 and get back to work.

The next few hours go by in a blur. Like what usually happens when I'm in deep, I lose all track of time and anything that isn't the code in front of me. In fact, my alarm is probably blaring for at least a minute before my assistant gets my attention to let me know it's going off.

I stare at the phone for a full thirty seconds before I remember why I set the alarm to begin with. I'm meeting Logan and Evander for dinner. I'm not sure if it's still considered a date. I'll have to ask them. Bleary-eyed, I look back at my screens. Is it reasonable for me to walk away for half an hour now? Typically, I never would. I would just work throughout the night until the problem is resolved. If I eat or drink anything, it's whatever my assistant manages to shove in front of my face without me having to look away.

But realistically, it'll be ok if I take a short break. Both of my assistants recently had one, so I know they can manage without me, and I'm not actively hacking right now. I successfully blocked their hackers from infiltrating us and discovered who was in their system. That was the hard part. Now, I'm just working on getting back in.

That has been made ten times more difficult since they are now aware of a previous breach. Of course they changed their systems completely, added firewalls and encryptions, and are on high alert. It's not impossible, of course, but it'll take some time. And despite what my boss may think, it can wait an extra half an hour.

I don't have time to get changed, but I do sneak into the bathroom to wash my hands and face. I remember last minute that River warned me to make sure I brush my teeth. I can't exactly do that, but I take a mint out of my bag and eat it.

I look at myself in the mirror and decide I'm presentable. My hair is a hopeless case right now, but there's nothing I can do about it. There's circles under my eyes, but that's nothing new. I smooth out my white button-down shirt to attempt to get some of the wrinkles out. Alright, good enough.

I grab my light jacket that's hanging over my desk chair, tell my assistant to call if anything comes up, and run out of the building. I pull up my group text I have with Logan and Evander to let them know I'm on my way.

I immediately get two responses back. The first is from Logan, and it's just a picture of a takeout bag sitting on a picnic table with the words *Hurry, Little Bird* underneath it.

I scrunch my nose in confusion. Logan has been calling me that a lot. The three of us have exchanged some texts throughout the week. Most of them have just been friendly conversations, getting to know each other. But Logan has called me Little Bird in those texts quite a few times. I'll have to ask him about that. I don't consider myself a bird. It's a strange nickname.

I push that thought to the side for now as I read Evander's text. It's another picture. This one is a selfie of him and Logan sitting outside at a table, a fire flicking behind them. It's dark, so I can't quite make out their faces, but they look happy and not at all annoyed by the change of plans.

Relieved, I quickly go out onto the New York City streets and take the short walk to the park.

NINETEEN
LOGAN

I spot Lake first as he rushes down the pathway toward us. As he gets close enough that I can make him out in the streetlights, a smile spreads across my face. Gods, he's so fucking adorable. His eyes are scanning the park, trying to find us. He looks distracted and a little stressed. His shoulders are hunched and nearly up to his ears. He has a light-gray jacket wrapped around himself, and the collar is pulled up. His hair is all mussed, and it's pretty obvious he's had a rough day.

Ev waves and calls for our man, and his face completely brightens when he sees us. Fuck, that smile. I would do anything to keep that smile on his face.

Ev stands up as Lake reaches us and instantly wraps the man in a hug. His body stiffens at first, but it seems to mostly be confusion rather than discomfort. He awkwardly returns the hug. When Ev pulls away, I step in. "My turn."

I turn Lake's chin and kiss him gently on the lips. I don't go overboard like I did this morning with Ev. I don't want to overwhelm Lake, and my little bird looks like he's on the verge of losing it.

I was never much of a kisser when it came to women. I did it, obviously, but it never did much for me. But in the last week, I'm finding out I'm fucking addicted to Ev's and Lake's lips. I don't know if it's just them or if it would feel like this with any man. Regardless, I can't get enough of either of them. Hell, I jerked off twice today to the memory of that fucking kiss with Ev in his kitchen.

"Hi, Little Bird," I say huskily.

Lake's face scrunches in a combination of puzzlement and disgust. "Why do you keep calling me that? I'm not a bird."

I laugh as I wrap an arm around both men and lead them back to the table. I'm starving. We can have this conversation while eating.

"No, you're not. But when I saw you that first night, it was instantly what came to mind. You're extremely intelligent, but a little wary and standoffish. You can be very perceptive when you want to be, but you often stay toward the sidelines and people may not pick up on that." I smirk at him. "Plus, you're small, like a bird."

Ev glares at me. "He's not small. You're just massive."

I grin and begin to take the food out of the bag. "Same thing."

Lake still hasn't sat down, like he's trying to process my words. "If you don't like it, no big deal. I don't have to call you that."

Lake blinks, like he's finally coming back to the present. "No, I like it. I've never had a nickname before."

Well, that makes me feel special. "I'm glad I'm your first."

"I think you and Evander might be some other firsts for me as well."

I'm so taken by surprise, my soda comes shooting out of my mouth and all over the table. Ev, who was mid-bite of a gyro, practically chokes as he tries to swallow without laughing.

Lake's eyes bounce back and forth between us. "What just happened?"

Ev recovers before I do. "Sorry, sweetheart. We just weren't expecting that."

"Expecting what?" Oh, my innocent little bird.

"Just you essentially announcing you are a virgin before I even finish my first gyro," I announce jovially while opening the plastic container with the Greek salad.

Ev shoves a plate full of food in front of Lake, who seems to be trying to process everything. "Eat, sweetheart. I know you don't have that much time."

Lake smiles at Ev. "Thank you. I'm not sure when I last ate today. I tend to forget when things like this happen."

I won't lie, I'm fucking curious what's going on, but I promised Ev not to say anything. And generally, I agree. Lake needs to trust us and this relationship more before he reveals everything. I'm just thrilled he told us anything, but I can't help that I'm fucking nosy.

"Well, next time you get caught up at work, I'll make sure to, at the very least, text you to remind you to eat if I can't see you. It's important not to forget."

The exchange warms my soul. Ev is always such a caretaker. He's always feeding people. I think he must've been an Italian grandmother in a past life.

Lake seems shocked, but he smiles. "Thank you. I was afraid the two of you wouldn't want to see me after this. I'm so relieved and honestly surprised you were willing to adjust."

I frown. "Have a lot of people given you a hard time about your schedule, Little Bird?" I honestly don't know why that upsets me so much. The same thing happens to me all the time, but I hate the idea of someone putting Lake down because of his career.

Lake shrugs as he eats a fry. "Not me so much. My family is very understanding, and I don't really have anyone outside of my family and River's friends that cares enough about me to worry about my schedule. But, a lot of my coworkers experience issues with their significant others."

"Yeah, we have a similar problem. Poor Ev, he's going to have to be very *flexible*." I wink at Ev.

Ev gives me a smoldering look, making it clear he understood my double meaning. "Oh, I can be flexible all right."

The joke seems to go over Lake's head. Gods, he is so fucking cute. "But, seriously," Ev continues, "it's not a big deal. Will it suck, and will I be worried about you two? Definitely. But I understand. I hope I never make either of you feel bad about your occupations."

Lake's head tilts to the side. "The way you're talking, are you considering this a more long-term thing?"

Ev shrugs, trying to look casual even though I know there's nothing casual about how he feels. "I'd like to see where this goes. There's no rush, but yeah. I think we could possibly be long-term."

"I agree. I feel something special with you two, and I want to get to know you better, Lake, and Ev better from a relationship standpoint, and see where this takes us."

Lake's eyes are wide, but he nods enthusiastically. "I think I'd like that. Just be patient with me. I may say things that aren't appropriate, and I don't always understand innuendos. But I try."

I want to get up and hug the man, but Ev is sitting on the same side of the table as him, so he's closer, and he wraps an arm around Lake's thinner frame and brings him close. He kisses the top of Lake's head, and I just fucking melt. What is happening to me?

"We like you for who you are, Lake."

Lake just smiles and continues eating. I'm on my third gyro, but I can't keep my eyes off the two men in front of me. I'm watching Ev's lips move as he eats, how his Adam's apple bobs as he swallows, and it's turning me on. I've seen Ev eat countless times before, but I never once imagined my dick being wrapped before today. Holy fuck.

And Lake. Those lips that are currently wrapped around a straw deserve to be worshiped. I can't help but fantasize about them wrapped around something other than a straw. I imagine both of my men would looking fucking delicious on their knees for me.

At some point, Lake's phone buzzes. "Oh, that's my alarm," he explains. " I need to head back."

Lake starts to stand, but Ev gently grabs his wrist and stills him. "Before you go, there's something we need to discuss quickly."

"What's that?" he asks quietly.

"What's our opinions on any type of sexual activity when the other person isn't present?"

It's a good question, and I have to think about it for a second. I personally don't care if Ev and Lake get physical when I'm not there. Honestly, it's kind of hot to think about: coming home and getting a play-by-play of their activities.

Since Lake seems unsure of what to say, Ev plows on. "I personally don't have a problem with it, but I think our first time doing anything more than kissing should be the three of us together."

That's smart. "I like that, especially since this will be my first time with guys. I want to be with both of you." I look at Lake. "How about you, Little Bird?"

"I would like both of you to be there the first time as well. After that, I don't mind."

Ev kisses Lake. "Perfect, sweetheart. That's what we will do. Do you plan to go back home when you're done tonight?"

I frown, really hating that idea. It's already nearly 8:30, and Lake clearly isn't close to being done for the night. I know he's a grown ass man and capable, but just the thought of him traveling back to Jersey at some godsforsaken hour sets me on edge.

"No. I probably won't be done till the middle of the night, and there will be no more buses going. I'll probably sleep in the office."

I like that only slightly more than the original idea. "Ev's place is only ten minutes from here. Would you be interested in crashing at his apartment for the night? I have to imagine it's more comfortable than your office."

Lake's eyes narrow. "It's going to be very late."

I step up and wrap my arms around both men. Man, do they fit perfectly. "We'll wait for you, Little Bird."

His face lights up. "Really? You would do that?"

"Absolutely, Lake," I say, kissing the topping of his head.

"Just let me know when you're on your way, ok, sweetheart? I'll send you my address."

Lake seems happy and relaxed in my arms and I love it. "I do have to leave. You can't come into the building, but would you at least walk that way with me? I don't want to separate from you two yet."

My smile is huge, and I can practically feel Ev's contentment as he replies, "Good, sweetheart, because we feel the same way."

TWENTY
EVANDER

"You sure you don't want to keep playing?" Logan asks me, holding out a Switch controller.

I blink sleepily at him. "Nah, I'm exhausted. You can keep playing on your own."

Logan nods and changes the settings on *Super Smash Brothers* so he's playing against the NPCs instead. I haven't played games in years, so I really enjoyed this time I had with Logan while trying to stay up and wait for Lake. We pulled out all the updated versions of the games from my childhood: *Mario Kart*, *Mario Party*, and now *Super Smash Brothers*. But it's way past my bedtime now, and I just can't do it anymore.

It's a little after 2 am and I'm struggling to stay awake. Logan's used to working overnight, so he's still going strong. I, on the other hand, am feeling like an old man that can't hang with the kids anymore, but I don't want to crash and miss Lake's message.

Logan glances over at me where I'm now lying down on half the couch, my feet resting on Logan's lap, completely wrapped in a blanket. "Babe, why don't you sleep for a bit? I'll keep an eye out for Lake."

"I don't want him to walk here by himself. I'm going to order him an Uber when he says he's ready. I'd offer for us to go meet him, but I don't think he's ready for that yet."

Logan smiles affectionately at me. "Such a caretaker." My cheeks flush. He's not wrong; it always makes me happy to look after the people I care about. Logan pauses the game and rubs my leg before pulling out his phone.

"I'll message him and tell him to tell us when he's about ready to leave and we'll order him an Uber. You get some sleep. I'll look out for him."

"Thanks, baby." Logan grins at the nickname. I have no idea where it came from, but in my sleepy state, it just seems right.

I can't hang on any longer, and before I realize it, my eyes are closed and I'm in a deep sleep on the couch. I don't wake up until Logan's phone buzzes and I feel him heave himself up and walk to the front door.

The door opens, and I manage to open my eyes in time to see Logan lean in and kiss the top of Lake's head. "Hi, Little Bird. Did everything work out ok with whatever you were working on?"

I sit up on the couch and check the time. 2:45 am. Jeez. It feels like I've been asleep for hours, but it's really only been less than 45 minutes.

Poor Lake seems exhausted and frustrated. "I have to go back in tomorrow morning. I insisted my boss call it for the night, though. Everything is stable for now, and my team and I are going to make mistakes if we're too tired to focus."

I walk over to my stressed-out man and wrap my arms around him. "Smart. C'mon, let's get you to bed. Like you said, you need some rest before you have to go back."

"Ok." He jostles the travel bag he's wearing over his shoulder. "I keep a change of clothes and some hygiene products at work for situations like this. Do you mind if I just freshen up a bit?"

"Of course, sweetheart." I guide him to the bathroom and point out the bedroom for when he's done so he can meet us in there. His eyes widen in surprise, and I'm wondering if he thought he'd be sleeping on the couch.

"Would you be more comfortable on the couch?" I ask, really hoping he says no.

"I-I don't know. I've never slept in a bed with another person before, let alone two. Will there be enough room?"

Logan smirks. "Trust me, Lake, there's enough room. Ev's got a bed big enough to host an orgy."

Poor Lake's face turns beet red as I scowl at Logan. "Don't worry, sweetheart. I've hosted no orgies. I just like having space."

It's true, though. My bed is huge, way too big for the size of my bedroom. As soon as it was delivered, I wondered what possessed me to buy a bed that big. Now I have to wonder if I somehow knew one day I'd have two men I'd want to share it with, and one of those men is built like the Hulk.

"I'd like to try, if that's ok? To sleep in the bed. I'm honestly not sure if I can. I need space sometimes, but I'd like to try."

I kiss Lake on the side of the head. "That's perfectly fine. Here, go wash up, and we'll meet you inside."

Lake nods sheepishly before entering the bathroom and closing the door. I grab Logan's hand, and we make our way into my bedroom. The room isn't much, but it's the place that feels most like home for me. My massive king-sized bed takes up most of the bedroom. I have a small bedside table on one side but couldn't manage to squeeze in a second one. My desk takes up the majority of the other half of the room. Thankfully, I have a large closet, because I don't have room for a dresser. I did get some drawers installed inside the closet that are easily removed when I decide not to renew my lease, so I have a place for things I don't want hung up, like socks and underwear.

Besides the lack of space, it's a warm and comforting place

that makes me relaxed. The walls are painted a deep hunter green, my favorite color, and decorated with some of my favorite art. Actually, I commissioned my tattoo artist to draw quite a few of the art pieces I have hanging up throughout my apartment.

As soon as we enter the room, Logan slips out of his gray sweatpants and throws them into the corner of the room. Gods, he is so fucking hot. I can't get over how this man, the fucking perfect specimen, is becoming mine. After years and years of wishful thinking, this is finally becoming a reality. Add in Lake, and this whole thing only becomes more special. Deep down in my soul, I know it's meant to be.

Logan pulls down the covers and climbs in the bed. He pats spot next to him with a sleepy smile. "Come here, babe. I want to snuggle with my men."

He doesn't have to tell me twice. I crawl next to him and settle down. Immediately, I find comfort within Logan's muscular arms. As the toilet flushes and the water turns on in the bathroom, I turn to Logan. "I know you're not homophobic or anything, but I keep waiting for you to freak out about all of this."

Logan chuckles as he plays absently with my hair. I usually keep it slicked back, but after my shower, I didn't bother putting any product in it, so it's all in my face and probably looks insane right now. But I do enjoy the hell out of Logan massaging my head.

"Honestly, me too. But, I don't know. Everything seems like this is meant to be, so why fight it? And it doesn't bother me at all if I'm attracted to men. I mean, sure, I thought I'd figure out my sexuality before thirty-two, but I know it doesn't always work out that way."

I don't want to make a big deal about it, but I have to ask. "And this thing with us? I mean, you've known me since we were kids, and suddenly you want more than friendship? I'm not complaining; I'm just trying to understand where it's coming from."

Logan is serious as he plays with the strands of my dark hair. "I really don't know how to answer that, babe. I don't know why I suddenly see you in a completely different light, but I do. Maybe it's because you were so far in the friend box for me, I had my eyes closed to any other possibility? Or maybe it's because I had no inkling of an attraction to men, and I was blind to the way I felt? All I know is it started when you were trying to find Lake, and then the day I saw you jacking off? Yeah, something snapped into place for me. I know that's a shitty answer, but that's all I got."

I know I can make a bigger deal about it, but I don't want to. I know Logan never meant to hurt me or string me along. Neither of us can change the order things happened in. We just have to make the most of the situation we currently have. And I'm more than happy to do that.

The door to the bathroom opens, and I hear Lake walk down the hallway and into my room. He hesitates at the door when he sees Logan and me in bed already. I lick my lips at the picture Lake is right now. He's wearing loose navy-blue sweatpants with a long-sleeve light-gray sleep shirt. His hair is mussed up like he's already been asleep, and he's barefoot. He has his bag strapped to his shoulder, but he's holding it tightly to his chest.

"Maybe I should sleep on the couch." Lake takes a step back, and I quickly disentangle myself from Logan and crawl to the edge of the bed so I'm closer to him where he stands by the door.

"Can you tell me why, sweetheart? If you're uncomfortable sharing, then of course, I'll help you get set up. But if you think Logan and I don't want you here, then I promise you that's not the case."

Logan raises his eyebrows and stretches his arm out welcomely. "Yeah, Little Bird, it's not the same without you. Come here and snuggle between us."

Lake bites his lip as he watches the two of us. "Are you sure? It might become too much for me. But, I'd like to try, if that's ok?"

I smile sweetly at this beautiful man and hold out my hand to him. "That's more than ok. Come sleep with us."

I take his overnight bag from him and place it on the floor near the door, and then I hold my hand out toward Lake as an invitation. Lake grins shyly and takes my hand. We get the man settled in between the two of us. Logan wraps one arm around Lake and puts his other hand over Lake's head. I reach out and take his hand and snuggle my front up against Lake's back. We're all connected, and it feels amazing—right. I swear to gods, I feel an actual spark run through me once the three of us are all connected. What this means, I have no idea. All I know is that this is where I'm meant to be, and I wouldn't want anything else.

I'm not sure what happened, but we must have all fallen asleep, because before I know it, I'm waking up to the weight of a person climbing over me. I don't even have to open my eyes to know it's Lake. Just the feel of his slim body against mine is so different than the solid muscular figure of Logan.

"What'cha doing, sweetheart?" I ask huskily without opening my eyes.

I feel Lake startle on top of me, and then I hear a crash as he falls to the floor. My eyes fly open. Lake is sitting on the floor, looking startled and rubbing his ass. I climb out of the bed and kneel beside him. "Are you ok, sweetheart? What were you doing?"

"I had to use the bathroom, but both of you were sleeping. I was trying to get around you without waking you." Lake flinches. "Sorry that didn't go as planned."

I chuckle quietly and glance at the bed. Logan has rolled over and opened his eyes, a mixture of amusement and concern there. "Is there a reason you're on the floor?"

I think there's very few things I love more than Lake's blush, and right now it's crawling down his neck. I help Lake to his feet and kiss his cheek. "Go on, sweetheart, and do your thing."

Rubbing my eyes sleepily, I ask, "What time is it?"

Logan looks at his phone. "5 am."

Ugh. Still too early. But I seriously doubt I'll fall back to sleep. I crawl back into bed, and immediately Logan opens his arms up for me. After a few minutes, Lake returns, and I tap the bed. "Come back to bed with us, sweetheart. You still have some time before you have to leave, right?"

Lake nods, his expression serious. "Yes, but I doubt I'll be able to go back to sleep. Usually once I'm up, I'm up."

I can practically feel Logan's smile from where he's spooning me from behind. His lips brush against my bare shoulder as they move. "I can think of plenty of other things we can do in bed that's not sleeping."

The innuendo is clear enough that even Lake understands it. The tip of his tongue points out between his teeth, his golden-brown eyes wide as he watches us. Lake's nervous and looks like he's seconds away from bolting. I have this all-consuming fear that he'll not only leave the room, but the apartment, and I can't bear the thought. So I do something I've never done before and will probably never do again. I palm the back of Lake's neck and kiss him. Without brushing my teeth.

And it's not just a peck on the lips either. The way Lake opens up for me so sweetly makes me lose control. He clearly did brush his teeth and tastes like mint. I can't get enough, and as Lake relaxes, I completely consume him.

From the corner of my eye, I see Logan shift and prop himself on his elbow. He doesn't want to miss the show. Eventually, we both need air and I pull away, but only far enough so we can breathe. I rest my forehead against Lake's, my hand still cupping his neck. We're both out of breath and hard as hell now. Lake is staring into my eyes, the reluctance gone and completely replaced with lust and need.

"I-I don't think I want to go back to sleep, even if I am able to."

Logan adjusts himself as he waggles his eyebrows playfully at Lake. "Why not, Little Bird? You want more kisses?" Wide-eyed, Lake nods. It's so fucking adorable. I know he's a grown ass man and nearly thirty, but right now, he looks so young and innocent. Logan's eyes darken as he continues, "How about more than kisses?"

A little bit of that apprehension returns, but I can tell he's interested. Lake nods.

"Only if you want to, Lake," I remind him. "There's absolutely no pressure. We can just snuggle if you'd rather."

He's quiet for so long, I'm positive he's going to back out. But instead, Lake surprises me and nods, his expression way too serious for someone who's about to have sex. "No, I want to. Please."

My eyes find Logan, and we're both thinking the same thing. How the fuck are we supposed to say no to that?

TWENTY-ONE
LAKE

I know I can be pretty clueless when it comes to certain things, but even I realize that Logan and Evander are referring to sex. Normally, I'd reject the idea outright, but I find myself getting excited. Especially after that kiss. The idea of kissing never interested me before. It seemed kind of gross, honestly. But, I feel anything but gross when Evander or Logan's lips are on mine. I know I don't know the men very well in many ways, but in others it feels like I've known them my whole life. It feels right.

I expect Evander to immediately drag me back into bed, but instead, he excuses himself and hustles into the bathroom. I look back at the door, confused. "Where's he going?"

Logan chuckles huskily, his voice still rough with sleep. "To brush his teeth. He hates morning breath."

"Oh." Yet, he just kissed me. I'm not really sure what to do with that information, so I just store it in the back of my mind for later. When Evander returns, he eyes Logan meaningfully and jerks his head toward the door. With a long-suffering sigh, Logan gets up to take care of his own hygiene.

It doesn't take long for him to return, though, and launch

himself on the bed like an offering, which is certainly fitting. Logan is big everywhere. His arms are practically the size of tree trunks. His chest is almost as large, and I find myself fascinated by his dark-blonde chest hair. I wonder if he'd let me run my fingers through it. Is that strange? Unlike Evander, Logan doesn't have a six pack, but he has no real belly to speak of either. There's more hair that leads down into his underwear. With the way he's practically bulging out of his boxers, it appears that he's as large there as he is everywhere else.

I accept Evander's hand as he leads me back into the bed. I was too tired last night to appreciate him or Logan, but now I find myself mesmerized by their bodies and wanting to memorize every inch. Evander is both shorter and more narrow than Logan, but he still has a bulk to him that clearly comes from the gym. His well-defined arms are covered with sleeves of tattoos. In fact, the tattoos go from his neck and down both arms. It's hard to make out individual drawings. They are so connected, it's like one massive piece of art. The tattoos also cover his chest, which just has a very light smattering of body hair. Surprisingly, his well-defined abs and legs seem to be tattoo free. He's still wearing his underwear, so I'm not sure if he has any that are currently hidden.

As he knee walks both of us so that I'm positioned in the center of the bed, I get a good look at the bars that go through both of his nipples. How many piercings does this man have? Once Evander has me where he wants me, which is in the middle of the bed with my one side right up against Logan, he leans down and kisses me.

"You taste so good," he mutters into my mouth, and I get more of those butterflies.

"Thank you," I reply. By the mild chuckle, I assume that's the wrong response, but I know Evander isn't making fun of me, so I let it go.

Logan's fingers run through my hair. "I wanna taste every part of you," he whispers into my ear, which makes me shudder.

"Can I take your shirt off, sweetheart?" Evander asks me as he kisses my jawline. I nod, unable to speak in complete sentences.

Evander slowly slides my shirt up my torso, and I lean up to help take it off all the way. I watch as Logan and Evander take a look at my body for the first time. I'm well aware of the face that I'm nowhere near as muscular as them, but by the heated gazes they are both giving me, it clearly doesn't bother them.

"Oh our sweet little bird is not as clean cut as he seems," Logan tells me as he nuzzles the tentacles on my kraken tattoo.

I snort and shift slightly so they can completely see my one and only tattoo. "I wouldn't go that far. River and I decided to get them when we were twenty. His is on his thigh."

"Is it a nod to your names?" Evander asks. He's moved on from kissing my face, and now his mouth is tracing my pecs. His tongue grazes my nipple, and a shiver wracks through my body. For the first time this morning, I feel myself getting a little hard.

"Y-yes," I manage to squeak out. Evander sucks the nipple into my mouth, and my eyes roll to the back of my head. Why had I not realized how good that can feel? "I-I can't tell the story when you're doing that," I tell him shakily.

Evander laughs and pulls off. "Sorry, sweetheart." His eyes are dark and full of lust.

I shake my head to clear my thoughts. "In school, we were always teased about our names. But our mom named us, and it's the only thing we could always carry with us that came directly from her after she died. So one day, someone pissed River off, giving him shit, and he convinced me to get the tattoo with him. It was a way of embracing our names and telling everyone we didn't care what they thought." I shrug, knowing how silly it sounds. "It made sense at the time."

"It makes perfect sense, sweetheart. I like it."

I smile and relax into the bed. I love that he loves it.

Evander continues his assault on my nipples, while Logan tilts my head toward him and begins kissing me. I'm completely overwhelmed by the sensations, and we haven't even done much yet.

Evander pulls away, his long fingers caressing my stomach and chest. "Can I take your pants off, Lake?"

I find myself blushing even as I nod. "Yes, but um, not penetration today, ok? I don't think I'm ready for that." Plus, I don't want to have an accidental pregnancy and not be able to be a surrogate for Zoe. I'm still waiting on news on that front, to see if I can get implanted with one of the embryos, and I don't want to jeopardize it in any way.

Evander's eyes light up like he's proud of me. "Of course, sweetheart. There's no pressure for anything. And also, I'm vers, so if you decide you never want to bottom, I don't have a problem with that at all." He glances at Logan. "I'm assuming you'll want to top?"

Logan nods. "At least for now. Until I get more comfortable with everything. But I don't mind waiting. Whatever we do is more than enough for me."

I feel comforted and warm inside by both of these men's declarations. I haven't been in many sexual situations. I've just had no desire to. The couple of times I have tried anything, I found that my partner was annoyed when I tried to put a stop to certain things. No one ever tried to force me, but I can still sense the irritation. I get none of that now.

Logan begins to kiss me again as Evander slides my pants off. I'm wearing a pair of sensible briefs, nothing special, but I hear Evander's breath catch once he sees me. "I think our boy was hiding something from us, babe," Evander says, his voice rough.

I narrow my eyes, trying to work out what he means. Logan pulls away and follows Evander's gaze, which is firmly on the bulge in my underwear. Looking down, I'm surprised to see there's a wet spot.

Logan licks his lips. "Oh, Little Bird, you're not really so little, are you? Can I get a better look?"

I'm still not exactly sure what they're talking about, but I assume he wants me to be naked. I've never had a problem with nudity, so instead of answering, I begin to push down my briefs. Evander helps take them the rest of the way off, his gaze hot.

Logan crawls down so that his face is practically in my erection. I realize then that both he and Evander are still covered.

"It seems entirely unfair that neither of you are naked but I am."

Evander laughs, while Logan nips at my hip. "Let's remedy that, then." Both men take their underwear off at record speed, and I get my first look at both of them completely naked. Evander doesn't have any tattoos on his legs or anywhere on his lower half, at least on the front side of his body. As I let my eyes wander, I catch sight of his erection, and I can't take my eyes off it. His cock is long and on the thinner side, though probably a little shorter than mine. I know I am a little longer than average. I was curious one day and did some research, and *oh,* is that what they were referring to, the size of my penis? I guess that makes sense.

Either way, even from my limited experience, Evander's is nothing to sneeze at, and as he takes his erection in hand, I can't help but notice the line of barbells that go up the underside of his cock. Leaning forward, I completely forget about everything else so that I can inspect the piercings.

"What is that?" I ask, my face only inches from his dick.

"It's a Jacob's Ladder piercing. Do you like it?"

I nod, completely distracted. "Do they hurt? Can I touch them?"

Evander laughs and makes eye contact with Logan above my head. I'm not sure what the look means, but I don't care much. I gently rub up along the piercings, feeling the cold metal under my fingers. Evander gasps and shivers.

"They're sensitive, sweetheart."

"Really?"

"Yes, I hear they feel amazing when I'm inside someone."

Hmm. I'd love to feel that one day.

While I'm busy exploring, Logan comes up behind me, his large body completely enveloping mine. I feel his very large erection as it rubs up against my bottom. He lays gentle kisses up and down my neck.

"Do you want to taste him?" Logan asks as he nips at my neck.

My own dick jumps at the contact. Why do I love that so much? I nod and look at Evander. "Can I?"

Evander nods enthusiastically. "Gods, yes. Please."

Evander adjusts himself on the bed so that he's lying down, his legs spread, giving me access. That beautiful dick bounces against his belly.

I crawl in between his legs and bend down. I start off slowly, unsure exactly how to proceed. Peeking my tongue out, I lick down the underside, very much wanting to see how those piercings feel.

A full-body shiver runs through Evander, and he grips my hair, though he puts no pressure. It's almost an assurance, letting me know he's there. Behind me, Logan grips my hips and pulls me up so that I'm on my hands and knees.

"What about me, Lake? Can I get a taste?"

"Y-yes." I'm not sure how he plans to get there until Logan lies on his back and somehow slides his large body so he's in between my legs. He grips my ass and puts slight pressure, and I realize he's telling me to sit back. I do so, and his mouth wraps around the tip of my dick.

"Oh!" I exclaim.

Logan smirks. "Go on, Little Bird, make Ev feel good."

His lips wrap around my length again, and it takes a second for me to remember what I'm supposed to be doing. He's a little hesitant, and I know it's his first time, but it feels amazing. I lean forward and take Evander inside my mouth.

I start slow, but it doesn't take long for me to want more. I open my mouth wider and hollow out my cheeks, attempting to go deeper and take more of Evander's length. Evander moans.

"Oh fuck, sweetheart, that's so good. Use your tongue. Yeah that's it." Evander is gently guiding me with his hand; I know I can easily pull off if I want to, but I don't.

My only issue is that Logan is a huge distraction. He seems to have gotten comfortable sucking off another man. His large fingers are biting into my ass cheeks, and I know he'll probably leave marks. He's using them to leverage me up and down into his mouth. He's able to take about half of my dick before he begins to gag, but it's turning me on in a way I've never experienced before. This is by far the wildest thing I've ever done sexually, and it feels perfect, like coming home.

Evander seems to sense my distraction. "Is Logan making you feel good, sweetheart?"

I nod around his dick. "Mmmhmm."

"I bet he is. Those lips were made for sucking dick."

Logan laughs around my cock, and the sensation causes a flood of pre-cum to drip out and into his mouth.

I pull off Evander. "Sorry!" I call, trying to look down to get a better glimpse of the bigger man. He's licking his lips and doesn't seem upset one bit.

One hand comes off my butt cheek, and Logan begins jerking himself off. At the same time, he pushes me back down inside his mouth, and I can't help the whimper that escapes me. I'm completely overrun by sensation, so I'm thankful when Evander takes over and guides my mouth back to his cock.

He's not being overly aggressive, and again, I can easily pull away, but I appreciate his guidance, because I definitely can't concentrate right now.

We continue this way for I'm not sure how long, all moans and gasps and garbled words until I realize I'm very close to reaching my orgasm.

I pull off just enough to say, "I'm going to come, Logan." Then I immediately go back to Evander.

Evander groans and pushes off the bed slightly, causing me to gag a little. He immediately puts his hips back down. "Me too, Lake. I'm coming."

I have a split second to decide if I want to pull off. I decide I don't, and just in time, too, because Evander's release spills into my mouth. The taste isn't as bad as I expected. A little salty, but I enjoy it more than I thought I would. I swallow as much as I can, though some escapes. Evander smiles lazily at me as he thumbs my lip, wiping the excess release and placing his thumb into his own mouth.

I'm not sure if that's what caused my own release, or Logan's mouth on me, or his gasp and shudder. Maybe it's Logan's release hitting my thighs and in between my legs, or maybe it's a combination of all of them. Regardless, I feel the pressure, and within seconds, I'm spilling into Logan's mouth.

He starts sputtering and quite a bit of spills out of his mouth and down his chin. I pull away, terrified I hurt him, but he immediately pulls me closer, my own spend rubbing onto my stomach as he rubs his face into my torso. He blindly reaches behind him for Evander, who immediately joins our sticky cuddle pile.

Normally, something like this would disgust me. The couple of times I've exchanged blow jobs with other people, I've immediately gone and cleaned myself off. But I find myself not wanting to move right now.

"Are you two ok?" Evander asks eventually, probably understanding how new this is for both of us.

I nod, completely content. "Yes, I'm perfect," Logan says, his words muffled as he speaks into my stomach.

"Are you ok?" I ask Evander. He grins at me and ruffles my hair. I'm sure it looks a mess right now.

"I'm amazing, Lake. That was incredible."

He's not wrong. I've never experienced anything like that before. He's contemplative before finally adding, "Maybe the idea of fated mates isn't so crazy after all."

I frown, considering that. I haven't actively discounted that theory since River met Cooper. It's obvious there's something special there. But is Evander implying that Logan, he, and I are fated mates? I wonder if that thought should concern me. But instead, it just leaves me with a feeling of warmth and belonging. A feeling of hope. A feeling of family.

TWENTY-TWO
EVANDER

My heart is pounding as I help chop vegetables with my dad. Today's the day of the big family dinner where everyone is going to meet. And I have to say, I'm nervous as fuck. The situation is weird. I don't usually meet the dad of the person I'm seeing before we even officially become a couple.

But, obviously, these aren't normal circumstances, and nothing has been typical. I wonder if Lake even told his dad about us yet. I should probably ask him. I don't want to act all coupley around him before Lake's ready for that.

My dad took it in stride, just like he does everything else. He not only didn't bat an eye that Logan and I are suddenly more than friends, but also when I said the three of us were all seeing each other. "I'm not going to pretend I completely understand how a relationship between three men will work, but then, I guess it's a good thing I'm not in that kind of relationship. You know all I've ever wanted is for you to be happy, Ev, and if this is what makes you happy, then you know I'm all for it." And then he continued to season his steaks like nothing happened.

I love my dad for that. It's a pretty similar response to the one I got when I told him I was bi as a teenager. Back then, I was almost annoyed. I spent so much time thinking about my speech and what I would tell him, and he was just like, "That's nice, son. As long as he or she treats you well, that's all that matters. Can you get the milk out of the fridge? I'm going to make French toast for breakfast." And that was it. So I guess I shouldn't be surprised he reacted exactly the same to this news.

It's also crazy how much I miss both men. I haven't seen either of them since yesterday morning after our amazing mutual blow job experience. I'm dying to return the favor and get my hands and mouth on both of them. My gods, how did I get so lucky to get two men so blessed in that department?

And let me tell you, while I'm not overly surprised Logan has a huge dick, Lake took me aback. I don't know why exactly, if it's his size or because he's an Omega, but I never expected that monster on him. I'm not gonna lie. I'm a little jealous Logan got the first taste.

After that experience, we all spent a few minutes talking to each other and checking in, but then both my men had to get to work. Lake's been swamped with whatever the emergency is. Logan and I got a couple of quick texts letting us know he's ok, that he's having no second thoughts, and that he ate both lunch and dinner last night. I texted him earlier to confirm he's coming tonight and got a simple, *yes*. I'm anxious to see him. Not only do I miss him, which is nuts since it's only been a day, but I just want to make sure he's ok. I know he said he's had a couple blow jobs in the past, but something special passed between us last night, and I hope he's dealing alright.

I also haven't seen Logan. He caught a case yesterday and has been working nonstop. He assured me he'll be here tonight, though he might be a little late. I also tried to check on him, it was his first sexual activity with a guy, after all, but Logan assured me he was fine. I guess we'll see tonight.

It's a little too cold to eat outdoors, so Dad cleaned off his big dining table for the first time in recent memory. I know he's nervous too. Not only is he meeting the family of the kid who's been so important to his change of life, but now he's also meeting the family of his son's boyfriend—or whatever he is to me.

When Dad gets nervous, he cooks. So tonight is going to be a full-on feast. I know Logan is going to be excited. He loves when my dad cooks like this. I still remember the first Thanksgiving he spent at our house. He actually cried when he saw the feast. I think that's when I realized just how bad his home life was.

A couple of hours later, my dad and I have made enough food to feed a small country, and people start arriving. Both Lake and Logan text that they're running late, leaving me with Lake's family without him as a buffer. At least he said that his dad knows we're seeing each other, so I don't have to worry about hiding that.

I wonder what he'll think of me, or the whole situation, and I find that I really want him to approve. I never cared much what my partner's parents thought of me. I know what I look like, and I've gotten a lot of judgment before they ever got to know me, but it's never bothered me before. This will be the first time I'm hoping a parent looks past my looks to see the person I am underneath. I hope Luke Simmons can see how deeply I care about his son, and how I can easily see myself spending the rest of my life with him.

"So, Ev, tell me about yourself. I'm not sure if Lake mentioned what you do for a living."

I swallow a drink of water, trying to gather my thoughts, which is dumb. I clearly know what my job is, but everything about Luke Simmons has me rattled. The man has been nothing but a gentleman since he got here, and he and my dad have been getting along like gangbusters. He even chastised his daughter and asked her to back off when she was giving me the third degree. There has been absolutely no indication that he's remotely upset about his son and me.

And yet, I kind of feel like a teenager on his first date being interrogated by his girlfriend's dad while the girl finishes getting dressed. I can't help checking my phone. Still no Logan or Lake.

"I'm an editor for a publishing company. I've actually recently switched from young adult to adult fantasy."

Essie's face lights up. "Oh really? That's so cool. I love fantasy novels. I wonder if you've edited anything I've read?"

The conversation switches to that, thankfully, and Essie and I go back and forth for a while with her naming books and me telling her if I had any part in their editing process.

I have to say, I love Lake's family. Despite my nerves and desire to impress him, I can tell Luke Simmons is a great man. It's clear how much he loves his kids, and how much they all love him. If I didn't know the story, I would have no idea he wasn't Lake and River's biological father. He treats them no differently than his biological daughter. Even in his fifties, he's still good-looking, a real silver fox, though there's enough dark brown peeking through the silver in his thick curls to tell what his natural color is. I know that there is no relation, obviously, but his build and demeanor remind me a lot of Logan, way more so than Lake. He has broad shoulders and a strong chest, and I have to imagine that Logan's going to look similar in twenty-five years since their body types are so similar and Logan stays extremely active, just with different and lighter features.

And Essie is such a breath of fresh air. She's outgoing and sweet and says what she's thinking. She's a spitfire wrapped in a 5'2" package, and she has a combination of looks between her brothers and her dad.

Despite my nerves, I'm so happy to meet them, and Dad is

thrilled. Nothing makes him happier than having a huge group of people to feed and fill his house with conversation and love.

Miri is sitting on Cooper's lap, happily sucking on a crust of bread. She's teething, apparently, and will gladly take anything she can get her hands on and shove it into her mouth. Her dads definitely have their hands full.

River shows us some pictures from when he was pregnant, and it makes me wonder what Lake will be like when he's expecting. As scared as I am regarding the possible risk for him, I love the idea of watching him grow large with child and being there during the entire process. Maybe one day, that will be our child in there.

Mr. Simmons leans back in his chair, a smile on his face. "I really appreciate you having all of us here, Eric. Next time, I'll host. My house is awfully quiet now that the kids are grown. It would be nice to fill it up again."

River frowns at his dad. "Dad, have you looked up the group I told you about?" I wonder what group he's talking about.

Luke shrugs, looking a little uncomfortable. "I don't know, Riv. I don't think that group is meant for me."

"It's not a grief group, Dad. It's more of a social club." Luke's eyes bounce around to all of the guests at the table who are all focused on the conversation. He's clearly a little uncomfortable with discussing this in front of all of us.

Realizing this, Dad turns toward Luke. "So what's your favorite memory of your kids growing up?"

River and Essie groan, River dramatically banging his head against the dining room table. "Ok, now I have to hear this story!" I grin, leaning closer to Mr. Simmons, desperate for information on the man I care a lot about.

Mr. Simmons smirks, his eyes full of mischief, and oh boy, this is going to be a good story. "Ok, so it was the first vacation I took with the kids on my own." He pauses for a moment, squeezing Essie's hand. Cooper takes River's hand and smiles sympathetically. Lake hasn't spoken about his mother much, but I learned back when I was in stalker mode that his mom passed when he and River were eleven.

Mr. Simmons clears his throat. "Anyway, I decided to take the kids down to the shore in Jersey for a few days. We all needed to get away for a bit, you know. Anyway, one morning, we're at the beach, and before the trip, I had been working 60-80 hour weeks, so I'm exhausted, right, and before I know it, I pass out on my beach chair." Luke chuckles. "Burnt the hell out of myself too. Well, anyway, the boys knew not to go in the water or to let Essie go in the ocean when I wasn't with them, but I guess they were bored." Even River has gotten into the story. I guess just seeing his dad's eyes light up with joy as he talks about his kids is enough to get over the embarrassment.

"So, like a couple hours later, I finally wake up, and at first, I can't find the kids at all. I go into sheer panic mode, screaming their names like a banshee. Then all of a sudden, little preteen River pops up a little way down the beach. He's beet red and so excited as he comes running up to me. 'Dad! Dad! Come see what we did!'" River groans again, his cheeks as red as his hair, but he's smiling as Mr. Simmons continues.

"River takes my hand and drags me down the beach. There I see little Essie using this giant bucket, and I still have no idea where they got it. She has it filled to the top and is dumping on what I first thought was just a giant pile of sand. Well, no. It turns out that underneath that mountain was Lake."

We all gasp, but River quickly adds, "His face was uncovered! We weren't trying to kill him!"

Mr. Simmons smiles fondly at his son. "No, but there's so much sand; I had a panic attack that it would collapse on him before we were able to get him out, not that you knew that as kids. Both of you were so proud of your Mountain Lake, as you called it."

I'm laughing so hard tears are falling down my face. A part

of me feels my heart clench, knowing that it could've gone wrong and Lake could've been seriously hurt or killed. But since the incident is in the past and everyone can laugh at it now, I can definitely find humor in it. Not to mention, the image of my serious, buttoned-up Lake completely buried in the sand is adorable.

"How did Lake feel about this? I won't lie; it's hard to picture him enjoying that."

River laughs. "Oh no, he was pissed. At first he reluctantly agreed, mainly because I got Essie to beg him and he could never say no to Essie back then. But after fifteen minutes, he was ready to murder me. He refused to talk to me for the rest of the trip."

We're all still laughing at the story when my phone finally buzzes. And thank fuck, it's a message from Lake. *I'll be there in twenty minutes.*

I must have a goofy expression on my face because River asks, "Is that one of your men?"

My eyes immediately flash to Mr. Simmons, who still hasn't mentioned anything to me, but they are still full of light and joy. No judgment or animosity is in sight.

I smile up at River. "Yup. It's your brother. He'll be here in twenty minutes."

"It's about time," Essie mutters.

"Es, you know his job can be unpredictable sometimes," Mr. Simmons replies, then his eyes immediately flash to mine. I can tell he doesn't know if I know anything about Lake's profession.

I smile warmly at them. "Lake hasn't told us his exact job yet, but I know that he may have long and unpredictable hours or long trips he has to take at the last minute. I'm happy to wait for him."

Mr. Simmons's eyes narrow with concern, and oh, here comes the interrogation. "I know everything is very new right now, but that's going to be hard on you, two men with careers that have nontraditional hours. I'll admit, I don't know much about editing, but I have to imagine your hours are more stable."

"It's a valid question. "Yes, sir. They are for the most part. I do work from home quite a bit, so I've been known to work at night or on the weekend when I'm close to a deadline, but yes, it's nothing like what Lake and Logan experience. And yes, it will be hard on me. I'm not going to lie about that. But I think it comes down to: do I think Lake and Logan are worth the worry and the frustration that will come with long nights waiting up for them and canceled and delayed plans? And the answer to that question is yes, I do believe they are. I know it may be crazy soon, but my feelings are strong for Lake, and I really believe this can be the real deal, for all three of us."

Dad is smiling at me, his eyes filled with pride. River's eyes are also shining, as well as Cooper's, who gives me a slight nod. It's clearly the right answer. Even Mr. Simmons seems to approve, but he's not quite there yet. Understandable. It is his son that will get hurt if I decide all of this is too much.

"I agree that it seems to be early for you to be saying that. I know you and Logan have history, but you barely know Lake. It's easy for you to say this now, but will you think the same thing six months down the road, or a year?"

I open my mouth to answer. It's hard to explain, but I'm all in on both of my men. I know there's going to be struggles and growing pains, but I'm willing to fight for them. But before I get a word out, the front door of Dad's house opens and we all fall silent.

"Hello?" Logan calls out, and I breathe a sigh of relief. Perfect timing. I think some of Mr. Simmons's concerns will be relieved if he hears it from both of us.

"Excuse me," I tell the table as I jump out of my chair to grab one of my men. I hope tonight I can prove how committed I am to these men and this relationship.

TWENTY-THREE
LOGAN

I'm practically running as I take the steps up to Mr. C's front door two at a time. I can't believe I'm nearly forty-five minutes late to my first dinner with my boyfriend's family. We haven't actually had a discussion about us being boyfriends yet, but I don't have another word for it. Well, I do, but I'm not quite ready to say the M word.

My only saving grace is that Lake is even later than me. Hopefully that'll take some of the pressure off me, not that I'm overly concerned about meeting Lake's dad and family. I could tell River liked both of us right from the start, after we stopped interrogating each other, at least. And from the little I know about Mr. Simmons, he's the kind of guy to support his children and their decisions even if he doesn't necessarily agree with them. I doubt he's gonna completely reject us, even if he's confused by the whole throuple thing. Fuck, I'm confused myself.

I hear some chatter as I pull out my key. Mr. C never took it back from me so I could always enter the house. But as soon as the door opens and I call out, it gets silent. What the fuck?

Before I get my coat off and step out of the foyer, Ev

practically flies into the room. What's going on?

I hang up my coat as I look at my oldest friend and new lover. I didn't get a chance to change, but luckily, I was wearing civilian clothes today, so I still look relatively presentable. "Ev, what's going on, babe?"

Without answering, Ev wraps his arms around me and kisses me. I immediately return the kiss, letting my man melt into me as I tug him tight to me. "I missed you," he whispers.

"I missed you too." And it's true. We picked up another doozie of a case, shocker, but all day I was distracted thinking of Ev and Lake—my bad boy who's a closet nerd and my buttoned-up man who I know has a wild side just waiting to break free. I can't wait to get them alone tonight.

"Ev, is everything ok?"

He smiles and kisses me one more time, reluctant to let go. But I don't blame him. I don't want to let go either.

"Oh yeah. You're gonna love Lake's family. His dad is crazy hot for an older man. And his sister is awesome."

"But, something is wrong."

"No, not wrong. Mr. Simmons is concerned that we might be taking on more than we can chew with Lake, especially with his job and, I guess, the surrogacy, though he hasn't mentioned it. Since I'm the one who's gonna be sitting here day after day while you two do your thing, he's particularly worried about me."

I frown as I tip Ev's chin up so he can look me in the eyes. "*Are* you ok with it? I know you've always dealt with it in the past, but it's different when it's your boyfriend, or both of your boyfriends. Especially when we don't even know what Lake really does, so we can't fully prepare for the danger or what might happen."

Ev smiles and the sincerity shines through his eyes. "I promise you I'm fine. I might struggle here and there, I'm human after all, but I'm committed to making this work."

I kiss Ev one last time. "Good, me too. Let's go prove that to Lake's dad."

Ev takes my hand, and we go into the dining room to face the fire.

Ok, Ev isn't kidding. Mr. Simmons is fucking hot. It's strange for me to say this, since I still haven't found any other men attractive except Ev and Lake, but there's something about Luke Simmons, and I'm not ashamed to say I have a little crush. Of course it's nothing compared to how I feel about his son; it's more like I want to be this man when I grow up.

I think Ev and I eased some of Mr. Simmons's fears, but I'm still not entirely sure if he's convinced about the relationship. He lets it go, though. I'm pretty sure he doesn't disapprove, but I know Lake has never had a relationship before, so it's only natural for his dad to be a little overprotective when he's suddenly seeing two men and we are all claiming that it's serious. But now, everyone is back to eating and chatting conversationally when the bell rings, and fucking finally, Lake's here.

I don't think any amount of words will convince Mr. Simmons we're genuine. The best thing we can do for him is to let him see us with his son. Ev and I jump up. "We'll get it," I tell everyone at the table. And ok, I do grab a piece of cornbread for the trip, but hey, don't judge me.

We open the door to Lake, and I'm surprised to see he's on the phone.

"Really, Zoe? And the doctors are ready to move to the next step? Yes, that's fantastic. And how about you and Avery? Are you ready right now? I know you weren't sure between the Broadway show and my job?"

"Oh, that's great! No, I'm definitely all in. I mentioned the possibility to my boss and he's willing to work with me. Or he was after I went above his head and threatened to file a complaint with HR as well as leak his sexist ways."

Lake seems to realize Ev and I are standing here for the first time. He offers us a small smile and cute little wave, but I can tell he's distracted. At least this seems like a good conversation. I glance at Ev, and I can tell he realizes what's going on. It looks like our little bird is gonna be a daddy. Or well, carry someone else's child. I'm still a little unsure about what this means exactly. I guess it's time for a conversation.

"Yes, I can come in then. I'm happy to speak to the counselor. I completely understand that there's going to be a lot of psychological components to this and I want to be the best possible surrogate I can be."

My heart melts and I squeeze Lake's hand in support. We're obviously taking too long because there's a lot of chatter in the dining room and then Essie and River pop into the living room, both with concern and curiosity showing on their expressions. River is carrying a gurgling Miri in his arms.

Lake is still working out the details with who I figure must be Zoe and doesn't realize he now has an audience. I walk up to his siblings. "I think that's Zoe on the phone."

Both of their faces light up, "Wait? Does that mean what I think it means? Are they going to do it? Are Avery and Zoe going to have a baby?" River blurts out, clearly ecstatic.

"It seems like that. I guess we'll wait and see." While Lake finishes his conversation, Ev takes his jacket and the overnight satchel he brought with him and hangs them in the hall closet next to my coat. It's late October now, and we finally need a jacket, not just a long-sleeve shirt or sweater. Apparently, he's planning to stay over too. Maybe we should go to mine or Ev's place. It's kind of weird to crash at Mr. C's place in Ev's childhood bedroom, right?

Lake finally hangs up, his whole face lit up like he's a kid on

Christmas. He looks at me and Ev, and the absolute excitement on his face hits me like a freight truck in my core. Gods, what are these men doing to me?

Since Lake still hasn't said a word, Ev takes the initiative. "So, what was that talk about?"

"I'm going to be a surrogate! Or well, we're at least taking the next step in the right direction. We have to sit through a counseling session first, and the doctor in charge of the Omega Project wants to go over the risks again, but if all of that goes well, then they're going to try and implant the embryo inside of me. Of course, there's always the risk it won't take, but I have to admit I'm relieved we even got this far."

I'm so thrilled for him. All of those concerns and worries I've had swimming in my head about Lake taking this on disappear. Ok, so disappear isn't the right word, but I decide that I can just deal with them. I'll manage any fears I may have and keep them dampened down if it means this much to Lake. I've never seen him so enthusiastic.

Grinning from ear to ear, I lift my man off the ground and spin him in a circle, not caring who sees. Lake is laughing as I finally put him down and plant a kiss on his lips. "I'm so happy for you, Little Bird. I know how important this is to you."

Ev sneaks into our embrace, kissing Lake and hugging him tight. "Sweetheart, this is excellent news. I know it's not going to be easy, but Logan and I are here for you."

I don't have anything to add to that, so I hug them both tight. "Come on, let's go share the good news with the rest of the family and see if there's any more food to snag before it's all gone."

"We already heard." I turn around and am completely shocked to see everyone crowded into the entryway, all grinning from ear to ear. Nosy fuckers.

Lake's eyes immediately find his father and siblings. I follow his gaze to see Luke Simmons watching the three of us, his eyes full of fondness and affection. "I'm so proud of you, Lake, for doing this. This is amazing."

Lake beams at his dad's praise, and I have to swallow a little bit of hurt. Usually, I never think about my piece of shit dad. I have more than enough paternal love from Mr. C. I don't need that asshole. And I know Mr. C is proud of me, but sometimes, just sometimes in weak moments like this, I wish my asshole sperm donor showed at least a tiny bit of love and affection for me. I would've loved to have him look at me the way Lake's dad is looking at him right now, just once.

I quickly swallow that all down. It doesn't matter anymore. And Lake knows all about shitty sperm donors, so I have no right to complain. We both got lucky.

After more hugs and discussions, we finally all make it back to the dining room. Thank fuck. I'm still starving. Lake sits between us while we finish up eating. Then we all help clean up and pull out the desserts. Surrounded by all these amazing people, I forget all about my dad and the little bite of jealousy. I'm surrounded by love, and that's all that matters.

Finally, everyone is getting ready to leave. The three of us walk Lake's family out. The baby, Miri, is sound asleep in her car seat and looking absolutely precious. As he walks out, Cooper squeezes mine and Ev's shoulders. "You guys are good for him. I'm glad he finally found his people."

I smile at the man. Seeing River and Cooper together is like a revelation. They are serious couple goals. We say our goodbyes. River gives his brother a big hug before hugging his dad and Essie goodbye. He kisses Mr. C on the cheek, which makes the man blush. "Thank you for having us, again. I'm feeling like part of the family."

Mr. C has tears in his eyes as he says goodbye to Lake's family. I know this is like a dream for him, and I couldn't be happier.

After everyone else walks out, Mr. Simmons lingers for a

moment. He whispers something to Lake as he hugs him goodbye, and then he walks up to Ev and me. It's strange looking eye to eye with another man. It's not something that happens often. "I have to apologize for giving you two a hard time earlier. I trust my son, and I should've trusted he'd pick excellent partners. I know your relationship is very new, so of course none of you know what will happen, but I believe in you three and couldn't be happier for you."

I feel kind of sheepish at the approval. "Thank you, Mr. Simmons," Ev says. "We both care about Lake a lot and just want to make him happy."

Mr. Simmons squeezes his shoulder. "Please, call me Luke, both of you."

With a mischievous smirk, Mr. Simmons—I'm sorry, Luke— leaves the house, and Ev and I standing there dumbfounded. I blink, getting my bearings, and turn to my men.

"Well, today was eventful. How about we celebrate?"

Lake squints in confusion, but Ev knows exactly what I'm talking about, his eyebrows raising in interest.

Mr. C clears his throat. Holy fuck, I forgot he was there. "Don't all three of you have your own places? I'm thrilled you found each other, but can you please celebrate elsewhere?"

And with that mic drop, Ev's pops turns around and walks down the hall. "Goodnight, kids!" he calls out before I hear his bedroom door shut.

The three of us look at each other before Ev and I burst out laughing, definitely feeling like teenagers again. "What is he talking about?" Lake asks. Fuck, he's the sweetest.

"Come on, Little Bird, my place is closest. We'll explain on the way."

I hold out my hand for him, and with a small smile, Lake takes it. Feeling absolutely thrilled, I lead him out of the house, absolutely ready to get my hands on these men.

TWENTY-FOUR
LOGAN

My place is small but close, so it's the logical choice. My bed is big enough for all three of us if we cuddle close, and that's the most important thing. I could really care less that the rest of my living space is the size of a sardine can. I chose this apartment because of its proximity to the precinct, as well as easy subway access to get to Ev's place. The other deciding factor was that the bedroom is the size of the rest of the apartment put together.

The station is only a block away from my apartment, and as we get off, Lake grabs my hand, stopping my progress. "I still don't want to be penetrated." I nearly choke on my own spit, not expecting those words. "Well, I do, but I want to wait until the embryo is implanted and I know I'm pregnant. I don't want to risk anything regarding this baby."

Ev takes Lake's other hand as I kiss the top of his head. I see a couple glances our way since we're standing in the middle of the street, but I don't give a fuck. "That's fine, Little Bird. There's absolutely no pressure. I'm pretty new to this whole gay sex thing, but I have to assume there's other things we can do besides anal."

Ev's smile is absolutely obscene. "Oh, there's *so* much more we can do. Besides, I'm vers, so if Logan's ready to experience something new, I'm game. There are so many other options we can do with you, sweetheart. We'll make you feel so good."

I hadn't thought much about anal with either of them yet, but I'm so fucking game. I've done anal with girls a handful of times, and I've always enjoyed it. I can't imagine topping Ev would be much different. In fact, it'll probably be better because I feel so much more strongly about Ev. Plus, his ass is fucking fantastic.

This seems to ease whatever concerns Lake has. We each take one of his hands and walk the block to my apartment.

"Sorry, it's probably a mess. I ran out this morning because we picked up a case. I have no idea the state it's in."

Ev laughs as we walk the three flights of stairs up to my floor. The elevator in my building is almost always on the fritz, so we all just got in the habit of taking the stairs. At least I'm only on the third floor and not the eighth.

As soon as I'm in my apartment and lock the door, I push Lake up against the wall and claim his mouth. "Ah, mmm," he mutters into my mouth before relaxing and allowing me to take control. My hands rub up and down over Lake's body, which is still completely clothed, coat and all. Ev is on top of it, though. He somehow already has his jacket and shoes off and is working on stripping mine off even as I continue to make out with Lake.

"You have way too many clothes on," Ev mutters as he throws my coat onto the couch. I force myself to pull away from Lake. He's already in a daze, his lips all swollen from my brutal kiss. I feel this wave of pleasure seeing Lake like this. It's possessive, like I claimed him as mine. My Omega. I've never been particularly possessive before, but all I want to do is mark Lake all over, letting the world know he's mine.

"Let's get some of these clothes off, Little Bird," I whisper huskily against Lake's ears as I help him take his jacket off.

It's suddenly a flurry of limbs and urgent undressing as we all work to take off our clothes. Shoes are kicked across the room, pants and shirts are left in a haphazard pile on the floor. When we're in nothing but our boxers, we make the slow journey into my room, but none of us can keep our hands off each other. Even Lake is taking initiative. He's wrapped his arms around Ev's neck and completely latched on. He's very tentatively kissing the side of Ev's face and his neck, almost like he's afraid Ev is going to reject him, which is never gonna happen.

I need these men in my bed *now,* so I tip Lake's chin in my direction and distract him with a kiss. When his grip is loose enough, I take the man and scoop him over my shoulder, causing Lake to let out a very undignified squeal.

Ev laughs as I wrap my other arm around his shoulders and essentially drag him with us. As soon as I'm in my spacious bedroom, I kick the door closed behind me and toss Lake unceremoniously onto the bed.

"Ungh," he mutters, but before he can set himself to rights, Ev disentangles himself from me and crawls onto the bed, immediately straddling Lake. His fingers tangle into that gorgeous auburn hair, and his mouth devours Lake's.

Before joining them, I just take a moment to watch and appreciate my men. They are so incredibly sexy, it's insane. Lake's creamy skin is a beautiful contrast to Ev's more olive skin tone. The tattoos covering the majority of Ev's skin seem to flow with Lake's almost completely unmodified body.

Ev has moved on from Lake's mouth and is now taking his exploration lower, licking and sucking his way down Lake's torso. Ev's ass is sticking out, and gods, I need to get my hands on it.

I shuck off my boxers as I take a quick little detour to grab condoms and lube from my side table. My cock is painfully hard and bounces up against my stomach once it's free from the confines of my underwear. I begin to stroke it as I throw the supplies onto the bed and climb in with my men.

    I lie on my side next to the two of them. I grip Ev's hair and guide his face to mine. A small gasp escapes as I claim his lips. Once he's completely breathless and lust drunk, I do the same to Lake. Then there's this moment of tranquility. None of us are moving, we all just stare into each other's eyes, and I know this is way more than anything I ever experienced before. It's hard to explain why, but I know we're meant for each other. I may not be all the way there yet, but my feelings are so strong for these men, and it will easily become love. Not the brotherly love I always felt for Ev, but more, so much more.

    And then the moment breaks, and I simply can't wait another damn second to get my hands on these men. I'm ripping Ev's boxers off at the same time he's taking off Lake's, quickly tossing them to the side so we're all completely naked. All three of us are cut, and I have a brief moment where I wonder how it would feel if any of us weren't, but I push it aside. I'm more than content with these two.

    Ev's gaze is heated as he looks down at Lake. "I didn't get to taste this beauty last time. Now it's my turn." And then he swallows Lake's length like it's fucking nothing.

    Now, I know I haven't seen a ton of cocks in my day, but I've seen enough to know Lake is above average, especially for his size. I'm thicker than he is, but not much longer, and that's saying something because I'm a big dude. I know that I wasn't even close to being able to swallow all of Lake's length when I had a go at it.

    Either Ev has had a lot more experience than I'm aware of or the guy has no gag reflex, because I'm not kidding when I say he takes the entire thing in one try. He grips Lake's hips, giving him some leverage as his nose nuzzles into the soft curls surrounding Lake's cock and balls.

    I'm left speechless as I watch, my hand surrounding my dick

but not moving, I'm just too impressed. And turned on. This has to be hottest fucking thing I've seen in my entire life. I'm finally able to shake the trance, and I kneel so I'm behind Ev, and I straddle his legs so his ass is in the perfect spot for me to play with.

I look at Lake over Ev's body. "Does that feel good, Little Bird? Our man is fucking talented, huh?"

Lake's pupils are completely blown. One hand is wrapped around Ev's neck, his nails biting into the flesh, while the other one is gripping my comforter for dear life, his knuckles completely white.

"Y-yes. Feels amazing."

I reach around Ev and grip his own cock. Oh yeah, he's hard as hell and dripping pre-cum all over my bedding. I probably should grab a couple towels, but I can't be bothered. That's what a washing machine is for.

"Look at you, babe. You're so hard for us. I guess you must like sucking cock, huh?"

Ev pops off Lake and turns his head to eye me. He grins lazily at me. "Oh yeah. Especially this one. Holy hell, Logan. Our man here had a nice surprise hidden for us, huh?"

Fuck, these men. Growling, I grip Ev's hair and devour his mouth. He tastes like Lake. I didn't think it was possible, but my dick gets even harder. Oh yeah, I clearly love this.

"You wanna know what you taste like, Little Bird?" I ask Lake, who's watching us through hooded lids. He nods sheepishly.

Ev and I lunge toward him, and suddenly we're in this sloppy three-way kiss. We eventually pull away, a mess of tangled limbs. I look at Ev. "If you're up for it, I'd like to try topping you."

The look Ev gives me is practically feral. "Oh, I am so *up* for it." His eyes drop to his cock, letting me know the pun was absolutely intended, at least on his part.

Laughing, I slap his ass playfully. "Cheesy fucker."

Lake is watching us carefully with that look he gets when he's trying to analyze the situation. Unsure of what the look means, I decide to check in on him, make sure he's comfortable with everyone. "Are you ok with that, Lake? No one will force you to do anything."

Lake nods. "I can watch, right? I know how penatrative sex works in theory, but I've never seen it in person."

Oh, the look Ev and I exchange with each other. I know neither of us can wait to share every new experience with Lake. We'll make it so good for him. I caress his torso, then very lightly trace my fingers across his nipples. Lake shivers, little goosebumps forming in my wake.

"Oh, you can definitely watch. In fact, how would you like if Ev climbs on top of you while I fuck him? That way you're right there with us and know how much we want you."

Lake's eyes widen and the tip of his tongue points out between his lips. Oh yeah. He likes that idea. My little bird nods his head, clearly too flustered to say words.

Grinning, I turn to Ev. He's lightly stroking his dick, waiting for me. "How about you give our little bird's balls some attention while I prep you? I bet no one has ever done that for him before."

By Lake's look, I know I guessed right. Ev sucks in his lip ring, a move he makes when he's turned on or thinking. "I think I love that idea. And you know what you're doing?" Ev asks me. I wonder if I should be offended, but I'm not. It's a valid question.

"I've had anal with girls before. Is it much different?"

"Besides me having a prostate? Not really, I don't think."

I get into position behind Ev and kiss his delectable ass cheek. His lower half is completely ink free, which I love. That means the only marks on his ass will be from Lake and me.

"Then I should be fine. Let me see you worship our boy," I

tell Ev. He glares at me, probably because I'm being bossy as hell, but complies. I can tell he secretly likes it. I've always been a little bossy in bed, but being with them seems to bring it out tenfold.

I watch as Ev positions himself better. One hand wraps around Lake's length. The way his head is angled, I know he's watching Lake's eyes as he slowly lowers himself. And then, fucking finally, he licks the side of one of Lake's balls before sucking it into his mouth.

Lake bucks off the bed, a guttural moan escaping his lips. Oh gods, that is so sexy.

I smirk at him as I reach over and grab the lube. He's going crazy, all of that rigid control gone as Ev's magic mouth does its thing. I'm gonna need to feel that mouth for myself one day. But, there's plenty of time. I've got better things to do right now.

"Is Ev making you feel good, Little Bird?" I ask before straddling Ev's legs again.

Lake nods, but his eyes are unfocused. Ev has moved on to his other ball now, and he's simultaneously jerking him off. "You look so fucking sexy like that. Both of you do. Babe, don't make him come. I want us to all shoot together."

Ev grunts his agreement. I look down at the delectable meal in front of me. I've never once rimmed someone but I'm overcome by this desire to taste Ev before I fuck him. I want to know every inch of both of these men, including what every part of them tastes like.

"Can I taste you?" I ask Ev. He pauses long enough to moan low and long before nodding.

"Yes, fuck yes. Please."

"Well, if you beg so nicely." I spread his cheeks with my fingers before sticking my face in between. Ev still smells good and pretty clean considering he probably hasn't showered since earlier today. It's this musky manly scent, with just a little bit of sweat, but not dirty.

Having sensed my pause, Ev pops off Lake. "I cleaned myself out earlier. I wasn't sure what would happen today, and I wanted to be prepared for everything."

I growl at his words. Like, actually fucking growl. I didn't even think that sound was possible for humans, but I guess it is. Ever since I got tested and learned I may have this new version of the Alpha gene, I've noticed some traits of a traditional Alpha, like this intense need to possess and protect my men. Also, I feel like my instincts might be more enhanced, but it's kind of hard to tell. I've always had good instincts. But until now, I never fucking growled. The way both Lake and Ev moan, however, shows that they really like it.

I don't hesitate this time and stick my tongue into his hole. Ev's body stiffens before a full body shudder racks through him. "Oh, fuck, Logan, that feels so fucking good."

"I'm gonna get you so wet, babe. Nice and loose and sloppy and ready for me."

Both Lake and River groan at that. I go back to eating Ev out. One hand snakes around him so I can take his length in hand. I'm jerking him off in slow, even strokes. I know it's driving him crazy, but it's not enough to make him come.

Ev has gone back to Lake's cock and is back to deep-throating him. We both continue like that for a while, but I know we'll all end up orgasming before I even get inside Ev if we keep going, and that's just fucking unacceptable.

I pull away and grip Ev's hair, pulling him back and off Lake with a pop. Ev's gaze is absolutely heated, and just a little combative. But I meet the stare and don't let go of his hair. His head is pulled back. I know I'm not holding him hard enough to hurt, but it's showing him who's in charge right now.

Lake is watching both of us. He's sucking his bottom lip, and I just know he's loving the show. Ev lowers his gaze, though there's still fire in it, but that's perfect. He's offering his submission for now, but I know I'll have to earn it every time. And I can't wait.

"Lake, slide up a bit so your head's resting against the pillows." Lake does what I ask without question. Damn, maybe I'm bossier than I even thought.

Once Lake is settled, I turn toward Ev and kiss him gently. I even allow him to get some control, knowing he needs it a little. "Babe, can you get on your hands and knees over Lake? I'd like your faces only inches from each other."

Ev sucks in his lip piercing again. "Oh, fuck. Yes, fuck, yes." Ev scrambles into position. I take another moment to admire them. It's such a fucking erotic image, and it does things for me, especially knowing I'm orchestrating it.

I pour some of the lube I'm still holding into my hand and spread it in between Ev's ass cheeks. He shivers. I start with one finger, slowly sliding it in. "I might've done it before, but I still need you to guide me if it feels wrong or you need more. I want this to feel amazing."

"Trust me, it fucking does. I'm good, though. You don't have to go slow. Add another finger."

I trust Ev, so I do as he asks. "Ungh!" he mutters as he closes the couple inches of space between him and Lake and begins making out with him.

My fingers are large, so I'm taking my time. "You're so fucking tight."

Ev pulls away from Lake with a breathless smile. "Curve your fingers and you can go faster."

I do as he asks and his whole body jerks. Oh, there it is: his prostate.

Because I'm an asshole, I hit his prostate a few more times until he's absolutely mad with need.

"Fuck, Logan. I need you. Get inside me, please!"

"So demanding," I tease, but honestly, I'm ready too.

Ev is probably loose enough, but I'm large, and the last thing

I want to do is hurt him, so after I put the condom on, I pour even more lube on my dick before stroking it roughly a couple of times and positioning myself over Ev.

"Babe, move so that your dick is touching Lake's. I want him to feel every stroke."

"Holy fuck, Logan. Are you sure you've never done this before?"

Well, that makes me feel fucking fantastic. "Not with men, no." But that doesn't bother me in the slightest as I press the tip of my cock against Ev's hole.

I start slowly, trying to get Ev used to the intrusion. But then my man surprises me by arching backwards, taking another inch or so of my length. "Please, Logan, more."

I lean forward and kiss his shoulder blade before pushing myself all the way in so that I'm buried deep. I pause again, letting him stretch around me. But Ev pushes back again. "Ugh, move, Logan! Now."

I smirk. "See, I was about to, but now I kind of just want to sit here. Use your ass as a cock warmer."

Lake gasps at the words, and something in his gaze makes me think he might like that idea. Something to explore later, maybe, when Lake is ready. Ev, however, is not so thrilled with this idea. "I swear to gods, Logan. If you don't fucking move—"

I laugh. "So, so, demanding." And then I pull halfway out and slam back in.

"Oh! Oh, fuck." I keep up that pace for a while. Every single thrust pushes Ev closer to Lake, causing his dick to slide against Lake's. I know the friction must be driving them both mad. I fucking love it.

Ev only allows me to control the pace for so long before he starts to meet every one of my thrusts with a backward push of his own. I'm not sure why, but this feels even better than any time I've ever had anal with a girl. It feels like coming home.

"Fuck, Ev, you feel so fucking good. Your hole is so tight,

squeezing me so good, like it was meant for my dick. And you and Lake lying under me like this? Gods, I feel like the luckiest man alive."

"We're all lucky," Lake manages to choke out. His voice is rough.

"Yes, Little Bird, we all are."

Our rhythm picks up, and I know it won't be long before I reach my peak. "Ev, can you get your hand around both of you? I want you to stroke both of you at the same time. I'm close and I want us to come together."

"Oh. Fuck," Ev mutters even as he obeys, his hand snaking in between his and Lake's bodies.

I know he manages to grip both of them when Lake's eyes roll in the back of his head. My thrusts get harder, and I know they're causing Ev to fuck his own hand.

"Gods, you two are so fucking amazing. I want to just spend the rest of my days in bed worshiping both of you. You have no idea how fucking sexy the two of you look from this angle. I want to capture this moment in my mind forever," I tell them, slightly out of breath.

"I'm coming!" Lake shouts before his hips thrust upwards and a low moan escapes his lips. This must trigger Ev who forces out an, "Oh, fuck," before absolutely squeezing around my dick as his own release shoots out of him.

That final squeeze is all it takes for me to be shooting my release in the condom. I can't wait to fuck them both raw, but we're not ready for that yet. This is more than enough for now.

Once I'm completely spent, I slip out of Ev and collapse, half on top of my two men, half on the side. I'm vaguely aware that poor Lake is probably getting crushed, but judging by the sleepy, satisfied look on his face, he doesn't appear to mind so much.

I finally get enough energy to remove the condom and tie it up. I throw it into the small trash can on the side of my bed. I know I should get up and get a cloth for my men, but I'm fucking worn out. I've never felt anything like that before.

They must be uncomfortable, and this overwhelming desire to take care of them consumes me. So using the last bit of energy I have, I climb out of bed, soak a couple washcloths, and make my way back to the room. Neither of them moved.

"Ev, babe, scoot over a bit so I can clean you both up." Ev opens one eye to glare at me but slips off of Lake enough that I can wash them both up, as well as myself. I kiss them both gently once we're all a little less sticky.

"Are you two ok?" Lake nods and snuggles up against my chest. I wrap my arms around him. Ev crawls up so he's on the other side of Lake. I'm not sure when it became a mutual decision to keep Lake in between us, but it has, and it's perfect.

Ev looks at me over Lake's head. "That was amazing, Logan. Thank you."

I shake my head. "No, thank you. Both of you."

Both men snuggle closer into me, and within minutes, they're both softly snoring. I stay up for just a little while longer watching them. I'm not sure what I did in my life to deserve these men, but I swear to never take them for granted.

Then with peace in my heart, I drift off to sleep.

TWENTY-FIVE
EVANDER

"And then I told my client I wouldn't accept anything under 300 grand and walked out," Jake, Kayla's date for the night, and a total d-bag if you ask me, says as he sips scotch.

When Logan asked if I wanted to go on a double date with Kayla and her new man, Jake, I jumped at the chance. Lake was invited too, of course, but he had work. And as much as I wish he were here and miss him, it's kind of nice to be able to go out with just Logan too. This is our first time out in public now that we've started seeing each other.

We would love to spend more time one on one with each other, and hopefully can start incorporating that more into our dynamic. But we've all been crazy busy, and it hasn't been easy. Since it seemed more important to focus on our triad and strengthen the bond between the three of us, one-on-one dates have kind of been pushed to the back burner.

So when Logan called and asked for me to meet up with them for dinner and drinks, I was excited. Plus, it's been a while since I've seen Kayla. I knew that she and Logan used to be fuck buddies, but it doesn't bother me at all. I'm secure in my relationship with him and Lake.

But, I really can't stand this guy. Kayla's such a badass, so I have no idea what made her start seeing him. I know it's not serious or anything, but ugh. He just skeeves me out. He's the kind of guy that attempted to make my time in high school hell but never succeeded because I honestly didn't give a fuck. Plus, Logan's always been big and protective, and it kept most of the bullies away.

Kayla doesn't seem to see it, though, and is laughing genuinely at this guy's story. I glance over at Logan and realize that he's staring behind Kayla and Jake at the big screen playing the football game. I laugh and squeeze his hand. He clearly gave up on pretending he even gave a crap.

Kayla looks down at our entwined hands. "I'm so glad you two have finally gotten your heads out of your asses and got together. You're welcome, by the way."

I laugh, genuine this time, and Logan checks back into the conversation with a warm smile. "Logan told me about your conversation. Seriously, thank you."

"I can't wait to meet your other man soon," she says as she leans into Jake.

Jake scrunches his nose and the disgust is obvious. He's been giving us the stink eye since we got here. I don't know if it's because we're two guys, or because of my tattoos and piercings, or if he knows Kayla's history with Logan, but the dickbag has been judging us from the moment he met us. With one little phrase, the mild disdain has transformed into full-on revulsion. Clearly, he's not a fan of poly relationships.

"Your other man?" he asks, trying to sound casual.

"Yeah, it's really new, but there's three of us. His name is Lake," Logan says, his voice deep and intimidating.

Jake does the nose scrunch thing again, and I don't know if it's because of the triad or Lake's name. Either way, it sets me on edge. Logan stiffens next to me, and I know the guy is annoying him too.

"There's three of you?" he asks, the disdain barely contained. "I thought you worked for the NYPD, Logan? I wonder what they'd think about that?"

Logan is vibrating with anger, and a growl escapes me. Even Kayla narrows her eyes at Jake. The threat in his words are clear.

Logan leans back, a deadly smile on his face. He casually drapes his arm around me, clearly unbothered. "My chief doesn't give a fuck. As long as it doesn't affect my job, he could give two shits about what we do in our personal lives. But you're more than welcome to call him and check. I can even give you his number."

Jake sniffs and straightens his back. He clearly doesn't have a response. Kayla glares at her date. "Jake, can I talk to you for a second?" She practically drags him out of the booth, and with an apologetic glance toward us, she pulls him out of sight.

Logan kisses the side of my face once they're gone. "Sorry about that. I didn't realize the guy was going to be such an asshole. Usually Kayla has better taste."

I shrug. "It's fine. I just wish our date night were a little more fun."

Logan's eyes brighten. "Well, it doesn't have to be over. How about we bail, once I make sure Kayla's ok, and go do something else?"

That could be fun. "Like what?"

"I don't know. How about bowling? I haven't been since high school."

"Oh man. You say that now because you clearly forgot how I can kick your ass at bowling. It's the one sport I'm actually better than you at."

Logan scoffs, "First off, kick my ass is a slight exaggeration. I'll admit you usually beat me, but it was close." I roll my eyes. I'll let him believe that if it makes him feel better. "Secondly, bowling's not a sport."

"Agree to disagree. C'mon, let's pay our bill, find Kayla, and bounce." I start to slide out of the booth and remember Lake.

"Wait, do you think this is something Lake would want to do with us? I don't want him to feel left out."

"He doesn't strike me as a bowler, but text him."

I pull out my phone and shoot Lake a text. I'm not sure he'll get it, but it doesn't feel right to do some kind of activity like that without checking in first. I know this is probably not sustainable and we'll need to make some guidelines that aren't sexual about spontaneous dates and other things that might come up when one of us isn't around. I want to be able to have a relationship with them individually as well as the three of us together. But, the last thing I want to do is hurt either of my men. So until we get a good handle on things, I'd much rather shoot a text to our missing partner and avoid hurt feelings or miscommunication.

Hey, sweetheart. How do you feel about bowling?

It surprisingly doesn't take long for Lake to respond. I'm not sure if I happened to catch him on a break or if he just always has his phone with him.

Bowling? Why? Did you want to go bowling? I don't mind going with you guys, but would you be offended if I didn't participate? Last time I bowled was when I was thirteen, for one of River's friend's birthdays, and let's just say it didn't end well.

I chuckle at his response and show the message to Logan. "There's clearly a story there."

Oh yeah, and I'll definitely be wanting to hear that story later. But another thing strikes me about the message. He called the mystery birthday kid River's friend. It's not the first time I've noticed that, either. When he is talking about friends, whether in the past or current, they are almost always River's friends. Does he have any friends he can purely claim as his own?

The thought makes me sad, but it's definitely not a conversation we can have through text while he's at work and Logan and I are planning on ghosting a double date.

I definitely will need to hear that story later. Our dinner isn't exactly panning out, and Lo and I are considering going to the bowling alley for a bit. Do you mind? If you want us to wait for you, we can do something else. No big deal. I finish it up with the smiley face emoji that has the little hearts surrounding it.

Lake's reply makes me smile. *No, please go bowling and save me that torture. I should be done around midnight. Will you two be back by then?*

Of course, sweetheart. I'll see you then. I add another smiley face.

Lake doesn't do the emoji thing, so he just responds with *a, See you then.* Smiling, I look toward Logan. "We're good to go."

Before we can leave, Kayla and Jake return to the table. I'm not sure what happened when they were gone, but Kayla's hair is all mussed up and both of their clothes are wrinkled and crooked.

"Good talk?" I ask, my eyebrow raised and an amused smirk on my face.

Kayla discreetly gives me the middle finger, which Logan catches and causes him to crack up.

"Sorry about that." Jake doesn't say a word, just slides into the booth.

"Don't worry about it. But actually, Ev and I are gonna head out. Long day tomorrow. Will you be ok?" he asks Kayla.

"I'm fine. Thanks for coming."

Jake doesn't say a word as we give Kayla hugs goodbye and head out. The whole thing is weird, but whatever.

Logan takes my hand as we hit the streets. "There's an alley on 12th Street with glow in the dark bowling. And tonight is nineties night. They'll be playing Britney Spears and boy bands all night."

Logan waggles his eyebrows at me, and I smack his arm playfully. I'm regretting admitting that my first crushes were Britney Spears and Justin Timberlake back in the day when they were dating. They were actually one of the confirming factors of my sexuality. But also, I'm totally here for a night of glow in the dark bowling, beer, and cheesy nineties music.

I lean up and cup Logan's face as I kiss him. I can feel him smile into the kiss as he clutches me closer. Logan has a tendency to dominate most sexual acts, even kissing. But this time, he allows me to stay in control. Which is good, because I might be smaller than him, but I need that control most of the time too.

He smiles at me as I pull away. "I guess that's a yes?"

I laugh. "Yes, it's a yes. Let's go. It's been too long since I've jammed to Britney anyway."

Holding hands, we walk the handful of blocks to the alley.

The strobe lights flicker above us, "Everybody" blasting on surround sound, and I relax back in my chair with a beer as I watch Logan get a gutter ball, *again*. I grin at him as he stomps back, cursing.

"Are you sure I was exaggerating about kicking your ass?" My hand flicks up toward where our scores are displayed on the screen.

Logan wraps his big arms around me and nips at my neck playfully. "I'm positive. I'm just warming up. It's been a while since I played."

I decide not to comment that it's been as long for me and I am, in fact, kicking his ass. I rub my scruff across his face, causing Logan to shiver. "Sure, we'll go with that. You just don't want to admit that I'm better than you are."

Logan scoffs but doesn't deny it as he sits next to me and drags me into his lap. I see a few eyes glaring at me, but I ignore it. While most people are certainly more open-minded in the city, there's always bigots. I'm hoping the rebirth of the Omega gene is also a rebirth in compassion and understanding, but I'm not holding my breath.

Logan and I cuddle together for a while, our game forgotten. "As fun as this is, I miss our little bird," Logan whispers into my ear.

"Yeah, me too. We'll have to do something like this with him one day. Maybe he'll be more enthusiastic about mini golf."

"Why do I seriously doubt that?" Logan replies. Yeah, he's probably right.

Leaning into Logan, I twist my head up so I'm looking at him. "Sometimes I have to pinch myself to remember that this is all real. That you're actually with me like this."

Logan's blue eyes are serious as he watches me. He's quiet for a long time before he gently kisses my head. "I'm sorry," he finally replies.

My throat closes. What is he sorry for? I'm not usually an anxious person, but I immediately flash through a thousand different scenarios where he's breaking up with me, even though I know it's highly unlikely.

"Why are you sorry?" I finally manage to say.

"That it took me so long to see what's right in front of my face. I think about that a lot, you know—what changed. And I don't really have an answer. It's just like one day the blinders came off and I saw you, like really saw you, and I realized I wasted the last eighteen years keeping us in the friend zone."

I grab his face and kiss him. I know we're in public, but I can't help it. I need to kiss him, to feel him in this moment. I get completely lost in his lips and his arms. It's like there's no one here but Logan. He's the only thing that matters right now.

Someone clears their throat. I know my cheeks must be bright red as we break apart, and Logan is laughing.

"Maybe that's a sign we should head home?" he asks.

Chuckling, I detangle myself from Logan's lap and move to

stand. "Yeah, that sounds perfect. Let's go home and wait for our man."

We take off our bowling shoes and return them. And then hand in hand, we make our way back to my apartment to wait for Lake.

TWENTY-SIX
LAKE

"I still can't believe you've never seen any of the *Lord of the Rings* movies, Lo," Evander grumbles as he shoves a handful of popcorn into his mouth. I try not to flinch as a few crumbs land on my sofa and carpet.

Since I've been spending so much time in the city and at their places the last couple of weeks, Logan and Evander decided they'd come to my place this time. And despite the crumbs getting everywhere, I love having them in my space. I never expected to find anyone I'd be comfortable with having in my space like this.

"Well, I blame you for that. The only movies I ever saw back then were when you showed them to me. So clearly, Mr. Lord of the Ring's Biggest Fan, you must not love them as much as you're claiming." Logan's tone is light and snarky, but I can tell there's some deeper emotion underneath that.

Logan hasn't spoken much about his childhood before meeting Evander. All I know is that his mom died when he was young, and his dad pretty much neglected him. I suspect there was some physical abuse as well, though neither he nor Logan have mentioned it. I don't push. He'll tell me when he's ready, if he wants to.

"Ok, so I didn't get into them until college, but that's besides the point. I thought you'd have seen them by now."

Logan just shrugs. "Nope, this is the first time."

We're all crowded onto my sofa, and I'm regretting not buying the sectional Essie tried to convince me to get. It seemed a waste at the time, but I'm sure we'd all appreciate a little more space. Logan's in the middle, since he takes up the most room. He has his feet propped up against my coffee table, and if I tell myself that it's ok enough times, maybe I'll believe it. I don't actually want him to move, so I keep my thoughts to myself. Maybe I'll buy an ottoman if they're going to spend a lot of time here.

Ev is on Logan's other side. He's half lying on Logan's broad chest and half sitting up. He has his legs kicked up over the edge of the sofa. I'm also leaning against Logan, but I'm sitting criss-cross applesauce. Logan has his one arm thrown over the side of the couch, his finger gently caressing Evander. His hand closest to me is palming my stomach, his thumb massaging a gentle pattern.

After a very long and tedious process, I finally was implanted with the embryo a little over a week ago. It's still too early to tell; I go for a blood test in a few days to confirm the pregnancy, but I don't need the blood test to know. The implantation took. Somehow, I just know I'm carrying Zoe and Avery's child.

It seems like, at least subconsciously, Logan and Evander know as well. Even if this baby has no blood relation to any of us and we'll basically just be more uncles to them, some kind of instinct must have kicked in. I find that without either of them realizing it, they are both constantly touching my stomach.

As the Omega gene becomes more prominent, the Omega Project keeps releasing more information. It seems like people with the gene are tapping into their more intrinsic instincts, something that hasn't happened in well over a century. They still have no idea why it's happening now or what's causing these significant changes, but it's being observed enough to be believed it's not a coincidence.

"I remember the first time I saw the first movie. Dad took River and I to the movie theater to see it. River and I were hooked. Dad fell asleep."

Logan barks out a laugh as he takes another huge handful of popcorn. "That's hysterical. I can see why he did that. I'm getting a little sleepy myself."

I stare at Logan, completely incredulous. Evander hits him with a pillow. "Shut your blasphemous mouth! The only reason you're saying that is because we're all talking. And because it's still early. Just wait till you get to *The Return of the King*. I promise you'll be hooked."

Logan dramatically throws his head back against the couch cushion. "That's like ten hours' worth of movie from now."

I laugh. "Are you always this dramatic?"

"Yes," both Logan and Evander say at the same time, and I'm smiling so hard it hurts.

It's been about a week since Logan and Evander's bowling date. They told me all about it before Evander insisted we all sit down and make some ground rules regarding things like dates. We already discussed sexual acts, but I know they were concerned that I'd feel left out. I told them as long as we keep communication open I think it will be fine. We agreed as long as we never hide things from the other partners and made sure to be honest if one of us starts to feel left out or gets jealous, that we don't need to get permission for every little thing we do together. Sure, I know it will take a lot of tweaking as we adjust, but I'm confident in our ability to make it work for us.

Since the night of the family dinner, and our first night truly together, we've only grown closer. Our schedules are continuing to be a problem, but we're making it work. On days we can't all be together, we text constantly and FaceTime when we can. We've also spent more time in pairs as well.

I spent the night with just Evander the other day, and of course, Evander and Logan had their date night. Logan and I have managed to meet for lunch or dinner together a handful of times as well. As much as I love these moments with all three of us, I also cherish the time we spend one on one.

While we've had plenty of sex, I still haven't tried penetration. Evander offered to bottom for me, but I have no interest. I've done some research, and it seems like an inherent trait among the old Omegas is that they strictly bottom. I wonder if that's the case with this new form of the gene. I tried to ask River about his preferences, but he got extremely uncomfortable.

Regardless, I know I'm ready mentally. I just want to make sure everything is ok with the baby before we take the step, and I haven't felt any kind of pressure or resentment from either of my men about waiting, which I'm very grateful for.

I'm lost in my thoughts as the movie continues. When the credits begin to roll, Logan yawns and gently removes himself from Evander and me. Despite all his comments, Evander's the only one who fell asleep. Logan carefully places him on the couch. Standing to his full height, he stretches, and I can't help but watch his muscles bunch as he moves. The man is just so muscular.

Logan catches my gaze. "You like what you see, Little Bird?" I nod as I swallow, my mouth suddenly dry.

"I'd love to let you show me just how much you love my body, but unfortunately, I gotta go into work soon, and I need to eat and shower before I do so. Do you mind if I make myself a sandwich or something?"

"No." I start to rise. "I can make it for you."

Logan just kisses me and lightly pushes me back onto the couch. "As long as you don't mind me rummaging through your fridge, I can do it. You've been working crazy hours. You need to relax when you can."

I'm not the only one who's been working crazy hours, but I don't say anything. Even Evander has been extremely busy, and more than once I've woken up to him sitting up in bed, on his laptop and working first thing in the morning. I'm starting to feel guilty that they still don't know exactly what I do, so I don't want to bring too much attention to it.

Neither man has made a big deal about it recently, but I know they're curious, and also concerned. I'm not in any danger, not really, but since they have so little information, I can understand why they're worried. I want to broach the subject with my boss so that we can start the vetting process, but I just had to pull strings regarding the pregnancy. I'm not quite ready to rock the boat yet again.

I ignore Logan's suggestion and follow him into my kitchen. He has the stuff out to make at least four sandwiches. I've been very curious about his eating habits. He's a big man, and very active, so it's logical that he eats so much. I'm sure he has a very high metabolism. But I have a feeling there's more to it than that, and since I know he had a hard childhood, I wonder if there's a connection.

I'm working on a non-offensive way to ask when Logan notices me staring. He gives me a sideways smile. "You can just ask, you know. I won't be offended. Not from you."

I feel some of the tension release, though there's still guilt. They're so honest with me, and I'm still hiding things from them.

"It's really not my business, but I was thinking about your eating habits."

Logan's face is serious, but he doesn't appear angry. He opens up his arm, gesturing for me to come close, and I hurry to his side.

"I don't mind telling you. You should know anyway."

Logan's not looking at me, his gaze fixed on the sandwich options.

"You know that my mom died when I was young, right?"

"Yes."

"And that I was basically adopted by Ev's dad when I was fifteen?"

I nod.

"Well, that time in between was rough. Most of the time, my dad wanted nothing to do with me. He'd leave me alone for weeks at a time as a kid, most of the time with no food in the house." Logan laughs harshly. "Sometimes the apartment didn't even have electricity or water, and he'd just disappear."

I squeeze his hand, sensing Logan needs support. Ev must have woken up at some point and made his way into the kitchen. I know he knows all of this already, so he remains quiet and just begins to finish making the sandwiches that Logan started. Logan looks at him with so much love my heart melts. I'm not at all jealous. I know he looks at me the same way. We may not have said the words yet, but I find myself thinking them often lately.

"Though honestly, that was better than when he was around. Even when he was home, he was stingy about feeding me. And if I asked, he'd just knock me around. I learned to stay out of his way pretty quickly and just fend for myself."

That I can understand, at least in part. River and I were lucky though. We always had each other and Mom, who tried her best to protect us from Seth. We also were never hungry. I understand now, as an adult, that my mom probably went hungry more than once to make sure we had food, but River and I never went without. Logan was all alone. I can't imagine how terrifying that must've been for him.

I don't speak, but just squeeze his hand. He smiles sadly at me. "I stole food when I had to. I rummaged through dumpsters, went to every church lunch I could find. I had to avoid shelters because they'd ask questions, but I learned who would just give me food and look the other way and who wouldn't."

Logan sniffs as he continues, "That all changed when I met Evander. I've never been more grateful for getting caught stealing someone's lunch than I was that day." He looks fondly over at Evander, his eyes wet. Evander meets his gaze, tears in his own eyes.

"I've never been more grateful to have my lunch stolen," Ev confesses, and Logan lets out a wet laugh. I find myself joining him. Ev continues, "You and Lake are the best things that ever happened to me."

I can't stand by myself anymore. I need to be touching both of them. I squeeze myself in the space between Logan and the counter and take Evander's hand, bringing him closer to the two of us. They both squeeze tight.

"What happened to your dad, if you don't mind me asking."

"For a long time, I didn't know. I basically moved into Mr. C's house shortly after meeting them. I only saw my dad a handful of times as I was finishing up high school, and when I did see him, it was like he forgot I existed. I didn't see him at all for about two years. After I graduated from the academy, I looked into him. I guess he got arrested for prostitution and sexual assualt. He ended up killing himself in prison."

Logan says the words like they are facts in a history book, and I can understand that. It's kind of how I feel whenever I speak about my childhood and Seth. I can sense he's done with the conversation. Ev kisses Logan's cheek. "You are so much better than him, Lo."

Logan just kisses both of our heads before shaking his and backing away. "Well, anyway. You wanna share these sandwiches with me before I jump in the shower? Which you should also share with me, just saying."

I glance at Evander who shakes his head subtly. I get the message. It's time to drop the subject. So Evander and I split one sandwich while Logan eats the others, and then we crowd into my shower, which is not meant for three people. Eventually Evander and I excuse ourselves so Logan can take an actual shower. As much as I'm starting to enjoy sharing mutual blow jobs, there's just not enough room for all three of us to do that. Plus, Logan really does have to get to work, so Ev and I go cuddle on the couch while we wait for him. We make plans to go over to River's and spend time with him, Cooper, Cam, and the baby after Logan leaves.

Twenty minutes later, he's dressed and ready to go. He comes and kisses us both goodbye.

"Be safe," Evander tells him.

Logan gives us a lopsided grin, his expression full of mischief. "Always."

Evander snorts and I roll my eyes. And while it's completely insane, I'm missing Logan as soon as he leaves. As much as I love spending time with just Evander, it feels like a piece of my heart is missing when one of us isn't here.

TWENTY-SEVEN
EVANDER

"I really appreciate you coming here early to help out. It's been a while since I've had to cook for this many people."

I look up at Luke from where I'm peeling potatoes. Our busy schedules have made it impossible to have another family dinner like we had at my dad's up until this point. So when Thanksgiving started to roll around, Luke insisted on having all of us at his house. And I mean all of us. He even invited Avery, Zoe, Cam, and even Lucy. Lucy, Avery, and Zoe are all having the holiday with their families, though they may stop by for dessert. Cam's family lives on the West Coast, but his grandma bought him a plane ticket to come visit, so he'll be gone for a while.

Cooper didn't say anything, of course, but I could see he was relieved to get their house back to themselves when he announced the unexpected trip. I met Cam a couple weeks ago for the first time, and I can understand how someone may need a little reprieve from the guy, even if it's clear how loyal he is to River

"It's no problem at all, Luke," I tell him genuinely. At first, it seemed weird to call him by his first name, but I got used to it.

Like with my dad, Logan fell into the habit of calling Luke Mr. S, and for some reason he gets away with it even when I don't. "I actually love doing things like this."

Luke looks at me with genuine affection as he chops carrots. "Maybe one day you'll be able to host a holiday at your house with Lake and Logan." He chuckles and shakes his head. "Though I'm not sure how helpful either of them would be."

I snort. He's not wrong. Any time Logan helps my dad and me prep for a meal, he picks on the food more than anything else. And Lake is pretty much useless in the kitchen. "That's ok. I love cooking for them, honestly. I think it's how I show my love," I say with a laugh.

"Nothing wrong with that."

I get back to work, but now the fantasy is firmly in my head: We wake up in our very own home on Christmas morning, the house all decorated and a large tree in the family room. Lake makes us coffee while I make French toast for us for breakfast, slapping Luke's hand away as he keeps trying to steal the strawberries I cut for on top. Lake's round with a child, ours or Zoe's, I'm not sure, but he's still rubbing his belly fondly as he hands me a mug of coffee.

Then later on, the whole family comes over to have Christmas dinner and exchange gifts. Everyone is laughing and smiling, completely content as I pull out trays and trays of food, Miri crawling around the living room, trying to open all the presents. It's a good vision I hope happens one day.

Both Logan and Lake had to work this morning so they'll probably show up just in time for Thanksgiving dinner. Essie came home from college last night, but apparently went out, so she's still sleeping. River and Cooper said they'd come earlier to help, but Cooper's sister Casey is on leave from Germany, so Luke insisted they spend time with her this morning. River and Lake have been concerned lately that their dad is lonely, so I volunteered to come early to help prep, and honestly, it's been a blast.

We spend the morning in easy companionship, and I learn that we work really well in the kitchen together. I also hear more stories about Lake growing up, and I tell him more about me. Luke even asks about my tattoos, but I don't feel like he's judging me, just genuinely curious. So, I gladly talk about them.

Finally, everything is prepped, the turkey has been cooking for hours, and we're ready to go for a while. It's right when the two of us have everything cleaned up from prep that Essie walks casually into the kitchen.

She looks around at the trays of food. "Oh, you guys are done already? I would've helped."

Luke and I look at each other and roll our eyes. Like I didn't use the same tactic when I was her age. Luke kisses his daughter on the cheek. "It's ok, honey, we got it covered. You'll need to put a new pot of coffee on, though. I think Ev drank it all."

It's funny how the rest of Lake's family embraced calling me Ev, when Lake only calls me Evander. Typically, I correct anyone who insists on calling me by my full name, but I like when Lake says it. He makes it sound sexy and sophisticated.

"Luke, do you mind if I use your bathroom to freshen up before everyone gets here?" I brought a change of clothes so I don't smell like onions and stuffing all day.

"Sure. If you wanna shower, there's towels under the sink in the guest bathroom."

"Thank you."

The guest bathroom is the kind that has a door out to the hallway but another two inside that go directly to bedrooms. Both doors are ajar when I enter. One is clearly Essie's room, so I close and lock that so she doesn't accidentally walk in on me. I peek into the other room, and I immediately wonder if I'm looking at River and Lake's bedroom when they were teenagers. There's two twin-sized beds in the room. One is a loft-style bunk bed, the kind with the bed on top, but underneath is a desk set up rather than another bed. The desk looks empty besides a small lamp. On the other side of the room is another twin-sized bed. Both beds have matching navy-blue plaid comforters on top of them. Another empty desk is pushed up against the foot of the bed. At first glance, it looks like most of the things that made the room theirs have been taken down over the years, but for some reason, I just know that's Lake's bedroom.

I don't really have time to explore right now, so I leave that door partially ajar and take a shower. I figure no one would be entering that room today anyway.

I feel much better once I dress in my dark jeans that make my ass look amazing and a navy-blue sweater. The look is a little preppier than I typically go for, but it works for a holiday at my boyfriend's dad's house.

While we've had discussions about being exclusive, none of us have said the mate word or that we love each other yet. I have no idea what any of us are waiting for, but any time I start to say it, I hesitate. No matter how I feel, it just seems too soon. And the mate thing? Even as scientists keep bringing out more evidence that it's real, it seems so far-fetched to me, I have a hard time coming to terms with the idea. I know Lake believes, which is understandable after witnessing what happened to his brother, but he hasn't forced the issue yet.

Instead of going out the main door and into the hallway, I cut through Lake's old bedroom. Ok, sue me, I'm fucking nosy. I nearly jump out of my skin when I see Lake sitting on the single bed, playing around on his phone.

"Fucking A, Lake, you just scared the shit out of me!"

Lake smiles sheepishly. "Sorry, I didn't mean to scare you. I was just waiting till you got out of the shower."

I walk over to him and tip his chin up to kiss him hello. Instead of sitting next to him, I straddle Lake's legs and sit on his lap. A few weeks ago, Lake would completely stiffen up and get awkward if I did something like that. Now, he just laughs and wraps his arms around me, burying his head into my chest.

I hug him back. "Is everything ok, sweetheart?"

He glances up at me with sleepy eyes. "Yeah, it was just a rough morning at work. But, at least I'm not late."

I push on Lake's shoulders, not hard enough to actually move him, but he willingly goes down so his back is on the bed. I climb up so I'm lying next to him and begin to play with his hair. "Do you want to bet on how late Logan's going to be?"

Lake snorts. "On Thanksgiving? I'm sure all the nuts are out. I'll be impressed if he gets here before dessert."

"Maybe we'll be nice and save him some." Lake smiles softly at me, both of us knowing full well that we'll be coming home loaded with tupperware, even if Logan does make it on time.

I'm not exactly sure how long Lake and I lie here, but at some point, he takes my hand and rests his head against my chest. I absolutely love when he takes initiative with affection, since I know it's not the easiest for him. I play with his hair with my free hand, and we just lie here enjoying each other's company.

Eventually we hear the doorbell ring and reluctantly separate from each other. The guests are starting to come.

"Thank you for having me, Luke," Dad says as he leans back on the recliner, patting his belly. "Everything was delicious."

We're taking a break between dinner and dessert, and everyone made their way into the family room to watch the football games. Well, Luke, Dad, and Cooper are. River and Essie are on the floor playing with Miri, who's rolling around on a giant play mat. Lake and I are cuddled together on the chaise lounge part of the massive sectional. Lake is lying halfway on me, and I have one hand cradling his belly while I lazily scroll through my phone with my other hand.

It's weird, but ever since Lake got the confirmation he's pregnant, I can't get enough of holding his stomach. It's not like I can feel anything yet, and he's not showing, of course. Hell, he doesn't even have symptoms yet, but it's this protective instinct to look after the child growing inside the man I care deeply about, even if it's not his or mine. Not that it matters, but I'd already gladly give my life for this baby, regardless of their biological parents.

"You're welcome, Eric. Your son is quite the sous chef."

My dad beams at that praise. "That was one of the first things we bonded over when he first came to live with me: cooking together. I'm glad we still have that experience together, and I'm happy he now has it with you."

I smile contentedly. This has been a perfect Thanksgiving. All that's missing is Logan. He texted Lake and I that something came up and he's not sure what time he'll be here. Of course Luke already put two full plates aside for him, not including the leftover containers, but still, I'd love to spend our first holiday together as partners and lovers with him. But we'll have more.

At some point, Luke gets up to start getting dessert on the table. I go to help, but he waves me away since Lake has now fallen asleep. Ok, maybe he is starting to have symptoms. He's definitely been overtired lately. River and Essie are busy with the baby, so my dad and Cooper get up to go help him.

They're in the kitchen getting everything ready when my phone rings. It's Logan. I answer. "Hey, babe, do you think you're going to be here soon? Luke's just getting dessert out."

Logan is quiet for a moment before answering, his voice serious. "I'm actually outside. Can you and Lake meet me out here, please?"

I sit up so abruptly, I wake up Lake who nearly falls off the couch. I distractedly steady him with an apologizing glance. "Logan, what happened? What's the matter?"

"I'll explain when you come out here. I don't want to discuss this in front of everyone. Please."

Fuck. There's a sense of dread forming like a ball in my stomach. "Um, of course. We'll be right there."

Everyone is watching me when I hang up. I ignore the gazes from River and his sister and focus on Lake, who's staring at me with concern. "Logan wants to talk to us outside. I don't know why."

I watch as Lake's expression completely closes off, and he nods once. I'm not sure what he thinks is about to happen, but he just stands up and starts to walk toward the front door. His reaction is almost more concerning than whatever is going on with Logan. Does he think Logan's breaking up with us? I know deep in my heart that whatever is happening, that's not the case, but I have no way to prove that, so I stop Lake at the door as he's shoving his boots on.

I kneel in front of him where he's sitting on the bench by the front door and cup both his cheeks in my hands. "Whatever is about to happen, I just want you to know I love you and you're not losing me, ok?" I want to say the same for Logan, but I know he won't believe me. His eyes widen, and I realize I said I love him for the first time. But it's true, and he needed to hear it.

"But, if Logan makes you choose, you're going to choose him," he says as if it's fact, and it breaks my heart. I don't know where to go with this, because I am so sure that whatever this is, it's not Logan leaving us.

"I can understand why you would believe that, but it's not true. I am confident that Logan will never make me choose, and if he does, he's not the man I always thought he was. I'm not going anywhere, Lake, ok?"

Lake nods solemnly. I know he doesn't believe me, but we quickly get dressed in our shoes and coats and head outside before we attract an audience. I'm actually surprised we don't already have one. Right before I open the door, Lake stops me. "This feeling is new to me, but I'm pretty sure I love you too." I kiss his forehead, and for just one second, we stay there like that. Reluctantly, I pull us apart. Logan's waiting for us.

When we walk outside, I see Logan pacing the sidewalk in front of Luke's house. I can't see his expression from here, but he's clearly on edge. Lake grabs my hand desperately, like it's the only thing he has left to cling to, and I kind of know how he feels.

Logan spots us and freezes. His eyes are focused on Lake, and oh fuck? Is he breaking up with us? I swallow down the lump of nerves in my throat. No, there's no way. I can't think of anything that could possibly happen that would make Logan do that. We may be be early in our relationship, but we're fucking solid.

It feels like I'm descending to the gates of hell as we make our way to Logan. He's standing completely still, not moving a muscle. I've never seen him like this. He always acts like nothing gets to him, and even though I know that's not true, it's not always so apparent.

I'm practically dragging Lake the last few steps to meet him. "Logan, what's going on?"

His eyes flash behind him to the house. "Let's take a walk." I look behind me, and sure enough, I see auburn curls peeking through the small opening in the curtain.

Logan starts walking, so reluctantly, the two of us follow. He doesn't say anything until we're about a block away. It's freezing out, but I don't feel the cold. All I feel is absolute dread.

Finally, Logan turns around and looks at us. Some of that intensity has leaked out of his eyes, but he's still on edge. He looks at Lake. "I have a few things I need to ask you. I know we said we'd give you time, but that time has come. I'm going to need some answers, Lake, and I kind of need them now. I bought some time and put myself on the line, but I can only do so much without knowing the truth."

What the fuck is he talking about? Lake swallows hard enough that I can hear him. He has a death grip on my hand. "What answers do you need?" His voice is shaky.

"I need to know what you really do for a living. Seth McIntyre got arrested again today for some really serious charges, and with his past, he's going away for a long time. He's throwing some heavy allegations your way about your job. Allegations my boss is believing. I bought some time, but I need to know what you really do before the full force of the SWAT team comes to your dad's house and tears down his door on Thanksgiving."

"What is he saying that can cause this kind of reaction?" I ask.

Logan rolls his eyes, and I relax slightly. That's the first reaction that looks like the Logan I know since he called me. It's clear whatever the problem, he's on Lake's side. I just hope Lake trusts Logan enough to see that.

"He's saying he's a spy. That he's working for the highest bidder as a hacker and giving out top secret information in exchange for a paycheck, including information on national security and biological weapons."

And then tension is back as I swallow down bile. I'm terrified to look at Lake, but he's actually laughing. "Oh, that's all? Thank gods, I thought for sure you were breaking up with me and going to make Evander choose between us."

Oh, ok, then.

TWENTY-EIGHT
LOGAN

The whole drive to Luke Simmons's house, my mind had been racing with different scenarios. I had no idea how Lake was going to take this news. I know deep within my soul he's not some black hat hacker selling secrets to the highest bidder. While I'm sure he does some things that don't exactly follow the letter of the law, I know Lake isn't a traitor. But I still wasn't sure how he'd take being accused of being one.

And then there was the whole thing with Seth getting arrested and once again trying to throw his kids under the bus to save his own ass. I knew I'd probably lose it if my dad were alive and suddenly started to throw my name around, trying to get out of trouble.

Of course, my lieutenant was pissing me off more than anything else. He's one of those extremists who's convinced that the Omega gene coming back is the sign of the Apocalypse or some shit, so he jumped on the chance of shining one of them under a bad light. I got extremely lucky that one of my buddies happened to be the one who collared Seth and heard enough of what was going on and came to me. Very few people in my precinct know about Ev and Lake yet, but he's one of the few.

And thank gods for that. Otherwise, we may have been totally fucking blindsided by this insanity.

Anyway, of all the possible reactions, Lake straight up laughing wasn't on my radar. I can't even think about that, though, because my brain is focused on the second half of that sentence. He really thought I'd break up with him and then make Ev fucking choose? What did I ever do to make him think that? One look at Ev confirms he didn't have the same fears, so that's something at least.

Lake goes to open his mouth, probably to tell me the truth, but I stop him with a finger on his lips. "Hold up a second. Did you really think I was gonna break up with you? *And* make Ev choose between us? You need to know that thought never fucking crossed my mind, not once. I can't think of one thing on this fucking earth that would make me give the two of you up. And if I did, I'd never ever force either of you to choose. Honestly, it kind of hurts that you thought that. I get we haven't known each other for that long, but fuck, Lake, I love you. I love both of you," I say, looking at Ev. "I'm more likely to burn the fucking world down for you than leave you. That's how fucking strongly I feel. Fuck, forget hurt, I'm actually kind of pissed."

Lake blinks, and I know he's trying to process everything I just said. "I'm sorry. I didn't want to make you feel like this. It's just—all of this is new to me, and it's hard to believe I actually can have this with you two. That I even want it. It's easier for me to believe you'll get tired of me and want to leave than anything else. I know I'm not the easiest person to be around."

Fuck, all the anger melts out of me as I squeeze Lake close. "I'll never get tired of you, that I swear to you, Little Bird. And honestly, I think you're better in social situations than you think. You're just so fucking smart the rest of us need a minute to catch up."

Lake laughs, his eyes a little wet. He reaches out for Ev's

hand, who automatically gives it to him. "I-I love you two also," Lake says quietly.

"Me too," Ev adds. "I love you both so much."

For a moment, I forget everything else and just hold my men. Ev is the first one to break the hold. "I hate to break up this tender moment, but it's fucking freezing, and I'd love for my boyfriend to not get arrested as a traitor and terrorist, so what's going on?"

"Oh, right. Yeah, no worries there. I'll handle it now." Lake looks up at me. "I'm going to tell you everything, but I have to call my boss first. He's going to want to get a handle on this before Seth actually manages to ruin the operation. I'm way too valuable to get rid of, so whenever he causes problems, it's always a scramble."

I nod, still unsure about what's going on. Lake pulls out a cell phone, but it's not his normal one. Since when has he had two phones? He immediately pulls up a number. The voice on the other end is loud enough I can hear everything he's saying.

"Specialist Simmons, you realize it's Thanksgiving, right? You better have a fucking good reason for calling me."

"Yes, sir, I'm well aware of that fact. Trust me when I say you want to take this call."

There's a heavy sigh on the line. "What the fuck did you do now, Simmons?" I'm ready to take the phone out of Lake's hand and let this asshole have it for talking to Lake like this. I realize he's probably some high-ranking government official or something like that, but no one talks to my man like that. Lake, however, doesn't even blink.

"It's my biological father, Seth McIntyre."

Another heavy sigh. "What's the issue now?"

"He apparently got arrested and is being held at the 31st precinct. The charges are serious so he's trying to gain leverage by working a deal. He's claiming I'm a spy selling secrets of national security to the highest bidder."

The man on the other line laughs. "No one is going to believe that shit."

"Actually, sir, someone is." Lake looks at me, his hand covering the phone. "What's your lieutenant's name?" he whispers.

"Gary Jirabaldi."

"Lieutenant Gary Jirabaldi does believe him, at least enough that he's mobilizing a SWAT unit to hit my father's property, where I currently am for the holiday dinner."

"What a fucking idiot. Ok, I'll handle it. You're so lucky that the director loves you, Simmons. I'd have you out on your ass by now."

"You say that, sir, but the entire department would fall apart without me, and you know that. By the way, I'm about to tell my boyfriends the truth. One is a detective with the 31st, which is how we found out. I won't say anything sensitive until they go through the vetting process."

Ev and I stare at each other, dumbfounded. I still have no idea what's happening, but I didn't expect that.

"You're a pain in my ass, Simmons."

"I know, sir." Again, Lake isn't at all phased by the way his superior is talking to him. Don't get me wrong, my superiors can be harsh and also brash, but I feel like this man is taking it to the extreme. Maybe I'm just overprotective.

"Fine. I'll handle this incident with the police. I expect the paperwork to begin the process for your boyfriends on my desk first thing Monday."

"Yes, sir, thank you."

There's a grunt and the guy disconnects, leaving us alone with Lake and completely astonished.

"He'll handle it. I'm sure you'll be getting a call in a few minutes, Logan, regarding the situation."

"Ok, sweetheart, can you tell us what's going on now?" Ev asks.

"Oh, right. I can't discuss much out in the open like this. I can tell you everything at my place, because I know the security is sufficient. Basically, I work as a white hat hacker for the CIA. Everything is government sanctioned, and I've never once gone rogue."

I have to say, I'm not even that surprised. Ev wraps his arms around himself. "That was kind of anticlimactic, actually."

Lake looks at both of us. "Really?"

"Yeah, I kind of suspected that. And a lot of things are starting to make sense now."

"You're not mad?"

I hug him close to me. "No, Little Bird. We're not mad. I understand how you wouldn't be able to tell us."

"No, sweetheart, I'm not mad. I definitely have some questions, but they can wait. "

Ev jerks his head in the direction of the house. "Can we head back now? It's freezing and I don't want to miss dessert. Your dad made the most bomb-looking apple pie."

"Apple pie?" I ask excitedly. Now that I'm not terrified, I'm fucking starving.

"My dad makes an amazing pie. I'm pretty sure that's how he convinced my mom to marry him."

We all laugh and head back to the house. Sure enough, before we even get there, I get a text from my buddy. The lieutenant got the dressing down of his life from the director of the CIA, and Seth is being sent to some maximum security prison where he'll probably be buried under red tape until the day he dies. Holy shit, my man can be scary when he needs something done.

I show him the text, and Lake just smiles. That's it. It makes me wonder why Lake never did this to Seth before now, but it's not the time to ask.

As we approach the house, we can see the whole family hovering on the front porch, freezing their asses off and waiting to see what's going on. I make sure it's clear that all three of us are holding hands so they know whatever happened, we're ok.

Lake kisses each of us before grabbing his brother and Dad and bringing them to the side. I know he's telling them Seth won't be a problem for a long ass time, if at all. I feel warm inside when they all hug each other, Lake and River in tears. Mr. C senses they need a minute and begins to usher the rest of us inside. It seems in the time we were gone, Zoe, Avery, and Lucy all showed up, resulting in a full house of nosy ass people.

But once we're inside, Mr. C is dishing out desserts, and everyone forgets about the drama.

Later, as I'm curled up on the couch with my two men, eating my third slice of apple pie, I'm left with a feeling of satisfaction. This is where I'm meant to be. They may not be my blood family, but they're my family all the same.

TWENTY-NINE
EVANDER

"Babe, are you opening up a bakery and just forgot to tell me?" I glare at Logan as he lets himself into Lake's house. He's just come from the gym and is wearing formfitting joggers that make his ass look incredible with a skintight Under Armour long-sleeve top. I scowl before turning back to my baking. It should be a crime to look that good coming from the gym.

I'm impressed we both ended up at the right house at the right time. Managing three homes has gotten old, fast. I find myself daily wondering if it's too soon to mention moving in together. Every day is a new mass text trying to coordinate who's going to be where and which house we're meeting at tonight. I'm freaking tired of having to pack bags and, even worse, looking for a specific pair of pants for the one day in two weeks I actually have to go into the office and realizing that those pants are in Jersey and I'm in Brooklyn at Logan's apartment.

Today, though, there's no coordination or argument, because we've known for weeks we're going to be at Lake's house. That's because Lake is getting his first ultrasound today. While a blood test confirmed the pregnancy early on, the doctors waited until he was over eight weeks to do the ultrasound. Unfortunately, Logan and I weren't able to go since we're not actually the fathers of this baby, but I'm still as anxious as a first-time father. Lake is so determined to do this surrogacy right, and I'm terrified something is going to go wrong.

This isn't why I've been stress baking all day. It didn't take long for me to discover that I need an outlet besides work and the gym when both Logan and Lake are working. And lately, Lake is always working. In the weeks since that debacle with his father, Lake's boss has been giving him the worst assignments. He's had to travel three times in the last few weeks, though thankfully, they have all been short trips. With Lake hidden away in some country I'm not even allowed to know the name of, and Logan out on the streets trying to find missing children, I found out quickly that I need something to distract me.

That turned out to be baking. Good thing it's almost Christmas time, because Logan isn't wrong. I baked enough to feed everyone in Lake's development.

"Shut up, Lo. It's not like you're not benefitting from this. Don't eat the pumpkin bread. I'm freezing it and giving it to Essie when she comes back for winter break next week."

Logan pouts like he's a small child but I refuse to be swayed. There's plenty for him to eat. "I made you two loaves of banana bread. You don't even like pumpkin."

"I never said that."

"You went on a twenty-minute rant about how pumpkin spice is the worst flavor you've ever had and you don't understand how it became so popular. I think your exact words were, 'I'd rather eat nothing but brussel sprouts for the rest of my life than pumpkin.'"

Logan sighs dramatically but finds the banana bread and begins cutting off a slice. "I was exaggerating."

"Clearly. But it's still for Essie. You have plenty."

"Ugh, fine."

I chuckle as I begin to wash dishes. "Do you mind helping me clean up once you're done eating? I don't want Lake to come home to a dirty kitchen."

"Sure."

For a few minutes, we stay in companionable silence before Logan breaks it. "You're really worried about him, aren't you?"

I shoot Logan a look. "Aren't you?"

"Sure, but I don't know. I have a good feeling. I think this appointment will go well."

"It's not just the appointment. It's work too. I know Lake's trying to let it play out for a while before he goes back to the higher-ups, but it's clear he's being punished, and it's taking its toll. He's exhausted, Lo. He needs his rest. Not to mention, the morning sickness started."

Logan puts down the tray of cookies he's packing up and closes the distance between us. He opens up his arms and I eagerly fall into them. There's something about being in Logan's arms that makes me feel safe and secure.

"It's bothering me too, Ev. But Lake's a grown ass man with a very successful career. You know we have to let him handle this on his own."

I sigh and rest my head against Logan's chest, breathing in his scent. He smells of a mixture of the faded scent of his cologne, a little bit of sweat, and bananas. On anyone else, it probably would've been terrible, but I couldn't get enough right now.

"Yeah, I know, but it doesn't mean I have to like it."

Logan laughs as he rests his chin on the top of my head. That used to annoy the shit outta me. I'm not even short, so how is it possible he can do that? But now, I kind of like it. I feel claimed, in the best way possible.

"No, you definitely don't have to like it."

Lake gets home shortly after we packed up and divided my stress baking spree, and we're now killing time watching TV while we wait. Logan has taken a shower but now looks even hotter wearing nothing but a worn pair of gray sweatpants. Lake looks entirely too serious for someone who's first ultrasound went well. And I know it went well because we had River spying for us. We figured Cooper would get the news right away, especially if it was good news, since he's Avery's best friend. So Logan and I asked River to text us if he heard anything, good or bad. That way we could be prepared. River texted us twenty minutes ago with a thumbs up emoji and an *all good*.

"Lake, sweetheart? What's the matter? Did something else happen at the appointment?"

Lake looks up, startled. It's like he just saw Logan and me for the first time since walking in the door.

"Oh, sorry, I didn't even see you guys. I was thinking."

Logan and I stand in unison and instantly enclose Lake in our arms. I have no idea what's going on in his head, but I know physically feeling our support will help him. When we first met Lake a few months ago, he seemed to shy away from too much physical touch, but as it turns out, from Logan and me, he can't get enough. He's always seeking us out, and I honestly can't get enough of it.

"Do you wanna tell us what's wrong, Little Bird?" Lake scrunches his nose in confusion.

"What would be wrong?"

"We don't know, sweetheart. You came home very contemplative. River told us the appointment went well, but is there something he doesn't know about?"

Lake shakes his head. His voice is a little muffled since he's squished in between us, but I can understand him just well once he begins to talk. "No, the appointment went perfectly. The baby is developing normally for a fetus at this stage. We were able to hear the heartbeat."

"That's fantastic, Lake."

"Yeah, hopefully one day, you'll be able to come to the appointment with us. I think you'll enjoy it."

"We'd love that."

"If it's not the appointment, whatcha thinking so hard about, Little Bird?"

Lake flushes, and I instantly know he's thinking about something sexual. It's the only time Lake gets even remotely embarrassed. "I'm just trying to decide if this is a good time to ask for penatrative sex."

"Fuck, Lake. Are you serious?" Logan's behind me and pulls me tighter, grinding into me. Since he's only wearing sweatpants, I can feel his bulge as it slides up and down my ass, even with clothes on.

"Yes. I now know the baby is healthy and there is no risk if we have sex. I want to try it . . . with both of you."

Oh, gods. I have to swallow to keep myself under control. Over the last few weeks, Lake has expressed more interest in butt play, but there's still no anal sex. He was, however, perfectly ok with our fingers, dildos, butt plugs, and even a memorable afternoon with a vibrator. So while he may not have ever had us, he has gained some experience and training. If he wants both of us, not at the same time, not for the first time, at least, but one after the other, I think it's very much possible.

"What's making you hesitate, sweetheart? You said you weren't sure if you should ask. Are you feeling sick? Or tired? It can wait, Lake. You know we'll wait as long as you need."

Lake shakes his head. "No, I actually feel pretty good. I know you two have been stressed out about my job lately, and I wasn't sure if you'd be in the mood."

Logan chuckles darkly as he takes Lake's hand in his and then places it over his bulge. "Feel that, Little Bird? That's just from this conversation, nothing else. I can 100% promise you I'm in the mood."

I kiss Lake's neck. "Same here. As long as you're ready, we're ready."

Lake is silent for so long, I begin to wonder if he changed his mind. Finally, he nods once to himself. "I'm ready. I'd like both of you to make love to me."

"Oh, Lake. We'd love to. We'll take such good care of you."

We each take one of Lake's hands and lead him up the stairs to his bedroom. While I'd argue Lake is far from a virgin these days, it's still his first time being penetrated by anything but fingers and toys, and that deserves to be special.

As soon as we get into his bedroom, I fall to my knees in front of him and begin to pull his shoes off. Lake watches me in awe with parted lips. As I take care of his bottom half, Logan begins taking off his layers on his upper one. It's early December, and it's been a cold one, and Lake is especially prone to the cold, so he always layers up. Logan takes off his outer jacket, followed by a zip-up hoodie. He's still pulling off the sweater underneath the hoodie when I already have Lake stepping out of his pants. I pause and sit back on my knees just to watch as Logan undresses him.

Part of the reason it's taking so long is that Logan is teasing him every step of the way: tickling his sides, nibbling at his neck, tweaking his nipples. And it's definitely turning Lake on, a small wet spot starting to form on his briefs. Which, fuck, begins to turn me on. I was already halfway there, but this teasing strip show is taking me all the rest of the way.

Finally, Logan gets Lake completely naked on the top. Lake stares back down at me as Logan grinds up against Lake from behind. Making sure I maintain eye contact, I finally slide Lake's briefs off, and he steps out of them. Despite me being on my knees in front of him, there's something extremely sexy about still being fully clothed and Lake being naked. Even Logan only has pants on, so it gives me this small feeling of power, and I'm kind of into it.

But I'm more into Lake's cock, which is standing out and proud right in front of my face, begging to be sucked. Surely, I can take a minute or two to indulge, right? I meet Logan's eyes and they're dark and filled with lust. I know he's as excited as I am.

I return my gaze to Lake. I don't take my eyes off him as I lean in and take his delicious cock into my mouth. Fuck, I can never get enough of either his or Logan's dicks. I'm a bit of a size whore, and I have no idea how I got so lucky to get not one but two men with monster cocks. It doesn't even bother me that I'm smaller than them in the size department. My dick is perfectly fine.

Lake moans and throws his head back onto Logan's chest. I grip Lake's ass, my fingers biting into the skin so I can get leverage. While I swallow my man down whole, Logan is tormenting him. He's biting and kissing up and down Lake's neck, shoulders, and upper back. At the same time, his hands are playing with Lake's nipples, alternating between pinching and caressing.

Lake is a mess under our ministrations. His eyes are practically rolled into the back of his head and he keeps jerking his hips, causing him to go deeper down my throat. Good thing I have no gag reflex. I'm the only one out of the three of us that can take both Lake and Logan the full way, and I'm completely proud of that fact.

"Evander, I'm going to orgasm, and I don't want to until both of you come inside of me."

Oh. Oh, holy fuck. "Inside you, sweetheart? Are you sure?" I pull off, a line of pre-cum and spit coming from my lips to his cock. I wipe my mouth and wait for his response.

"Yes. All three of us have been tested and are with no one besides each other. I can't get pregnant right now, so I am very sure."

Fuck, this moment couldn't get any hotter. Logan has clearly lost his patience with waiting after that moment and unceremoniously scoops up Lake and drops him onto the bed. We both strip at record speed and crawl onto the bed with him.

"How do you want to do this, Lake?"

"I'd like you to go first and then Logan." That makes sense. Since I'm smaller, I can stretch him out and get him ready. There's definitely something sexy as fuck about that.

"Can you turn on your stomach for me, sweetheart? I want to prep you."

"I've already cleaned myself and stretched some."

"Fuck, Lake. You're killing me here," Logan says as he lazily strokes his dick. He's lying on his side with a heated gaze, ready to take in the show.

Since Lake is still not showing, he can lie comfortably on his stomach. I set him up by sticking a couple of pillows under him so his ass is a little higher and he can relax more.

Once Lake is settled, I kneel and straddle his legs, palming my dick. Gods, his ass is a delight. I want to stick my face into it, but I know if I do, we'll never make it to the main course. I look over at Logan. "Can you get me the lube, babe?"

Logan nods, his eyes hooded, and reaches over into the drawer, pulling out the lube and tossing it to me.

I spread Lake's ass cheeks and pour some lube directly over his hole. Lake shudders. "Are you ok, sweetheart?"

"Y-yes." Logan reaches under the pillows and grins when his hand gets on Lake.

"Oh yeah, he's definitely good. Our little bird is enjoying himself." Lake moans as I begin to breach his hole, sticking a finger into it. He did prep himself. My finger goes in much easier than I expected, though he's still tight as hell. It's not long though before I'm adding a second. I scissor my fingers, and ok, I'm an asshole because more than once, I peg Lake's prostate, knowing it's driving him crazy. Logan is still lazily jerking off both Lake and himself, but it's not enough as Lake begins to hump the pillow, thrusting his ass up to get my fingers deeper.

"Evander, I'm ready."

I lean down and kiss in between his shoulder blades, right on the tip of one of the kraken's tentacles. "Not yet, sweetheart. I want to make sure you're nice and loose." Plus, I just like to play.

I slide a third finger in, and Lake goes nuts under me. Logan takes advantage and cups Lake's face, bringing him in for a bruising kiss.

Finally, I take pity on Lake and pull my fingers out. He thrusts back at the lack of intrusion. "Don't worry, I'm not done yet."

Logan eyes me. "It's about fucking time." I grin at him. Apparently, I'm torturing all of us.

"Lake, are you absolutely sure you don't want a condom?"

Lake nods. "Yes. Yes, I'm sure. Please, Evander. Please, get inside me. Please, fill me up."

Fuck, how can I say no to that? I quickly add a little more lube to my hand and stroke myself a couple of times. Once I'm nice and coated, I begin to slide in.

"Fuck, you're tight." I groan as I grip his hips and slide in, inch by tortuous inch.

Once I'm fully seated, Logan asks, "How does that feel, Little Bird?"

"G-good. Full."

"Oh yeah, you're full alright. Completely stuffed with Ev's cock. Are you ready for him to start moving?"

"Yes! Please. Please move."

"How does that fucking sexy piercing feel, Lake?" Logan continues, his voice deep and raspy. "Do you feel it as Ev makes himself at home inside you?"

Both Lake and I moan at the same time, and he pushes his ass up so I go even deeper and drag against his prostate.

"Yes, I-I feel it. The sensation, it's making it hard to stay in control."

"Oh fuck, sweetheart." I thrust into him and we both groan. "You're killing me here."

I start slow, but it doesn't take long to see that Lake is going nuts and I need to pick up my pace. Besides, Logan's waiting. I find a good rhythm as my fingers dig into his hips, and I know I'm leaving bruises. Lake is completely gone, and I'm afraid he's going to come.

"Easy love, you didn't want to come until both of us fill you, remember?"

Lake shakes his head. "I changed my mind."

"No, Little Bird. That's not how this works. Unless you tell us you want Ev to pull out or you're not ready for me, you have to wait for your release. Ev's almost there, right, babe?"

"Oh yeah, I'm so fucking close. You're milking my cock in this tight ass, sweetheart."

"I'm a little jealous now. I think I might want a taste of how those piercings feel soon." Logan says huskily. "Must feel amazing."

Oh fuck. I have to hold myself back so I don't come right now. Logan seems like he's exclusively a top, and I'm totally fine with that. I love both. But, now the image is in my head, and I don't think it'll be leaving anytime soon.

"Mmhm, so good." Lake groans and clenches his ass, and fuck, that's enough to bring me right to the edge. "I'm coming, Lake." A couple more thrusts and I'm suddenly screaming out my orgasm. My hips jerk as I fill Lake to the brim.

"Holy shit, that was so fucking hot," Logan mutters, his eyes wide with amazement. I collapse to the side, my dick sliding out with a slurping sound, cum leaking everywhere.

I'm face-to-face with Lake, who looks ready to take a nap. "Are you ready for Logan, sweetheart?"

"Yes. Logan, please, I need you too."

I can barely move I'm so fucking tired, but I manage to lean forward enough to kiss Lake. "I love you," I whisper.

"I love you too," he tells me. Lake twists his head and looks at Logan. "I love you too."

"I love you both so fucking much." Logan is already positioned behind Lake.

"Are you ready for me, Little Bird?"

"Yes."

Logan doesn't waste any time before he slides right into Lake. He's larger than me, but Lake is so fucking wet right now, he has very little resistance.

LAKE POV

Logan feels different than Evander. Both are amazing, but Logan is both longer and thicker, and I can feel the difference. By now, I'm so far gone that I don't care. I love it.

I know I have been putting off anal sex, but now I regret waiting so long. I had my reasons, but this feels like where I'm meant to be. I've never felt so relaxed before, so floaty. Logan is fast and rough, and I know he's desperate, but so am I.

"Are you ok, Little Bird? You went quiet on me." I was so lost in the feelings that I didn't realize Logan slowed down. As a response, I tilt my ass up, driving him deeper inside of me.

"I'm good. Keep going."

Evander chuckles and kisses my shoulder. "You get bossy when you bottom."

That's just because I know what I want. And right now, I want Logan to pick up the pace. I'm so desperate for my orgasm. Logan gets the hint and suddenly he goes from grazing to pegging my prostate every time.

"Oh, uhh, oh, my gods."

"That's it, Lake. You can take it. Ev, start jerking him off, please. I'm close."

LAKE POV

Evander mutters something along the lines of *Lake's not the only one bossy in bed*, but he still grabs my cock and begins jacking me off to the rhythm of the thrusts. That's because despite all his complaining, Evander likes when Logan gets bossy in bed, and so do I.

"I'm going to come!" I choke out, so lost in the ecstasy of the moment.

"Fuck, me too, Lake. Come with me, Little Bird."

Just as Logan's thrusts become erratic and I feel his load start to fill me, my own orgasm storms through me. I've never had one so violent before, and I'm completely breathless as my release soaks the pillows below me.

I know Logan has already cum, but instead of feeling him begin to soften, he seems to be getting harder and wider.

"L-Logan?" I ask, unsure of what's happening.

"I-I don't know Lake. I'm stuck."

"You're what!" Evander shouts, scrambling to a sitting position.

Logan sounds like he's about to panic. "I don't know. I'm fucking stuck. I can't pull out."

Both of my men are on the verge of a panic attack, but I just feel relaxed and satiated. Sure, it would be nice if I could go shower, but this is pretty great too. I'm so full, and I'm surrounded by the men I love.

"He expanded after the orgasm," I tell Evander calmly.

"What do you mean, he expanded?"

"He's bigger. I could feel it. I think it's a knot."

"What the fuck do you mean, you think it's a knot? No one knots anymore, and I've never had one before, so why now? Hell, wouldn't my dick start looking different? I've seen those pictures in museums of the Alphas of old, and they always had the knot at the base of their dick even when it wasn't expanded. I don't have a fucking knot."

They're beginning to stress me out. "Logan, can you please

come lie down with me. You're not going anywhere for a bit, and I think stressing will make it worse."

"Shit, sorry, Lake."

With the help of Evander, we manage to position ourselves so Logan and I are lying on our sides and he's basically spooning me from behind. Besides the overwhelmingly full feeling, it's kind of nice. Ev is lying on his side but facing us, so we're all together.

"How can you be so calm, sweetheart?"

I shrug. "Honestly, it's just instinct. Remember the doctor said the more this gene mutates and evolves, the more changes we'll all begin to see, and we'll have to rely on our instincts. My instinct is telling me this is the modern version of a knot, even though it's his whole length, and that it's perfectly fine."

"I don't get it though," Evander says quietly, "Why now? And why when you're already pregnant. I always thought it was a reproduction thing?"

"Maybe it's because Logan never penetrated me, and I'm an Omega. The next time he fucks you, we'll have to see if the same thing happens. And I don't know why it's happening while I'm pregnant. I'll have to do more research on the knotting process of the past."

"Fuck, can I please just go down this time first before we're worried about next time or research?"

I chuckle. "Please, relax. I know this is ok. There's nothing wrong."

Logan kisses the back of my head. "Ok, Little Bird, I trust you."

Shortly after Logan finally calms down, he begins to go down, and soon, he can slip out of me. I've never felt better. Yes, I'm exhausted, and sore, and covered in our cum. But my first time couldn't have gone more perfectly.

I can tell both Logan and Evander are still freaked out, but I'm too tired to worry about it. I barely stay conscious through

LAKE POV

the bath they draw for me, and they have to wash me and hold me up. Once Logan changes the sheets, I crawl into bed and immediately begin to crash. Around me, my two men are still whispering, but I tune it out. Usually, I'm the one researching and hypothesizing, but that will have to wait till tomorrow. Today, I just need sleep.

I tug on both of their arms. "Think tomorrow. Cuddle today."

Evander chuckles and wraps his arms around me. "I like that. I'm going to start using that all the time. Get some rest, sweetheart. You're right, we can figure everything out tomorrow."

"Love you," I mumble. I hear two more I love yous as Logan joins us in bed. It's completely perfect. We have a lot of struggles coming ahead of us as our relationship grows . . . and a lot of questions. There are still so many things unanswered and unknown about the Omega gene, and I know we will have our battles to face. But together with my mates, because despite their reluctance to use the word, that's what we are, I know we can handle anything. With that, feeling completely secure and safe, I fall asleep with the men I love surrounding me.

The End

Don't worry, this is only the beginning of our favorite trio's story. Part Two of Surrogate Omega coming soon!

BOOKS BY JACEY DAVIS

Caldeon Brothers Series:

Stian's Sacrifice

Ronan's Redemption

The Unexpected Omegas

The Unexpected Omega

The Surrogate Omega Part One

Knotty or Nice: An Omergaverse Holiday Anthology (The Very Merry Omega)

The Surrogate Omega Part Two (Coming Soon)

RAM Securities:

Surviving the Storm

Saving His Sunshine

ABOUT THE AUTHOR

Jacey is a true East Coast girl, born and raised in New Jersey. After a brief stint in North Carolina, Jacey is back in NJ with her husband, two young girls, and a black lab mix.

Jacey writes MM romance. Her first series, Caldeon Brothers, was a dystopian romance, but it just expanded from there. When she's not writing, Jacey can be found reading smut and steamy MM romances, watching Netflix, and trying to tame the chaos that is raising two little girls.

She loves all things PNR, Marvel, and fantasy. Jacey is always looking for new books and shows recs, so feel free to share. She is also working on becoming more active on social media. So please follow her for up-to-date information, conversation, games, and overall good times.

Facebook: Jacey Davis
    Facebook group: Jacey's Juicy Jaunt
    Instagram: @JaceyDavis_author
    TikTok: @JaceyDavisauthor

Want More Unexpected Omegas Content?

Click here to sign up for my Newsletter to receive an exclusive bonus NSFW knotty scene with River and Cooper! Plus additional freebies, giveaways, up-to-date information, and more.

Made in the USA
Middletown, DE
22 February 2023